England,
their England

A. G. MACDONELL

PICADOR

First published 1933 by Macmillan and Co. Ltd

First Pan Books edition published 1949
in association with Macmillan London Ltd

This edition published 1983 by Picador
an imprint of Macmillan Publishers Ltd
25 Eccleston Place, London SW1W 9NF
Basingstoke and Oxford

Associated companies throughout the world

ISBN 0 330 28041 4

19 18 17 16 15 14 13 12 11

A CIP catalogue record for this book is available from
the British Library.

Printed and bound in Great Britain by
Mackays of Chatham plc, Chatham, Kent

To J. C. Squire

The English Poet

chapter 1

The events which are described in this book had their real origin in a conversation which took place between two artillery subalterns on the Western Front in the beginning of October 1917.

But although this first short chapter has to be devoted to the circumstances and substance of that conversation in order that the rest may be more intelligible, and although the words of the conversation were spoken upon the slopes of the Passchendaele Ridge, no one need be afraid that this is a war book.

From Chapter 2 to the end there will be no terrific descriptions of the effect of a chlorine-gas cloud upon a party of nuns in a bombarded nunnery, or pages and pages about the torturing remorse of the sensitive young subaltern who has broken his word to his father, the grey-haired old vicar, by spending the night with a mademoiselle from Armentières. There will be no streams of consciousness, chapters long, in the best style of Bloomsbury, describing minutely the sensations of a man who has been caught in a heavy-howitzer barrage while taking a nap in the local mortuary. There are going to be no profound moralizings on the inscrutability of a Divine Omnipotence which creates the gillyflower and the saw-bayonet, and Shakespeare and Von Mackensen (or, as in the translations, Unser Shakespeare and Ferdinand-Foch), on the lines of the Ode to Baron von Bissing which borrowed, and rightly borrowed, Blake's famous question, 'Did He who made the lamb make thee?'

And, finally, there are going to be no long passages in exquisite cadences and rhythms, shoved in just to show that I am just as good as Ruskin or any of them, about the quietness of life in billets in comparison with life during a trench-mortar bombardment, and about the blue spirals of smoke curling up from the tiny French hamlet nestling in the woods which have echoed and re-echoed the thunderous footsteps of the army of Charlemagne, which have waved their green leaves above Hugh Capet and Louis the Saint and Henry of Navarre (always a sure card), which have screened the rustic lovers and the wheeling hawks and the marching Emperors, and so on and so on and so on.

In a word, after this first chapter there will be, to borrow the name of an ardent society of left-wing pacifists, No More War.

The conversation between the artillery officers took place in one of those rectangular, reinforced-concrete, frog-like boxes with which the German military engineers sprinkled Flanders in 1915 and 1916 in order that their effete and pampered infantry, unlike the more virile troops of Britain, of Belgium, and of Portugal, and of one French corps, should not have to sleep in six inches of water under a quarter-inch sheet of corrugated iron.

It was in 1917 that the British High Command got wind of the existence of these structures, or 'pill-boxes', as our irrepressible combatant-soldiers had christened them when they first appeared. It is thought that the news reached G.H.Q. in its peaceful little backwater of Montreuil from an agent in Berne, who had it from an agent in Amsterdam, who had got it from a journalist friend in Rio de Janeiro. But some people believe it was the special illustrated supplement in the *Chicago Tribune*, giving pictures of twenty-seven different types of pill-box, that first put our Intelligence Service, admittedly the finest in the world, upon the track. But whichever it was, there is no doubt at all that by February 1917 British G.H.Q. had decided, in principle, that a good way of checking the alarming wastage of man-power through influenza, frost-bite, and trench-feet, with all their accompanying opportunities for malingering, would be to house the front-line troops in pill-boxes. There was some opposition, of course, from the tougher-fibred, harder-bitten school of fighter, who maintained, at Montreuil, that nothing sapped the morale of troops so quickly as temporary security from shell-fire. The only way one could steel the nerves, this school argued, was to expose oneself all the time to shell-fire, until one got so accustomed to it that one simply did not notice it at all. This weighty argument was only silenced in the end by the production of the influenza-statistics and, especially, the estimated malingering-statistics.

But the High Command, having decided in principle that pill-boxes were, on the whole, desirable, was not so foolish as to make a present of them to the already over-mothered infantry. There is no maxim so true as the one about gift horses and their mouths. Small boys despise free seats at cinemas and unearned chocolates, and fighting soldiers are very like small boys. And the High Command at that moment was still smarting from a painful experience of the truth of this maxim. For, in a moment of warm-hearted, impulsive generosity, it had decreed that combatant officers might in certain circumstances be considered to be entitled to as much as half the amount of leave which every staff-officer always got, and the reception of this free gift had not been so full of enthusiastic gratitude as the High Command had expected, and had been justified in expecting.

The infantry were to have pill-boxes – good. But they were to get them for themselves. In this way a double purpose would be achieved. The pill-boxes would be appreciated, valued, and kept clean, and the infantry would get further practice in the art of offensive warfare. And, besides, Montreuil was a little uncertain how to set about making pill-boxes. And, besides, Montreuil had only just mastered the art of making deep dug-outs, invented by the Germans in late 1914, and was reluctant to dabble in new mysteries.

So during the month of August, in which it rained three-quarters of the time, and during September, in which it rained half the time, and October, when it rained all the time, the infantry were busily employed in getting hold of these pill-boxes, and, at the end of the three months, at the cost of a good many lives and a good many shells, they had acquired several hundreds of them.

It was true that they smelt most vilely of stale cigars and that the entrances all faced the wrong way and that the mud was inclined to ooze into them when no one was looking. But, as the Fifth Army staff-officer said who was detailed to make a report upon their structure, composition, thickness, seating capacity, field of fire, siting, and shell-resistance, and who examined what he thought was one of them through a powerful telescope from the roof of the Château des Trois Tours, behind Brielen, 'After all, you can't have everything.' With which eternal verity upon his lips, the staff-officer handed the telescope to one orderly, dictated his report to another, stepped into his motor-car and departed on leave. But he was well rewarded for his hazardous toil, for in the drawing-rooms of Mayfair and Belgravia he was now able to add enthralling accounts of his experiences in the Front Line, almost, to his predictions about the trend of forthcoming campaigns and the plans of forthcoming battles, on which he had previously had to rely for the captivating of feminine hearts. And a few weeks later he received a well-merited bar to his D.S.O.

Upon the slopes of the Passchendaele Ridge, about two hundred yards east of the Steenbeck river (when I say 'east' I mean on the wrong, or German side, and when I say 'river' I mean a ditch about nine feet wide at its widest) and about two hundred yards west of the front line, there stood a pill-box so large, and with walls so thick, that it served as the headquarters for two adjoining battalions, and as no battalion headquarters ever dreamt of stirring a yard without the company of an artillery subaltern, there were consequently two gunners in this particular box.

The reason for the indispensability of these young gentlemen – for they were seldom more than twenty or twenty-one years of age – was a curious one. It had been discovered long before, right away back in the almost pre-war days of the early days of the war, that by some mysterious freak of Providence no infantry soldier, of whatever rank or with however long a row of campaign medals, can distinguish between shells that are fired from in front of him and shells that are fired from behind him. Whenever, therefore, a heavy artillery barrage fell upon their trenches, the infantry, their natural optimism damped by interminable digging and carrying, always assumed as a matter of course that it was their own artillery firing short. Indeed there were times at the beginning of the war when it was difficult to convince them that the German artillery ever fired at all, and the fact that a British six-gun field battery of eighteen-pounder guns had a strict ration of thirty-six shells, all shrapnel, to last them for an entire week, was held to be no proof that it had not plastered our front line with a thousand six-inch high-explosive shells in two hours.

The result was that a young artillery gentleman had to be attached to each battalion headquarters in the Line, whose duty it was to point out the fundamental difference between east-bound and west-bound projectiles and thus soothe the fighting-troops into a feeling of partial, at any rate, security.

The two battalions, of which the colonels, adjutants, signal officers, runners, batmen, and general hangers-on were housed in this long, gloomy, dank, cigar-smoky, above-ground tunnel during the second week of October 1917, were the seventeenth battalion of the Rutland Fusiliers and the twenty-fourth battalion of the Melton Mowbray Light Infantry. The artillery officers were Lieutenant Evan Davies, tenth East Flint Battery, Royal Artillery, Territorial Force, who was attached to the Rutlands, and Lieutenant Donald Cameron, thirteenth Sutherland Battery, R.A., T.F., attached to the Melton Mowbrays, each for a period of four days.

The East Flint artillery belonged to a Welsh Division, the Sutherland to a Scottish, but it was the usual practice to leave the gunners in the Line while their infantry was out at rest, thereby doubling the artillery strength of the Line, and sometimes, when divisions were plentiful, trebling and quadrupling it. It is true that this practice had its drawbacks, and a perspicacious civilian, a temporary major, who had by an error of drafting been placed in quite a high-up position in the Montreuil backwater, pointed out that it meant that the artillery never got a rest at all. The perspicacious major – in happier times a professor of Greek, a man of subtle intelligence, and great learning, and a capacity for working seventeen hours a day – was duly transferred to the command of a Chinese Labour battalion, and spent the rest of the War in building a wharf at a fishing village near Finisterre, which was to be used as a base for the British Army in the event of one of Von Ludendorff's brisker drives capturing Le Havre. But though the major had gone, the dilemma remained. If the artillery strength in the Line was to be doubled, trebled, or quadrupled, the artillery personnel would get no rest. The ultimate solution was simple, as all ultimate solutions are, and consisted of the words, 'Oh well, it can't be helped,' and everyone was delighted, except, of course, the artillery personnel.

Mr Davies and Mr Cameron naturally gravitated towards each other in the corner of the pill-box furthest from the door

– artillery officers always seemed to drift into the corner of the pill-box furthest from the door – and in a short time were deep in conversation. They discussed the usual topics, the general bloodiness of the war, the shocking hold-up in the leave-rotation since the Passchendaele offensive first began, the tragic sublimity of the Staff, and the foulness of the weather. They compared the number of consecutive days on which their respective batteries had received marmalade in their rations instead of jam – the East Flint battery apparently was leading by a hundred and eighteen days against ninety-six – returned to the general bloodiness of the war, and then settled down to discuss, in discreet whispers, their infantry hosts and, finally, the general characteristics of the nation from which both Rutland Fusiliers and Melton Mowbray Light Infantry were recruited.

'I've lived for five years in London,' said Davies, a big, pleasant man whose five-and-thirty years were an exception to the general youthfulness of liaison officers, with steel-rimmed glasses and a heavy black moustache, 'and I must admit I find the English are extraordinarily difficult to understand.'

'I was never in England before the War,' replied Cameron, 'so I've really only seen them as soldiers. I've been in London for a day or two when I was on leave, of course.'

Donald Cameron was a boy of about twenty, slender and fair-haired with a small fair moustache and small hands. He was about five feet nine or ten, and even the changes and chances of war had not battered his natural shyness out of him. He spoke the pure, accurate English of Inverness-shire.

'What do you think of them as soldiers?' asked Davies.

'They're such an extraordinary mixture,' replied Cameron. 'The last time I was liaison to an English battalion was about a month ago. It was a battalion from Worcestershire or Gloucestershire or somewhere. The Colonel wore an eyeglass and sat in a deep dug-out all day reading the *Tatler*. He talked as if he was the Tatler, all about Lady Diana Manners and Dukes and Gladys Cooper. We were six days in the Line and he had the wind up all the time except once, and that time he walked up to a Bosche machine-gun emplacement with a walking-stick and fifty-eight Bosche came out and surrendered to him. What do you make of that? Do you suppose he was mad?'

'I don't know,' replied Davies, puffing away at a huge black pipe. 'We had an English subaltern once in our battery who used to run and extinguish fires in ammunition-dumps.'

Cameron dropped his cigarette. 'He used to do what?'

'Used to put out fires in shell-dumps.'

'But whatever for?'

'He said that shells cost five pounds each and it was everyone's duty to save Government money.'

'Where is he buried?' asked Cameron.

'In that little cemetery at the back of Vlamertinghe.'

'I know it.'

Donald Cameron lit another cigarette and asked:

'Why do the English always laugh when Aberdeen is mentioned?'

'Heaven knows,' replied Davies. 'Why do they have a Welsh Prime Minister and a Scotch—'

'Not Scotch. Scots. Or Scottish.'

'Sorry. —A Scottish Commander-in-Chief and a Scottish First Sea Lord of the Admiralty, and think it funny?'

'Lord knows.'

'And here's another thing, Cameron. The English pride themselves on having always beaten the French except at Hastings.'

'Yes.'

'Then why is it that the French Army is so much more successful in this War than the English?'

'The French staff-work is supposed to be miles better.'

'It must be, I suppose. Because the English soldier, the chap who actually does the fighting, is amazingly good.'

'Why do the English,' asked Cameron, 'crack up the French seventy-five as being the most marvellous gun in the War? Our own 18-pounder is just as good.'

'If not better.'

'Exactly. If not better.'

'But then why does the average Englishman,' said Davies, 'pretend he is a perfect devil with his fists when really he is the most peaceable soul in the world, and then, in spite of his peaceableness, suddenly turns into a first-class soldier?'

'Yes, but then why does the Englishman—'

'Oh, for Heaven's sake!' cried Davies laughing, and hauling a great flask out of his pocket, 'this is going to drive us mad. Have a drop of Scotch. I beg your pardon! Have a drop of Scots or Scottish.' They each had a good swig of it, and then Davies went on: 'I'm a publisher by profession – I've got an office near Covent Garden – and the more I see of the Englishman as a business man, or as a literary man, or as any kind of man, the more bewildered I become. They're the kindliest souls in the world, but if they see anything beautiful flying in the air or running along the ground, they rush for a gun and kill it. If an earthquake devastates North Borneo, they dash off to the Mansion House and block up all the traffic for miles round trying to hand over money for earthquake relief, but do you think they'll lift a finger to abolish their own slums? Not they. If you assault a man in England and bash his teeth down his throat and kick him in the stomach, that's just playfulness and you'll get fourteen days in jug. But if you lay a finger on him and pinch his watch at the same time, that's robbery with violence, and you'll probably get eighteen strokes with the "cat" and about three years in Dartmoor. You can do pretty nearly anything you like to a stag or a fox. That's sport. But you stand up and say you approve of bull-fights, and see what happens to you! You'll be lucky if you escape with your life. And there's another thing. They're always getting themselves up in fancy dress. They adore fancy dress. Look at their Beef-Eaters, and their Chelsea Pensioners, and their barristers' wigs, and their Peers' Robes, and the Beadle of the Bank of England, and the Lord Mayor's Show, and the Presenting at Court, and the Trooping of the Colour, and all that sort of thing. Show an Englishman a fancy-dress, and he puts it on.'

'They sound rather fascinating,' murmured Donald.

'They're fascinating, all right,' replied Davies. 'I love them. I don't understand them, but I love them. I've got a theory about them, which I rather want to test some time, if I can extract myself unpunctured from this bloody Armageddon.'

'What is it?'

'I've got an idea that all their queernesses and oddities and incongruities arise from the fact that, at heart, fundamentally, they're a nation of poets. Mind you, they'd be lurid with rage if you told them. Imagine what Colonel Tarkington over there would say if you told him that he was a poet.'

Colonel Tarkington was the C.O. of the Melton Mowbrays. He was a cavalry major who had transferred into the infantry for the sake of promotion – a neat, dapper little man who ate sparingly in order to keep his weight down for post-war polo.

'I'd rather like to write a book about them some day,' said Cameron thoughtfully.

'It's a book that wants writing,' replied the Welshman. 'Come and look me up after this bloody war is over, and we'll discuss it.'

'Seriously?'

'You bet your life I'm serious. I told you I was a publisher once, and I hope to be a publisher again. That's a bargain. If ever you want a job in London, come to me and we'll talk it over. You'll find me in the telephone-book, Davies and Llewellyn Glendower, Henrietta Street.'

Cameron made a note of it in his gun-registration book, and in his turn produced a large flask.

Evening was drawing on. The rain was falling steadily, in grey sheets, hour after hour. The German artillery was tuning up for its evening performance, and an occasional thud shook the pill-box when a shell pitched near. But it was not the shells that worried the two gunners. They were in the corner furthest from the door, and both knew that the reinforced concrete was twenty-eight inches in thickness, for both of them had measured it independently as soon as they had arrived, and both knew perfectly well that nothing short of a direct hit from an eleven-inch or eight-inch howitzer, both fortunately rare in Flanders mud, or repeated hits on the same spot from a 5.9, which was unlikely, could do them any real harm. The real danger was that the infantry might get agitated, and ask for an S.O.S. to be sent to the protecting artillery.

The two gunners shuffled their feet uneasily, and tried not to watch the Colonels and their staffs at the other end of the pill-box. A lot of talking was going on at that other end, and runners kept on arriving with messages. The air was now throbbing and thudding and hissing and quivering, and the pill-box was filling up with orderlies and signallers, taking cover from the thickening barrage. The atmosphere was heavy with smoke and the smell of wet macintoshes and sweating runners and the bitter fumes of a shell which had pitched at the entrance. The adjutant of the Rutlands came elbowing his way towards them through the crowd. Davies saw him coming and sighed.

'Hell! Now we're off,' he murmured. 'Retaliation wanted. Five pounds to a bun that my wire is down.' He stretched out for his gas-mask and tin-hat.

'All the wires will be down,' said Cameron. 'Listen. It's a regular corker of a barrage.'

'Have you got any rockets?' asked Davies. 'Mine were blown into a shell-hole on the way up.'

'Four. Two red and two green; we might try them first.'

The adjutant reached them, with the usual request for an S.O.S. "It might be an attack,' he explained.

The two gunners struggled through the mob to the door, carrying their clumsy rocket-apparatus. Outside was a maelstrom of noise and mud and death.

'God Almighty!' exclaimed Davies as he peered out. 'If they don't see the rockets, Cameron, one or other of us will have to run for it. No one in the world could mend a wire in all that.'

'Let's hope the damned things work,' said Cameron, feverishly propping the rocket-stand against what was left of a parapet. A moment or two later the first rocket soared up into the dripping twilight and burst into a rain of green stars. The second, the red one, followed at once and failed to burst.

'Damnation!' exclaimed both gunners simultaneously. The S.O.S. signal was green followed by red. Green alone would not be enough. They fitted the other red rocket, and then the matches wouldn't strike. The matchbox was soaked. Cameron rushed inside and came out with another box. The rocket spluttered and soared away and broke into a beautiful red shower.

The two gunners crouched down behind the broken parapet and waited. Davies counted the seconds aloud from his wristwatch. If the rockets were not seen by the artillery, one of the two subalterns would have to try to cross the open mile and a half to the nearest battery, with a five-hundred to one chance against getting through. And if he failed, the other would have to try. It was of some considerable importance to them, therefore, that the rockets should be observed. The seconds passed. At seventy-five, Davies made a cup of his hand and shouted into Donald's ear, 'It looks like a wash-out.' At ninety he held up his ten fingers, and at a hundred, he half-turned to Cameron and yelled, 'We'd better toss. Will you call?' He spun a franc and Cameron shouted 'Heads' and at that moment a gun fired from behind them, and then another gun, and then five or six together in a straggling salvo, and then like a giant thunderbolt the whole of the British artillery sprang to life and the western sky was a blaze of yellow flame. The iron curtain was down.

With a huge grin across his face Davies sprang back into the shelter of the pill-box. Cameron paused to retrieve the franc from the mud and a 5.9 high-explosive shell pitched beside him, and he woke up a fortnight later, suffering from concussion and shell-shock, in the Duchess of Westminster's Hospital at Le Touquet.

chapter 2

One of the routes by which shell-shocked officers progressed from the base hospitals back to health was via a temporary row of huts in Palace Green, two enchanting private houses on the top of Campden Hill, and finally one or other of the monster hydropathics in Derbyshire or Scotland. Donald Cameron travelled this route, and ended in a monster hydropathic in Scotland, where the chief, indeed, the only, qualification of the Commandant for solving the three hundred separate psychological problems entrusted to him by the War Office was an unrivalled knowledge of the drainage system of the insalubrious port of Leith. But even this expert was unable to do much for Donald beyond applying his universal remedy for all shell-shock cases. This remedy was simple. It consisted of finding out the main likes and dislikes of each patient, and then ordering them to abstain from the former and apply themselves diligently to the latter. For example, those of the so-called patients

– for the Commandant privately disbelieved in the existence of shell-shock, never having experienced himself any more alarming manifestation of the power of modern artillery than the vibrations of target-practice by invisible battleships – who disliked noise were allotted rooms on the main road. Those who had been, in happier times, parsons, schoolmasters, journalists, and poets, were forbidden the use of the library and driven off in batches to physical drill, lawn tennis, golf, and badminton. Those who wished to be alone were paired with horse-racing, girl-hunting subalterns. Those who were terrified of solitude had special rooms by themselves behind green-baize doors at the ends of remote corridors. By means of this admirable system, the three hundred separate psychological problems were soon reduced to the uniform level of the Leith drainage and sewerage, and by the time that a visiting commission of busybodies, arriving unexpectedly and armed with an absurd technical knowledge and jargon, insisted upon the immediate sack of the Commandant and his replacement by a civilian professor of psychology, it was estimated that the mental condition of as many as two per cent of the patients had definitely improved for the better since admission to the hospital.

Donald was not among the fortunate two per cent. His natural shyness had been increased by the concussion of the high-explosive shell on the Passchendaele Ridge, and the Commandant's system, which had made Donald president of the Debating Society and compulsory speaker at all debates, had had the unfortunate effect of assisting rather than countering the efficient work of the German militarists and munition-makers. Indeed the professor of psychology, a man who not only believed in the existence of the subject which he professed, but also read books about it written by foreigners, and Germans at that, allowed more than a year and a half to elapse before he felt that it would be safe to send Donald out into the world of civil life from which he had been so suddenly and so strangely excluded for six years. It was not until 1920, therefore, that Donald was furnished with a document which said that he would only be forty-hundredths of a normal man for the next seven years; that his physical rating for the rest of his life as a potential soldier in any future war that might elude the influence of the Great War to end War was C2; but that on the expiration of the seven years he would, unaccountably, become once again a hundred per cent citizen with no further claim upon the finances of his country. Such was the mathematical exactitude of prophecy with which the Ministry of Pensions was endowed in those years that immediately followed the War, and it is believed to be the first successful poach by Aesculapius upon the preserves of the Delphian Apollo. To this document was attached a statement that the missing sixty-hundredths of Lieutenant Donald Cameron were worth £85 a year – a mortifying comparison with the value put upon his services at that desperate crisis in world affairs when General von Kluck, the subject of so many admirable rhymes, was advancing nimbly upon Paris, and Colonel Repington was beginning his diary.

The £85 per annum was to be paid in half-yearly instalments and was subject to income-tax. Income-tax was to be deducted at the source.

Donald packed his valise for the last time, saluted a major for the last time, shook hands affectionately with the professor who had so unpatriotically called in Herr Freud to redress the balance of Frau Krupp, and departed in a first-class carriage, for the last time for many years, to Aberdeen, and from Aberdeen by slow train to the country district of Aberdeenshire which is called Buchan. His father, Ewan Cameron, was the proprietor of a farm in Buchan called the Mains of Balspindie, and Ewan was known as the best singer, the best violinist, the champion whisky-drinker, the story-teller *par excellence*, the scholar who could out-talk the minister, the quickest-tempered, the kindest-hearted, the handsomest old man, and the worst farmer, from the Mormond Hill to the foot of the Lecht. Ewan Cameron had not always been a farmer. He had once owned a small distillery near Edzell in Angus, but the distillery had failed because of the owner's sentimental attachment to his own wares. He could not bear the thought of other people drinking the precious fluid. At another period of his life, Ewan Cameron had kept a general store in the village of Forres, but this too had failed. For Ewan contracted a habit of putting up the shutters earlier and earlier every week in order to indulge his passion for fishing, an art in which he was a complete master, as even the pundits of Deveronside and Spey admitted. The result, of course, was that as the creel filled the till emptied, and Ewan Cameron packed his belongings, filled his silver snuff-mull – it had a huge cairngorm on the top – and moved on. Tomintoul, highest village of Britain, saw him for a month or two. In Charlestown-of-Aberlour he stayed two years, nominally as factor to a small laird, but actually spending all his days and a long part of his nights in making violins, which he offered for sale to those who could not play the violin and gave as presents to those who could. In Fochabers he taught Latin in the school for a while, but neglected his school hours in order to argue with the parish priest about the Infallibility of the Pope, a subject in which he was greatly interested at the time; and in Knockando for six months he drove the straightest furrow that had been seen in those parts for many a long day. His hair gradually silvered, his face grew wrinkled and old, but no amount of whisky and no length of nocturnal discussion and no fall from comfort to poverty could dim the brightness of his eye or roughen the clearness of his tenor voice, or shake the nimbleness of his fingers upon the violin-strings or the chanter. Only on two subjects he would never talk, and those were his father and his father's father. All that Donald knew about his great-grandfather was that he had 'come over the hills' in about 1790 and that he was a very silent man; and all that he knew about his grandfather was that he was the most skilful poacher, although an amateur, from Donside to Fort George, and that he too was a very silent man.

In 1921 the farm in Buchan was gradually going the same way as the distillery and the shop and the schoolmastering and the rest of them had gone. Ewan Cameron did not care. His wife had been dead many years; his only son had been supported by the Government since 1914, and he had just discovered Dante. He had no cares in the world. A weird machine which the English call a char-à-banc, and the French an autobus, had begun to ply between the district of Balspindie and Aberdeen, and twice a week the old man went to plague the life of the librarian of King's College in the Old Town by demanding obscure Continental books of which the librarian had never heard, and to chase the lecturer in Italian of Marischal College in the New Town. His conversation with lecturer and librarian was as learned and dignified as his repartee in the char-à-bancs was lewd and swift. 'Auld Balspindie' or 'the auld deevil' was respected and feared and admired in that countryside of lewdness and learning.

When Donald went home in the spring of 1921 with his £85 per annum, the old man was surprised.

'This is no place for a young man,' he said, looking sternly at his son from under his white eyebrows and pouring out two whiskies. 'I won't say I'm not glad to see you for my sake, because I am. But not for your sake. Balspindie is for old men.'

'And what for young ones, Father?' asked Donald.

'The world,' replied the old man sharply, draining his glass and refilling it.

'But I've seen quite enough of the world for the time being,' protested Donald.

'Ay,' Ewan Cameron nodded, 'I thought you might be thinking that. It's the child's instinct. You've been hurt and you run home to your mother. Your mother's dead and Balspindie has to do in her place. Well, you're welcome here. And you can stay till you're well again. But after that, it's the road for you, my boy. Come back here to die, if you like. But go out there,' he flung his arms wide as if he was King of All the Spains and Emperor of All the Indies, 'go out there to live.'

'I don't know that I want to,' replied Donald timidly. He was feeling that he never wanted to stir five miles from Balspindie again for the rest of his life. By some amazing series of flukes he had escaped the Germans, the Staff, disease, and even the sewage-expert from Leith, and his instinct was to settle down and live a quiet life. He had no desire whatever for further adventures and experiences, and he said so, diffidently.

His father did not argue. He nodded repeatedly and said finally:

'You're not cured yet. When you are cured you'll leave me. Not because I tell you to, but because you'll want to. Meanwhile, there's plenty to do here.'

There was plenty to do, and Donald did it. He got up early and went to bed early. He worked in the fields, and in time he ploughed a furrow that was quite creditable.

'I might have ploughed that one myself,' said his father admiringly on one occasion, 'if I'd been blindfolded and short of one arm and with a team of horses that rocketed about like steeplechasers.'

For several years father and son continued their queer, incongruous partnership until the senior partner dissolved it by dying. Ewan Cameron made as little fuss about dying as he had made about living. He went to bed at about six o'clock one evening in late summer, windless and warm and scented with the scent of corn-stooks, and told the dairymaid to go out into the fields for Donald. When Donald came in, breathless from running across stubble, he found the old man lying on his side in a doze. He knelt down on the stone floor beside him, and Ewan Cameron opened his great black eyes and smiled a smile that Frans Hals might have painted.

'I'm for off, boy,' he said, in the only Buchan phrase that Donald had ever heard him use. And then: 'Lochaber no more. Go to the Gordon barracks in Aberdeen tomorrow and bring a piper who can play a Cameron lament.' He stopped and shook his great head a little and then went on. 'I was a Catholic once. Go away from Buchan. It's not our country. Don't be afraid, I won't gabble of green fields. If ever you meet Lochiel, give him a peat. The snuff-mull was carried at Culloden.' Then he sighed and said, 'I'll not see Achnacarry again,' and then he shut his eyes and died.

Donald Cameron fetched a piper from Castlehill barracks, and all Buchan came to the funeral and listened to the Cameron lament and there were no dry eyes for 'Auld Balspindie'.

On the day after the funeral, an advocate from a firm of advocates in Golden Square, Aberdeen, came out in a motor-car with the news that Ewan Cameron had left just over seven thousand pounds to his son Donald, on condition that he spent no more than one month in the year north of the Tweed until he was fifty years of age. Where the old man got the money no one ever discovered, but it must have been a long time before, the advocate said, for the original sum had been about thirty-five hundred pounds and had been lying in Aberdeen at compound interest for over twenty years.

At first the advocate frightened Donald a good deal, for he

had not spoken to a man of the world since leaving the military hospital, until it came out in the course of conversation that the man of feus and fees had himself commanded a battalion of Highland infantry in the War and that they had many battle-field friends, and had once had many more, in common. To this small, dry man, once a leader of desperate attacks and com-mander of a thousand incomparable soldiers, Donald entrusted the fortunes of the Mains of Balspindie, and a week or two later, having packed his military valise with his civilian clothes and procured two or three introductions from the librarian of the University Library and the lecturer in Italian to friends in the southern part of Britain, he set off once again for London, for the first time in his life making the twelve-hour journey in a third-class carriage. It was very uncomfortable.

chapter 3

Donald Cameron had no qualifications for any profession ex-cept the ability to drive a moderately crooked furrow and to direct the fire of a six-gun battery of eighteen-pounder guns, and so he resolved to try his fortune as a journalist. There seemed to be no other profession which required neither ability nor training. He was fortified in this resolution by the fact that his letters of introduction from the lecturer and the librarian were all addressed to literary men, the former having several times corresponded with editors about rejected articles and the latter being a member of the Librarians' Association, a body that occasionally came into touch with those who write books as well as those who read them.

But the double set of introductions led to a small difficulty at 7.30 on the morning of the day when the Aberdeen express drew up at King's Cross station and decanted a tousled and sleepy Donald from his third-class corner. For the lecturer in Italian had warmly recommended Chelsea as the only possible region in which a literary man could live, whereas the librarian had repeatedly affirmed that no one who was anyone lived further away from the British Museum than an average athlete at the Aboyne Games could throw a stone. Donald's own experience of London consisted of an intimate knowledge of Reggiori's restaurant opposite King's Cross station, the few hundred yards between the Palace Theatre and the Piccadilly Hotel, and the leave-train platforms of Victoria Station; and in consequence Chelsea and Bloomsbury were all one to him, both as residential districts and as Movements in Art. To him Chelsea was 'the Quartier Latin of London', and as for Bloomsbury, he had heard of Virginia Woolf but not of Miss Sackville-West.

It was the spin of a coin upon the arrival platform of the London and North-Eastern Railway's terminus that directed his taxi in the direction of Chelsea, and by tea-time of the same afternoon Donald was installed in a bed-sitting-room on the second floor of a Carolean house in Royal Avenue, just off the King's Road. The landlady was an elderly dame with a roving eye, who looked as if she had had her fling in her day, forty years before. Her daughter also had a roving eye, and looked as if she was ready to have a fling at any moment. Her name was Gwladys and she terrified Donald. She was tall and ladylike and full of little ways. Every morning Donald met her at the door of the bathroom, for his descent, at whatever hour he made it, invariably seemed to coincide with her entrance or exit – screaming modestly in a flurry of pink dressing-gown and lace-topped nightgown. And often when he was going upstairs to bed he would meet Gwladys on the stairs, and she would tell him all about her fiancé, a naval commander who was killed at Jutland and who was very fond of port wine. Donald shyly sympathized with her loss and put forward the opinion, nervously, that port wine was infinitely preferable to Jutland. Gwladys' view was that in any case the present was better than the past.

Donald's first letter of introduction was to the literary editor of a well-known weekly paper which had leanings towards a mild form of intellectual Socialism. No one would have been more alarmed and bewildered than the literary editor if a sudden swing of the political pendulum had brought about the nationalization of the Means of Production, Distribution, and Exchange which his newspaper so elegantly advocated. For the literary editor was an Irishman who, if he despised money and made very lethargic and intermittent efforts to acquire any, nevertheless was heartily fond of many of the things which money can buy. He was a brilliant critic, a vile editor, and a superb luncher-out. He went to a lunch-party every day of the week, was always the first to arrive and the last to leave, and was always welcome. For his converastion was not only easy, witty, learned, universal; it was enchanting as well. The man radiated charm. Charm was his capital and conversation his income, and both were inexhaustible. His name was Charles Ossory.

Donald presented his letter of introduction to Mr Ossory's secretary, a small, dark lady of incredible sharpness and efficiency, one afternoon at 3 p.m., and the sharp little lady examined him briefly and explained that Mr Ossory was out. She added that she had full authority to make appointments for Mr Ossory, and that if Mr Cameron cared to come along at 4.30 on the following afternoon, Tuesday, it was possible that Mr Ossory might by that time have come back from his lunch.

'From his tea,' corrected Donald mildly.

'From his lunch,' snapped the sharp little lady, and she turned to a gigantic card-index in a way that suggested only too plainly that the conversation was over. On the Tuesday afternoon Donald presented himself nervously at the dragonlet's den and waited until, an hour later, the butler of a Dowager Marchioness telephoned to say that Mr Ossory was not going to return to his Bureau that day.

On the Wednesday afternoon it was the lady secretary of a Cabinet Minister's wife who did the telephoning, only she called it 'his department', and on the Thursday it was a Countess whose quarterings were unimpeachable but whose income did not run to a telephonic intermediary, and so had to do it herself. On Friday Mr Ossory went away for his usual week-end, returning on Tuesday just in time not to go to the office, and it was only by chance that a hasty visit on the Wednesday afternoon, to correct the proofs of a wise and witty article about Molière, happened to coincide with one of Donald's vigils. Charles Ossory came into the office in a great hurry and stayed, talking to Donald enchantingly, for an hour and a half, his eyes twinkling away and his lovely sentences tumbling out in his lovely soft voice. He was no longer in a hurry. His engagements were forgotten. In vain did the dragonlet dart in and out of the office, ordering him either to correct his proof or to go to Whitehall Gardens to have tea with Mr Bernard Shaw. Mr Ossory, with enchanting blandness, refused to do either, and Donald thought it was the most flattering thing that had ever come his way. But that was all from Mr Ossory that did come his way, except the task of compiling a list of autumn novels for a book-supplement of the mildly Socialistic weekly, for which he received three guineas; that, and a piece of information. For Mr Ossory told him, in his soft lovely voice, that the literary profession was grotesquely overcrowded, and that it was only possible for men of exceptional talent to enter it, and then only if they had been already in the profession for years. Unless they had been in it for years, he pointed out, how could they show their exceptional talent?

It says a great deal for Mr Ossory's charm that he made this sound quite reasonable, and it was not until Donald had returned home to Royal Avenue and pondered deeply over the position that he decided to give up Mr Ossory as a potential Maecenas and to try his second letter of introduction.

This was from the librarian of King's College Library, and was addressed to Mr Alexander Ogilvy, LL.D. of St Andrews University, and editor of the *Illustrated Planet*. Mr Ogilvy's business habits were different, apparently, from those of Mr Ossory, for he made an appointment with Donald for 8.30, and at 8.31 received his visitors. 8.31 is a difficult time of the day for any but the hardiest of spirits, and Donald's shyness was even more overpowering at that hour than later on. He had breakfasted much too early, so as not to be late for the appointment, and he had spent a cold half-hour in a dark, stone-flagged waiting-room at the office of the *Illustrated Planet* between 8 o'clock and half-past, his courage sinking with his temperature, and a hungry feeling competing with a nervous feeling for supremacy in the neighbourhood of his lower waistcoat buttons. The sudden jarring of the electric bell at one minute past the hour of the appointment came like the whistles of the platoon commander at zero hour, and his eyes were all blurred when he shambled through a glass door into the presence of the great Mr Ogilvy.

When the haze had cleared away, he saw that an extraordinary person was staring at him from a distance of about three feet. Mr Ogilvy was a small man – a very small man – and he had an enormous head. Seated at his office table, he looked like an eccentric giant who preferred to sit upon the floor so that only his head appeared above the polished surface, for there was little of Mr Ogilvy visible except his mammoth cranium. But when he jumped up smartly and held out his hand, his full length of about five feet – four feet of which were body and legs, and one of which was head, became apparent. Donald sat down opposite him and an embarrassing silence followed. Donald glanced round the room, looked at the floor, his finger-nails, the shiny top of the table, and finally shot a furtive glance at Mr Ogilvy. This glance gave him a profound surprise, for he had imagined at first that the hugeness of the little man's head was his most important feature. Now he saw that this was wrong, for the giant skull, dwarfing as it did the four-foot body, was itself dwarfed by a chin that was shaped like a Spanish spade-beard, like the front end of a torpedo boat photographed in a dry dock, like an instrument for bashing in the gates of medieval cities. It was a regular Cyrano among chins, and the little man was evidently as conscious of his panache as the Gascon was of his. For as he looked at Donald during the embarrassing silence, he thrust it forward in a rather menacing way, just like the pictures of the mythical Captain Kettle. Donald, by now a-twitter with nervous palpitations, wondered if the little man's first words would be a rasping command to Marshal Soult to attack the Russian centre, or a single word which would unleash the Old Guard up the slopes of St Jean. As it was, Mr Ogilvy's first words were unintelligible.

'Erracht, Mamore, or Fassifern?' he barked.

Donald started, and swept a large glass inkbottle to the floor, where it shivered into ten thousand splinters and flung its blue-black contents into every corner of the room. Mumbling apologies and perspiring freely, for the cold feeling had been suddenly superseded by intense heat, Donald fell on his knees, upsetting his chair with a clatter, and started to mop up the flood with his handkerchief. Somewhere in the distance, about two miles away, the electric bell rang again, and an office-boy, miraculously covering the two miles in a second or so, appeared with mop and brush and pan, and Donald, purple in the face and blue-black on the hands, reseated himself on his righted chair.

Mr Ogilvy waved away his apologies, and Donald perceived that there was a kindly look in his eyes and a gentle tone in his voice which did not harmonize with the terrific aspect of his chin.

'I was asking you,' said Mr Ogilvy, in a very broad Lanarkshire accent, 'to what branch of the Clan Cameron you belonged?'

'I—I don't know exactly,' stammered Donald. Mr Ogilvy's kindly expression vanished and the Austerlitz manner reasserted itself.

'It's a poor Highlander who doesn't know his own chieftain,' he observed coldly.

The blood ran to Donald's forehead at this, and he astonished himself by replying sharply, 'We have no chieftain. Lochiel's our chief.'

Mr Ogilvy lay back in his chair and smiled a friendly smile; his huge head nodding up and down slowly, as if it was afraid of overstraining the neck by which it was precariously supported.

'All right, Mr Cameron – all right, all right. I'm not so gyte as to ask questions that need not be answered. Do you know what "gyte" means?'

'N-no.'

'Where are you from, Mr Cameron?'

'Balspindie, in Buchan.'

Mr Ogilvy pulled out a vast scrap-album from a shelf of vast scrap-albums and examined it attentively. Then he said:

'Was Ewan Cameron your father?'

'Yes.'

'Ah! Then your mother was a Gordon from the family of William Gordon of Kinaldie? And William Gordon married an Allardyce who was the second cousin of the first wife of one of the Macleods of Assint? Let me see. Your father's father married a Kennedy from the region of Drumnadrochit, and she was half-sister to one of the Laggan Grants, the one who was drowned, you remember, in the great storm on Loch Lochy. Dear me! that's very interesting. And his father – your great-grandfather, Mr Cameron, was believed to have been born during or just after the rebellion—'

'The what?' exclaimed Donald, starting up.

'I beg your pardon, Mr Cameron. I profoundly beg your pardon. I should have said the Forty-Five. And that's all that is known about your family, except that your great-aunt Mary, who married a Fraser from Strathcarron, was so proud of her beautiful voice that she used to go to Mass late, in order that the congregation might notice the difference between the singing before and after her arrival.'

Mr Ogilvy closed the big album with a bang, just saving his chin from being caught by the clashing covers like the Argo escaping the Symplegades, and carefully replaced it on its shelf. Then he turned back to Donald and said:

'Well, Mr Cameron, and my good friend Mr Greig of the College Library tells me that you want to enter upon a literary career.'

Donald squirmed on his seat. The phrase 'a literary career' seemed to make him out to be a pretentious prig, especially when it was endowed by the Lanarkshire accent with more *r*'s than appeared phonetically possible. He had come south to try to support himself by 'writing', a much simpler and homelier ambition than the carving of literary careers. Mr Ogilvy went on.

'Mr Greig says that he is sure you have all the makings of a literary man.'

Donald squirmed again. Mr Greig was a highfalutin ass. But Mr Ogilvy's next words brought things to earth again.

'Well, maybe you have and maybe you haven't,' he went on drily. 'But there are two ways of finding out. Either go home and write something good – if it's good it will be published. There's a notion that publishers neglect good writers. They don't. They know their job. Either do that, or start in as a journalist.'

'That was my idea,' murmured Donald.

'Very good. Then you must try and get a job on a paper.'

'I thought of free-lancing,' said Donald, his voice sinking almost to a mumble. Again there was something priggish about the word 'free-lancing', an affectation of romantic, individualist dash, like a captain of Free Companies or a cavalry leader.

'Very good,' said Mr Ogilvy decisively. 'Free-lance and starve. Get a job and live. That's the rule in Fleet Street. Don't go and be silly. Now, I've been asked to find a man – an apprentice – for a paper, and if you like you can have the job. It'll be a good start for you.'

Donald opened his eyes. To stumble upon a journalistic job within the first few weeks of coming to London was an amazing bit of luck. Free-lancing could wait. He leant forward eagerly and murmured some words of gratitude.

'It's a small job,' said Mr Ogilvy, 'but it's a beginning, and in a few years, say three or four, you'll be qualified for a rise in the world. It's the usual thing – apprentice-reporter. That's how we all started. Would you like it?'

'I would love it,' replied Donald fervently.

'Good. It's on the *Glossop Evening Mail*—'

'On the what?' said Donald, his jaw dropping.

'The *Glossop Evening Mail*. Glossop. Town in Derbyshire.'

'But – but – I thought you meant a job in London,' faltered Donald.

'Young man,' replied Mr Ogilvy, 'London is half-way up the ladder. You must start on the lowest rung. Your niche is Glossop.'

Except for this mixing of metaphors, Donald remembered nothing more until he found himself on the stairs of the Carolean house in Royal Avenue, watching a swirl of pink ribbons and silks retreating swiftly – yet not too swiftly – into the modest shades of Gwladys' bedroom.

chapter 4

The third and last of Donald's letters of introduction was from the Italian lecturer to a Mr William Hodge, editor of the *London Weekly*, a paper which was entirely devoted to the Arts and, unlike Mr Ossory's, rigidly excluded politics from its pages. Before going to keep his appointment with Mr Hodge, the hour fixed by Mr Hodge's secretary being 'any time between 11 o'clock and five minutes to 1', Donald bought the current number of the *London Weekly* in order to make some sort of estimate of the character of the man he was going to meet. So far, he only knew Mr Hodge as the author of several books of poems, exquisite in words, severe in style, lofty in thought – a fastidious genius who published a poem seldom, a bad poem never. Donald was even more nervous at the prospect of meeting the poetical Mr Hodge than he had been at the prospect of meeting the enchanting Mr Ossory and the practical Mr Ogilvy. The former had only asked for an audience, an enchantee, so to speak; the latter had only wanted a victim for the altar of Glossop. The poet would require intelligence in anyone who was to gain his approval, and perception and intuition and fastidiousness. Donald wished he could quote Shakespeare aptly, or better still, Milton. Milton was more impressive, but fearfully difficult to do aptly. Shakespeare often came down to earth, Milton so seldom. But as Donald could quote neither, the difference between them hardly mattered. The best thing to do was to sit quiet and let Mr Hodge do the talking. But there again, there was a difficulty about that. Poets had an infernal habit, so Donald had always understood, of probing into people's characters, looking into their souls, 'laying bare their inmost thoughts', as a lady critic had once finely said of Coventry Patmore in the *Aberdeen Press and Journal*, and, in fact, asking a lot of difficult questions and expecting answers to them. Mr Hodge would be exceedingly angry and justifiably angry – if he took the trouble to lay bare Donald's inmost thoughts and found that Donald either resisted the process or, alternatively, had practically no inmost thoughts worth laying bare.

'The only thing to do,' said Donald unhappily to himself as he began to turn over the pages of the *London Weekly*, 'is to hope for the best.'

But his hopes, never very high, were diminished by his study of the journal. Each contribution to its columns added to his perplexity, and, at the end, he lay back in his chair in a daze. So far from arriving at a clear notion of Mr Hodge's personality, he was now completely befogged, and the only conclusion he could come to was that either Mr Hodge was away holiday-making, leaving behind him a most erratic staff, or else that the editorial chair was occupied by a syndicate to which Mr Hodge simply lent his name. Take the poetry, for instance. What consistent policy was there in printing three Shakespearean sonnets by one of the major Victorian Survivals, then a weird affair in chopped-up lines and no capital letters, all about violet-rayed bats in a-minor belfries, and then a ballade on the severe French model but with the refrain, 'I made a century in Zanzibar'? Or consider the prose articles. A critical commentary upon the new edition of Dryden was admirable; copiously footnoted, obviously authoritative. A page upon the new Shakespearean discovery in the Record Office (made by an American professor of course; only American professors ever go into the Record Office) was in the best vein of scholarship, even though the discovery itself – that Shakespeare's father had once sold a bale of hay to a man called Browne and had not been paid for it – was not of the first importance. But how could those two weighty contributions be followed by a short story of extreme flippancy about football? A page describing the developments of post-war Nordic architecture was good. But to devote a page and a half immediately afterwards to an apparently serious estimate of Mr Edgar Wallace's novels, in which Mr Wallace's technique was favourably compared to that of Dostoievsky, Mallarmé, and Pascal, seemed to the serious-minded Donald to be lunacy. To deplore the modern tendencies of the drama was one thing; to inveigh passionately against the proposed changes in the rules of billiards was surely another. And finally, the *London Weekly* was apparently doing its editorial utmost to raise funds for two causes – firstly, to save Stonehenge from being converted by a kind-hearted, sentimental Government into a canteen for welfare-workers among the neighbouring barracks; and secondly, to provide a purse which would enable a gentleman called Young Billy Binks to face all-comers at, or under, eight stone six at the National Sporting Club.

At the foot of the back page was this statement: 'Printed by the London Weekly Press, E.C.4, and published by Mr T. Puce. Subscription rates, Two pounds twelve shillings per annum. A subscription implies that this journal will be sent to the subscriber until one of the three expires.'

Donald mopped his brow, read the whole paper through again, and then went to bed and dreamt that he was lost in a maze of trenches in a thick fog on a cold winter's day. Next morning he dressed himself very carefully for his interview with the poet. He put on a very old pair of grey flannel trousers with a hole at one knee, a pair of purple woolly socks specially bought for the occasion, a pale blue jumper, and the old coat in which he used to farm the Mains of Balspindie, a big bow tie and a big black felt hat; and, on surveying himself in the glass, he decided that he looked exactly like the ladies and gentlemen who sat upon the high stools in the Cadogan Arms, King's Road, and asked each other in loud voices across the saloon bar whether Augustus John had been in lately. And what was correct for painting and sculpting obviously could not be far wrong for poetry.

A No. 11 omnibus took him from Sloane Square to Fleet Street, and at twenty-five minutes to 12 he presented himself at the office in Bouverie Street of the *London Weekly*.

'Go right in,' said Mr Hodge's secretary, a tall young lady with fair hair and pleasant manners. 'First door on your right.'

Donald timidly opened the door, was met with a clatter of voices, and hastily closed it again.

'I'm afraid Mr Hodge is engaged,' he ventured.

'Shouldn't be surprised,' replied the secretary indifferently. 'Go right in,' and she began to type with great dexterity.

'I think I'd better wait till he's disengaged,' he murmured. He had no desire to be introduced to what was probably a brilliant group of poets and essayists as a 'young man with literary aspirations' – for thus had the infernal librarian, who had seemed at the time to be so civil and appreciative – described him in the letter of introduction.

'Just as you like,' said the secretary absently.

After a few minutes Donald plucked up sufficient courage to ask how long it was likely to be.

'How long is what likely to be?' shouted the secretary above the clatter of the typewriter.

'Before he is disengaged?' said Donald, raising his voice a little.

'What?' roared the secretary, typing faster than ever.

'Before he is disengaged?' bellowed Donald bravely. Unfortunately the secretary, who was a kindly soul and perceived the young man's diffidence, stopped her manipulations of the keyboard just as Donald let out his gallant stentorianism and his shout echoed wildly through the building, rattling the windows and setting the electric light bulbs a-quiver.

'Wot's up?' said the office boy, shooting through the door like a rather grubby cherub in a religious play.

'Get out! ' said the secretary.

'Coo! ' said the cherub, getting out.

A small, neat, wizened man with a bowler hat cocked rakishly over one ear and a salmon-pink tie, poked his head round another door and observed roguishly:

'Six to four the field, eh? I'll have a dollar each way on Jolly Boy for the 3.30. Bung-o, young Isaacs,' and with this cryptic statement the wizened man winked twice and vanished.

Donald, blushing scarlet at his unfortunate predicament, was in far too great an agony of mind to grasp what the man had said, and the secretary obviously did not think it worth while grasping, for she tossed her head disdainfully and said:

'That's only Puce. Don't you mind him. As for William, he's never disengaged, so you might as well go in now as wait for a year.'

And before Donald could resist or protest, he was shoo'd and shepherded through the first door on the right into the presence of one of the first poets of the land. The room in which he found himself was long and narrow, uncarpeted and unfurnished except for a desk at the far end and three chairs. Four men were grouped round the desk, one lounging against the mantelpiece, one sitting on the desk itself with dangling legs, and two kneeling on two of the chairs. The third chair, a large leather-padded swivel, was occupied by Mr William Hodge himself, and the other men were obviously the circumference of a circle of which he was the centre.

Mr Hodge was a man of about forty. He was of medium height, squarely built, rather stout, a little bald, and he had a pair of brown eyes behind enormous horn-rimmed, powerfully lensed glasses. He was clean-shaven, or rather the last time he had shaved he had been clean-shaven. He was wearing patent-leather shoes, striped trousers, a morning coat, a grey waistcoat, a grey bow-tie, a huge pink carnation, and a grey bowler hat, and, at the moment when Donald came shuffling through the door, he was lying back in his swivel chair laughing uproariously. Indeed, all the men were laughing uproariously, and at the sight of the newcomer the laughter died away into a silence that made Donald wish he was dead. But the next moment he was saved by Mr Hodge himself, who jumped up, threw his grey bowler into a waste-paper basket, and came down the room to meet him.

'Mr Cameron,' he said, beaming at him through his colossal glasses. 'Come and sit down. How is my good friend of King's College Library?'

'He's sent you a letter,' stammered Donald, fumbling in his pocket, but Mr Hodge would have none of it.

'Don't bother about that,' he said. 'Letters of introduction are always silly and usually lies. "A friend's friend" is all that ever need be said. Let me introduce Mr Cameron, Mr Smith, Mr Walter, Mr Wilson, Mr Harcourt. Mr Cameron is another of these infernal Scotsmen. And I rather fancy he comes from the neighbourhood of Aberdeen.'

'I'm afraid I do,' admitted Donald, and the five men laughed heartily.

'There was once a man from Aberdeen——' said Mr Smith and they all laughed again. Donald joined in politely, being anxious not to appear provincial among these metropolitan wits.

'Well,' said Mr Hodge, 'the real question of the moment is not whether you have recently been engaged in your fellow-citizens' favourite pastime of outdoing Jews in business deals, but whether you play cricket?'

'Cricket?' said Donald, blinking.

35

'A game played with dice and counters,' put in Mr Harcourt. He was a tall, thin youth of twenty-four or five, and his poems were already famous.

'Shut up, Rupert,' said Mr Hodge benevolently. 'Do you play cricket, Mr Cameron?'

'I used to play years ago,' began Donald, and was interrupted by loud applause from the others.

'Splendid!' said Mr Hodge warmly. 'You're just the man we're looking for. I'm raising a side to play a village in Sussex. Saturday week.'

'But I haven't played for ages.'

'That doesn't matter two straws. A motor-bus will be at the Embankment entrance of the Underground Station at 10.15 on Saturday week. Do you bat or bowl?'

'Well, not really either—'

'Splendid. And now, what about a drink?'

'I've been saying that every five minutes since they opened,' said thin Mr Harcourt bitterly.

The party formed a sort of bodyguard round Mr Hodge's grey bowler hat and flocked downstairs. The poet paused beside his secretary's table and said, 'I'll be back in a quarter of an hour.'

'No you won't, William,' she replied without looking up.

'I assure you—' he began and then gave it up, and followed the others.

The Black Cat public-house was already crowded, although it was not yet 12 o'clock. Not since he had left the Army had Donald had a drink at such an early hour. Mr Harcourt appeared to think that much valuable drinking-time had been lost since 11.30.

Mr Hodge's party, appreciating the immense power of an organized minority, formed itself into a compact phalanx and quickly pushed its way to the counter, where it deployed to the right and left of the grey bowler, annexed all the available stools, and got down to business.

Donald, a pint mug in his hand, edged away to the extreme left of the line. The others were already deep in an argument about the comparative merits of two Rugby three-quarter backs, neither of whose names was familiar to Donald, and he was not anxious to push himself forward into the conversation. Gazing round through the already smoky atmosphere of the bar, his eye was caught by a figure which seemed familiar. It was the figure of a middle-aged man with a heavy iron-grey moustache and a heavy jowl. He was sitting by himself in a corner, drinking a whisky-and-soda and leaning his chin upon a large stick and gazing at the company. The more Donald looked at him the more certain he was that he had seen him before. This certainty was confirmed by the man's small but palpable start of surprise the first time that their eyes met. Donald quickly looked away, but on venturing a quick glance round the edge of his tankard a minute or two later, he saw that the man was no longer gazing at the company but was sitting back and frowning at the ceiling. Round of drinks succeeded round, and Donald had just disbursed the sum of seven shillings and a penny for five double whiskies for the five literary men and fourpence-halfpenny for a half-pint of beer for himself when he saw that the thick-set man in the corner was no longer frowning at the ceiling or anywhere else. He was smiling to himself in a complacent way, as a man is apt to do if he has accomplished something of which he is rather proud.

At 1 o'clock the bar of the Black Cat was filled almost to bursting-point, and thin Mr Harcourt announced that no gentleman could drink in such a damnable place, and suggested 'an adjournment' – a curious Parliamentary phrase, thought Donald – to the Pink Mouse in Something-or-other Alley. The others heartily concurred, and being now in the midst of a vigorous discussion about the language that Charlemagne spoke as his native tongue, they did not notice that Donald unobtrusively slipped away from them in the crowd and made for another exit. He had drunk quite as much beer as was good for him, and besides, it was looking as if it would be his privilege at the Pink Mouse to produce another seven shillings and a penny for his new friends and, if so disposed, another fourpence-half-penny for himself, so swiftly did the turns come round. And he only had elevenpence left in his pocket.

After the smoke and beer, the fresh air of Fleet Street, such as it was, hit him like a cold douche on the back of his neck, and he stood for a moment on the pavement, taking deep breaths of it. A pleasant voice at his elbow observed, 'I don't remember your name, but we shared a pill-box at Passchendaele.'

Donald spun round and faced the thick-set man.

'You're Davies,' he said at once, the whole scene coming back to him.

'That's right. How clever of you! And now I'm going to be clever. Your name's come back to me. It's Cameron.'

They shook hands warmly, and Davies carried Donald off to lunch and listened to the story of his experiences. At the end he said:

'You don't remember my suggestion in that infernal pill-box, I suppose?'

'I got concussion that same day,' said Donald apologetically, 'and I can't remember things very clearly.'

'I'm a publisher,' replied Davies, 'and I suggested you might try a book about England for us. England as seen through the eyes of a Scotsman. Would you like to have a shot at it? We could fix up for you to meet people – you know the sort of thing – typical Englishmen.'

'I'd love to have a shot at it,' said Donald doubtfully.

'Splendid. When can you start?'

'At once.'

'Good man. And look here,' added the publisher, 'I've got a small dinner-party tonight – just the sort of people who might be useful. Will you come along? Eight-fifteen?'

'I should like to very much.'

'Black tie. 74B Mount Street.'

And so it was arranged.

Just as they were parting outside the restaurant, Mr Davies said:

'Oh, by the way, since I saw you last I've found out something about the English. There are two things you must never, never rag them about. One is the team spirit in cricket. You must never suggest in any sort of way that there are any individuals in cricket. It's the highest embodiment on earth of the Team.'

'I must remember that on Saturday week,' said Donald. 'I'm

going to play for Mr Hodge. And what's the other thing you mustn't rag them about?'

'Lord Nelson,' said Mr Davies earnestly.

There were four other guests at Mr Davies' dinner-party that evening, and each of the four took a kindly interest in the diffident young stranger. Sir Ethelred Ormerode, M.P., vaguely invited him to play golf at Sunningdale; Sir Ludovic Phibbs, M.P., vaguely invited him to play golf at Walton Heath; Miss Perugia Gaukrodger devoted an hour and three quarters to him after dinner, describing with a wealth of minute detail the story of her rise to world fame, each step being measured in the net sales of her novels; and Lady Ormerode, M.P., firmly invited him to spend the following week-end at Ormerode Towers in the county of Surrey.

chapter 5

Next day Donald started to collect material for his book, and he decided to make a beginning with a study of Mr Hodge and his circle of friends. It was comparatively easy to find them every day, for Donald soon discovered that there was a definite tendency among them to rendezvous at one or other of the many taverns of Fleet Street between the hours of 11.30 and 1.30, and he found that with a little perseverance he could usually run them to earth. Once he had done so, he had only to perch himself unobtrusively upon a high stool on the outskirts of the group, and he could listen as long as he liked to the conversation of a brilliant circle of Englishmen. But the oftener he sat upon his high stool, drinking the small tankards of beer which were lavishly thrust upon him, and occasionally standing a round of drinks himself, the less he discovered about the genius of the English race.

Sometimes he tried, very timidly, to turn the conversation to subjects which would afford an opportunity for these men to illumine themselves and their race, but each time the result was a failure. It was not that they consciously dried up or avoided the mild traps which Donald baited for them. It was rather that one or other of them was absolutely certain to say something flippant about any subject within fifteen seconds of its being introduced, and the moment one became flippant they all became flippant, and the conversation fell into a chaos of laughter.

There was only one occasion on which Donald met a man who was not only prepared, but was eager, to talk seriously, and it cannot be said that Donald learnt from him anything that helped to clear up the fog in which he was groping.

It happened that one morning Donald entered the Dragon hostelry in Fleet Street at about a quarter to 12 and found one of Mr Hodge's group leaning moodily against the counter. He was a man of about thirty-five, a thick-set man of medium height, with a red face and red hands and an irresistible combination of vitality and impertinence. Donald had met him once or twice but had hardly ever spoken to him. The man recognized him, however, in a gloomy sort of way, and said, 'Have a drink. Flaming fish! but this is a stinking country.'

'A half-pint of bitter,' said Donald nervously. He was nervous partly because he thought the man looked positively ferocious, and partly because, for the first time since he had acquired the Fleet Street habit, Donald saw that he would have to bear a responsible part in the conversation.

'A half-pint of bitter,' said the man across the counter to no one in particular.

'A half-pint of bitter,' he repeated in a louder voice, and then, in a sudden whirl of rage, he seized an enormously thick walking-stick, or rather cudgel, which leant against the counter beside him, and struck the counter a terrific blow which set the glasses jumping and rattling, and shouted, 'Stinking fish! Is there no one here to serve a gentleman?'

A man in a black coat and striped trousers came up and said severely:

'You can't do that here, sir.'

'Can't I, by God!' was the spirited reply of the red-faced man, and he struck the counter another resounding blow. The managerial-looking person smiled a forced and sickly smile, and faded away.

'Scum!' said the red-faced man. 'Filthy, lousy, herring-gutted, spavin-bellied scum!'

Donald was surprised.

'What on earth is spavin-bellied?' he inquired.

'A disease of horses, common in all fog-ridden, disgusting, beer-drinking countries.'

'But I've never heard of it,' protested Donald.

'Do you know anything about horses?' demanded the man.

'I've done a good deal of farming—' began Donald, but the other interrupted him.

'Then in God's name let's talk about something else. Do you prefer crocodile or suède for fog-horn containers?'

'For what?' faltered Donald.

'For fog-horn containers. I've just lost mine beside the Mitcham Gasworks, and I've put an advertisement in the *Dog-Lover's World* and also in the *Battersea and East Putney Philatelist* to say that the Finder may keep it.' He gazed at Donald with tragic intensity.

Donald's brain began to go round in circles.

'But surely that was a waste of money,' he began. 'I mean, was it necessary to advertise, and why in a philatelic newspaper – I mean—'

The red-faced man looked as if he was about to burst into tears.

'You think the *Amalgamated Assistant-Laundrywomen's Gazetteer and Boomer* would have been a more attractive medium?' he asked lugubriously. Then he suddenly brightened, and went on before Donald could collect himself sufficiently to say anything: 'You are going to dispute my implied suggestion that any medium can be attractive. I think you're perfectly right. I hate all spiritualists myself.' He guffawed loudly and shouted: 'Beer! Steward, porter, miss, two gallon mugs of your perfectly beastly beer. What! no gallon mugs? God! What a country. All right. Two pints.' He turned again to Donald. 'I can't think why any of us live in this foul land. You can't get decent beer. You can't get decent food. You can't buy soft roes on toast after 8.15 or hard roes on biscuits between midday and

3.15. You can buy grated carrots after 11 but not mashed carrots, or sliced carrots or pinched carrots—'

'What is a pinched carrot?' asked Donald faintly.

'A carrot that has been pinched, of course,' was the answer, in a tone of dignified reproof. 'You can buy orange marmalade at dog-fanciers' shops, but not lemon marmalade. You can get synthetic Burgundy out of penny-in-the-slot machines in all tunnels under the Thames, but not synthetic Bordeaux. In short, England is a country of madmen, and only madmen live in England.'

There was a pause in the conversation while the man lowered his tankard of beer down his throat, and ordered two more, and waved aside Donald's proffered money.

'This is on me,' he said. 'It is the anniversary of Roland's death in the Valley of Roncesvalles. The world came to an end on that day. It has never really existed since. We must drink to my fellow-countryman who saved Europe in the Pyrenees a thousand years ago, just as that other fellow-countryman of mine saved Europe in the marshes of St Gond on the River Marne in 1914.'

'Do you mean Sir John French?' asked Donald.

The red-faced man became apoplectic. He swelled like a frog and his eyes appeared to become bloodshot. A queer, hoarse croaking issued from his lips. At last he managed to say, 'I mean Ferdinand Foch, Marshal of France,' and he stood to attention.

'I beg your pardon most profoundly,' said Donald in great distress. 'I had no idea – I mean your English is so perfect – is it really possible that you are a Frenchman?'

'My family name is Hougins,' replied the man with superb dignity. 'And there were Hougins in the Channel Islands a good long time before Duke Robert of Normandy cast his eyes upon the tanner's daughter.'

'No wonder that you are proud of your descent,' twittered Donald, anxious to make up for his unfortunate error, 'and of your fellow-countrymen too.'

'Yes,' replied Monsieur Hougins, 'when I consider how the French Army, the French nation, alone, single-handed, met the whole power of Germany, resisted it, drove it back, and finally destroyed it, I think I am entitled to be a little proud.'

'Single-handed?' said Donald, puzzled.

'Practically single-handed,' replied Monsieur Hougins negligently. 'There were some English troops on our left, I remember, and a Portuguese division somewhere in the centre, but I can't recall any others. Were there some Belgians?' He wrinkled his brow.

Donald began to feel angry.

'What about the British Navy?' he demanded.

'Ah yes, ships, to be sure,' said M. Hougins, as if he were talking about toys to a child. 'There were ships. They fought a battle too, so far as I can recollect the facts.'

Donald's warm retort was fortunately never uttered, as Mr Hodge and a bevy of talented youth came pouring at that moment through the swing-doors of the bar. Half an hour later Donald found the opportunity to ask Mr Hodge about the singular Frenchman. Mr Hodge laughed.

'Frenchman?' he said. 'He's no more French than I am. That's only Tommy's lunacy.'

'But he said his family name was Hougins.'

'So it is, in a sense. It's Huggins. Tommy Huggins, and he comes from Bolton. His great-grandfather was Mayor of Bolton about a hundred years ago.'

'But he sneered at the British Army,' protested Donald.

Mr Hodge laughed again.

'That's a favourite pose of his,' he said. 'He went to the War as an infantry Tommy and performed prodigies of valour.'

Donald went home thoughtfully. The problem which Mr Davies had set him to answer was deeper and darker than he had ever imagined. Indeed, if Mr Huggins was a representative Englishman, the problem was utterly insoluble. After some hours of concentrated thinking, Donald came to the conclusion that he must dismiss the pseudo-Channel Islander, and everybody like him, from his considerations. Mr Huggins must be a freak. If he isn't a freak, thought Donald, if all Englishmen are like that, I shall go mad. So, greatly relieved, he wrote down Mr Huggins as a freak and made up his mind to see as little as possible of him in the future. But if Donald had finished with Mr Huggins, Mr Huggins had by no means finished with him.

*

Donald was due at Godalming station at midday on Saturday, to be motored thence to Ormerode Towers, and at a little after 10 o'clock that morning he was standing in his room in Royal Avenue in a state of some perplexity. It was the packing that was the trouble, for he did not know what he was likely to need in addition to his evening clothes. While he was still puzzling over each individual item of his scanty wardrobe, he heard a loud shouting in the street, and, putting his head out of the window, saw that the great-grandson of the Mayor of Bolton, and descendant, perhaps, of a long line of Channel Islanders, was standing below.

'Hell's eggs!' cried Mr Huggins as he came up the stairs, 'but this is a flamingly lucky chance. I was roaring down the King's Road just now, pushing buses aside and stamping great holes in the pavement, when I saw a shop which advertised Corsican wine. Look!' he shouted, pushing his way past Donald into the bed-sitting room and producing a bottle of wine from each side pocket of a disreputable overcoat, 'Fleur de Maquis, by the bones of the Ramolinos. What are you hanging about for? Jump to it, lad, jump to it.'

'Jump to what?' asked Donald. He found it difficult sometimes to follow Mr Huggins' conversational methods.

'Corkscrew, boy; corkscrew and glasses.'

'But we can't drink at 10 o'clock in the morning,' Donald protested feebly.

Mr Huggins stared at him in amazement.

'Got a touch of the sun,' he observed in a meditative way. 'Very rare thing in London in early May. Must write to the *Lancet* about that,' and he pulled out a huge note-book and made an entry. Then he went back to the door and roared down the stairs, 'Hi! Mother Hubbard! Gloria Swanson! Garbo! Bring two corkscrews and a glass. Or two glasses and a corkscrew. Whichever you like.'

Gwladys, all of a flutter at the powerful masculine voice, came pattering upstairs with a tray, while the doors of the other bed-sitting rooms opened an inch or two, and nervous spinsters put out their heads to see if anyone was offering murder, arson, or rape.

44

Mr Huggins poured out two tumblers of Fleur de Maquis and drank one at a single gulp and refilled it.

'By the sun of Austerlitz! ' he cried, 'but that is the stuff. Hallo! What are you doing here?' and he gazed round at the confusion of haberdashery. Donald explained his difficulty, and Mr Huggins immediately drank off his second tumbler and became portentously serious.

'It's a very, very lucky thing for you,' he said, 'that you've got me here to advise you. I am probably the most expert adviser on week-end procedure between Staines and Burton-on-Trent; or, if you look at it from another angle – which you are fully entitled to do if you want to—' he added in a burst of generosity, 'between the Vale of the White Horse and Walton-on-the-Naze. People tell you one thing and people tell you another. But I'll tell you right. Now take Bill Hodge. He goes to week-end parties in his football shirt and white flannel trousers and pumps, and sends out the footman on Sunday morning to knock up the local chemist for a razor. Not right, Cameron, not right.'

Mr Huggins shook his head lugubriously and refilled his tumbler, and then uncorked the second bottle of Fleur de Maquis.

'Then there's Guy Mitcham – you know Guy? Ah! well, you haven't missed much – he takes a pale-blue dinner-jacket and diamond studs for the evening, and jodhpurs for the daytime though he's never been on a horse in his life. And Bobby Southcott, the boy novelist, takes a cold ham in case he gets hungry between meals, and a book on birth control.'

Mr Huggins' queer sense of humour was beginning to lose command of itself under the mellowing influence of the warm South, and he went on in a kind of sing-song chant: 'Verona Mimms, lady novelist, only takes a cold ham. She's younger than Bobby, but she's more experienced. Wilhelmina Poddleton, lady novelist, takes a lock of Freud's hair and a sea-green velvet gown. Ernestine Bunn, lady novelist, takes Young Woodleys and goes home sad on Mondays. Ravenna Rust, lady novelist – I say, Cameron, what on earth are you talking about?' he exclaimed with some warmth and slipped suddenly to the floor, where he remained as if nothing had happened.

'I hope you don't mind my interrupting you,' he went on, 'but I am in rather a hurry as I have an important engagement. I have to sit up tonight with a sick friend.'

'But don't you think – I mean, don't let me keep you – if your friend is unwell.' Donald was distressed at the thought that he might be trading upon Mr Huggins' good nature.

'Oh, he's all right now,' responded that gentleman airily. 'He won't be sick until he knows that I'm going to sit up with him tonight. To return. Pass me the Fleur. Thank you.' He settled himself comfortably against a table leg. 'Cameron, be guided by me. The crux of the week-end is the servant. Do you follow me?'

'N-no. Not quite.'

'I should have thought I had made my explanation foolproof,' said Mr Huggins severely, 'but apparently I haven't. Listen carefully. Get at the rich man's servant before he gets at you. Treat 'em rough and they're lovely. Treat 'em humble and they're hell. Attack, attack, attack, as my famous fellowcountryman observed at the something or other. You can fool all the lackeys all the time. That's what Foch told Aimée Semple McPherson at the Oddfellows Ball. Good-night, old chap. Thank me another time.' And Mr Huggins fell asleep with his head upon one of Donald's three clean dress-shirts.

'But you haven't told me what clothes to take,' cried Donald in despair, shaking him vigorously. Mr Huggins woke up and struggled uncertainly to his feet.

'I will now recite,' he remarked a little thickly, 'that soulstirring, tear-provoking epic, "The Dog that took the Serum to Alaska". Hullo! what's all this? My dear chap! Why didn't you ask me before? Clothes! that's the problem. And I'll give you the solution. Take all the clothes you've got. The more the better. Take one suitcase; the butler sneers, the footmen giggle, the under house-parlourmaids have hysterics. Take fifty and they'll treat you like the Duke of Westminster.'

'But I've only got two small suitcases,' objected Donald plaintively. 'I brought all the rest of my things from Scotland in a trunk and a valise. Besides, some of my things are so old that I couldn't possibly take them.'

Mr Huggins was seized with demoniac energy. He drained off Donald's glass. He routed out the two small suitcases. He rushed out of the house and roared at a passing taxi so that the windows shook, and rushed back in ten minutes with twelve second-hand suitcases that he had bought at a shop in Sloane Square, and a bundle of enormous labels and a pot of red paint, and started to pack all Donald's belongings into them. Donald's protests were overridden tempestuously. For instance, when he pleaded almost tearfully, 'I can't take a pair of grey flannels with a hole in the knee,' the invincible Mr Huggins whipped out a pair of scissors and instantly converted the trousers into shorts, exclaiming as he did so, 'There you are! Shorts for otter-hunting. Put them in the otter-hunting suitcase.'

An old football outfit was packed with the description, 'Beagling kit'. A battered bowler hat, two frayed dressing-gowns, a broken umbrella, odd shoes, books, newspapers, bits of rope, ornaments dearly beloved by Gwładys and her mother, photographs and pictures, were all crammed into another suitcase and labelled by Mr Huggins 'Amateur Theatricals', and one entire suitcase was filled with old newspapers and solemnly corded up and sealed and labelled, in huge scarlet letters, 'Dispatches; Secret'. It was useless for Donald to protest, for Mr Huggins paid no attention to him whatsoever. Nor was it possible to escape from this appalling accumulation of luggage by depositing it in the cloakroom at the station, for Mr Huggins insisted upon accompanying him to the station himself, and caused poor Donald agonies of embarrassment and confusion by engaging two porters to carry the Secret Dispatches, in addition to two others for the remaining packages, and by addressing Donald deferentially but loudly, all the time as 'Excellency'. Nor were Donald's apprehensions allayed by the last mysterious whispered words of his self-appointed and unwanted ally as the train steamed out, 'I'll fix that bloody butler. Trust me.'

chapter 6

If there is one social custom which distinguishes the Anglo-Saxon from the Latin, from the Slavonic, from the Basque, the Turanian, and the Greek, it is the Saturday-to-Monday hospitality in the country. In what are now usually called the spacious days before the War – indeed, they appear to be becoming almost as spacious as those presided over by Queen Elizabeth, which are well known to have been the widest on record – the hospitality lasted from Friday until Tuesday. But that is rare nowadays because everyone works on Saturday mornings except stockbrokers, and even they lose on the roundabouts. For their attendance upon mysterious things like kerbs, tickers, spot-markets, and contangos is always required so soon after dawn upon Monday mornings that they usually have to leave the week-end party on the evening of the Sunday. So that in the long run the Stock Exchange gains nothing even on the Foreign Office, even though the latter hums like a lodge of beavers from 11 to 1 on Saturdays. For the political world may blow up in a storm of cataclysmic convulsions between 1 on Saturdays and 11 on Mondays and the Foreign Office will take no official notice. Eleven o'clock is their hour for opening – like the pubs in Knightsbridge – because in the pre-railway days, also comparatively spacious in their own way, the couriers from Dover, however hard they spurred their horses and however often they changed their mounts, could never arrive in Whitehall with the Paris mail before 10.30 in the morning. So the letters, which were sorted at twenty to 11 and distributed to the departments at five minutes to, were ready for persual at 11 o'clock. And the routine which defeated the ungentlemanly General Bonaparte was good enough to defeat anyone else.

There are three main sources from which the student of sociology may learn about the English week-end, and Donald had, of course, examined them thoroughly. In the gospel according to the lesser lady novelists, he learnt that the Saturday-to-Monday period was invariably devoted by the entire house-party to profound and brilliant and soul-searing self-analysis. It seemed, from these works, that the English *fin-de-semaine*, when spent in sufficiently rural surroundings, was of an inspissated gloom, a tenebriferous melancholy, that made Strindberg's studies of demented lighthouse-keepers seem regular rollicks. Nothing ever happened except a fearful lot of heavy thinking and, from time to time, symbolical downpours of rain which gave scope for some beautiful English prose.

Donald had also learnt much about country-house life from the second source, the books of astonishingly brilliant young men, mostly about one-and-twenty years of age. These books, for some reason, were always on the same model. They began with life at Eton, or Harrow, in the proportion of about eighty of the former to twenty of the latter, and the first part invariably contained two descriptions. There was always a rather sardonic description of the Harrow match, or, in twenty per cent, the Eton match, and always a description of a small boy being whipped by a larger boy. It is only fair to say that the whippings were usually put in at the urgent request of the publishers; for it is a well-known fact that a really good piece of flogging in the early chapters of a novel sells between four and five hundred extra copies.

After these two routine preliminaries, the scene automatically moves in these books to the week-end party, and there the hero, his contempt for cricket having been duly flaunted and his injured posterior healed, finds himself in surroundings that are worthy of him and his brilliance. Arriving at the Norman manor of Faulconhurst St Honoré at midday on Saturday, he drinks absinthe cocktails and exchanges dazzling epigrams until luncheon with others of his own age and brilliance, all about the Hollowness of Life, the Folly of the Old, the Comicality of the War, the Ideas of the Young, the Brilliance of the Young, the Novels of D. H. Lawrence, the Intelligence of the Young, the Superiority of Modern Photography over Velazquez, and the Futility of People of Forty. After luncheon, which consists of quails and *foie gras* and sparkling Burgundy, with sherbet for the teetotallers, the pomegranates and persimmons and a glass of Advocaat, there are more epigrams until cocktails again at 4.30, and finally the exhausted epigrammatists retire to their virtuous couches at about 3, to rise again at noon on Sunday for a breakfast of aspirin and absinthe, and another day of brilliance.

And finally, Donald had studied the third school of week-end novelists, one of whose leaders was the Mr Southcott to whom Mr Huggins had so disrespectfully referred. Mr Southcott's idea of a country-house week-end was very different from the school of Analysis, or of Aspirin and Absinthe. According to Mr Southcott, life from Saturday to Monday in great country mansions was quite another affair. There were no deep thinkers, wondering 'what it all meant'. Nor were there young men and maidens – or indeed by the Monday morning any maidens – who sat up in billiard-rooms and mah-jong-rooms and smoking-rooms, wasting precious time in verbal felicities. All the young ladies were slim, all were exquisitely gowned, and all had lovely long legs 'encased in the thinnest of silken stockings'. All were seductive, and all were, in due course, seduced. Never were there such goings-on, in the immortal words of Mr George Robey, as in these weekends; never were there such soft words, such blandishments, such delicate, and always successful, woo-ings; never were there such white shoulders or bright eyes, never such satiny chemises, such crumpled gardenias, such bouncings-about upon tiger-skin divans.

Mr Southcott's sales were enormous, and his school of admiring imitators did pretty well too.

Lady Ormerode was a remarkable figure in Society. A Canadian of humble parentage (or rather it was humble until old Milton Carraway, an ex-saloon-keeper, brought off a capital merger in light beers miles away back in the nineties, and retired with a packet), Adelaide Carraway had taken London Society not by storm, but by sapping her way from bastion to bastion, from trench to trench, enfilading, undermining, breaching, and always consolidating each barbican, ravelin, redan, counterscarp and glacis before moving on to the next, conscious of her own magnificent blonde beauty, and pinning her faith to her undauntable tenacity and her seven million pounds. Thus between 1902, the year when she opened her parallels, to continue the Vaubanesque metaphor, and the time of Donald Cameron's timid arrival in London, Addy Carraway had achieved a lot. For one thing she had married in 1903 Sir Ethelred Ormerode, a gay young baronet from whose unflagging pursuit the Gaiety Chorus had only turned away a contemptuous galaxy of noses because of the extreme shortness of his purse. For another, she had redeemed the mortgage on Ormerode Towers, a superb mansion in which not merely Elizabeth, but Bloody Mary herself had once passed the night, and had startled England with the quiet luxury of her entertainments in that majestic pile. Then she had pushed Sir Ethelred into Parliament, into the Athenaeum, into the local Ruri-Decanal Conference as parish delegate, on to the Royal Commission on the Sterilization of the Insane, on to the Commission of the Peace, and, during the War, into the Chairmanship of a Recruiting Tribunal. For all of which activities Sir Ethelred got an M.V.O. 3rd class, a C.H., and, after the War, an M.B.E.; and, of course, a good whack at the seven million pounds. Lady Ormerode had financed Grand Opera; she had 'backed' highbrow plays; she had her portrait painted every year by the newest R.A. She hunted, shot, fished; she raced at Cowes and Newmarket; she subscribed to charities; and during the War she equipped a hospital for officers and received a D.B.E., a French medal, a Belgian medal, six Serbian, one Greek, and one Roumanian medal, and a Silver Garland from one of the Central American Republics, the Minister of which took refuge in the hospital, which was situated near the Admiralty Arch, on the occasion of one of the Zeppelin raids upon Sheerness.

After the War, the redoubtable Addy had conquered new fields. She herself entered politics and won a seat in the House of Commons as a Die-hard Conservative. But she soon found that there was more scope for originality in championing, from time to time, the working classes, and she startled many of those who had thought that they knew 'dear old Addy' inside out, by declaring publicly that she was against the shooting of all those who had led the Coal Strike of 1926. But dear old Addy lost no friends by this outspoken Bolshevism. Indeed it was not until she went too far and said, at a garden fête to raise funds for a local Conservative Association near Farnham, that she was also against the policy of shooting Mr Gandhi, that her right-wing friends felt that they could no longer meet her upon the same old terms of friendly intimacy.

But if Addy shed her Winstons in ones and twos, she picked

up her Epsteins and her Gauguins in scores by her unceasing and open-handed and catholic patronage of the arts.

No one could deny that she was catholic. Lady Ormerode, M.P., was not the one to entertain narrow prejudices. She gave a thousand guineas to a fund to buy yet another Titian for a National Gallery that has already plenty of Titians, and, in the same week, financed a one-man exhibition of sculpture at the Leicester Galleries by a Kaffir from the Belgian Mandated Territory of Ruanda-Urundi, in which the now-famous group of three interlocked triangles of varnished ferro-concrete, representing Wordsworth's Conception of Ideal Love, was seen for the first time in London. The masterpiece of the exhibition was a vast cylinder of Congolese basalt which was called, and rightly called, 'The Spirit of Bernhardt', and which was dedicated to the President of the French Republic, and which, furthermore, was formally unveiled by the French Ambassador in the presence of eleven London correspondents of provincial papers, a man from the Press Association, the editor of the *Quarterly Sculptor*, and the Liberian Chargé d'Affaires. And no one could say that it was Lady Ormerode's fault that this work of art was described in the catalogue as 'The Spirit of Bernhardi', thus causing dismay and despondency upon the Latin bank of the Rhine and jubilation upon the Teuton, where the name of General Bernhardi occupies an honourable place among the experts whose prophecies, theories, and preachings about the art of war have long been completely discredited.

Nor did the French, usually so gallant, come well out of the subsequent controversy, for the only counter which they could find to the Teuton argument that the spirits of Bernhardi, of Hindenburg, of the Vaterland itself, are all like solid cylinders of basalt, was that Madame Bernhardt, in her later years, was just as solid a cylinder as any dirty little Prussian general.

In the same spirit of catholicity, Lady Ormerode in one year paid for the entire regilding of the roof of the Albert Hall, for the mending of all the broken windows in the Crystal and Alexandra Palaces, and offered to stand the whole racket of 'doing up', in her own good-hearted words, 'the Stones in that Henge of theirs that they're always talking about'.

Such, then, was the Lady of Ormerode Towers who was to be Donald's hostess for the weekend.

A Rolls-Royce met the train at Godalming, and Donald felt like bursting into tears as suitcase after suitcase emerged from the station. He was too miserable to notice the subtle increase of deference with which each piece of luggage was greeted by the chauffeur and footman. The station-master himself attended with his own hands to the Secret Dispatches, murmuring discreetly in Donald's ear, 'I was warned by telephone, my lord, from our Head Office.' He was charmed by Donald's unassuming manner and his half-crown.

Just before it reached the front door of Ormerode Towers, the Rolls-Royce loosed several melodious toots upon the summery air, obviously a prearranged signal, and half a dozen flunkeys came tumbling down the broad steps followed, with great majesty, by the butler. As Donald disentangled himself from the huge fur rug with which the chauffeur had insisted upon enveloping him, and scrambled out of the mammoth automobile, the butler sidled up to him respectfully and whispered in his ear, 'The Secretary of the French Foreign Ministry rang up, sir, and Budapest has also been on the line. Budapest is to telephone again, sir.'

Donald was completely staggered by this information until he reflected that this must be Mr Huggins' amiable method of 'fixing that bloody butler'. He wondered, with a sinking heart, what other steps that eccentric individual was likely to take in order to smooth his week-end path, and he heartily cursed the entire family of Huggins, whether from Bolton or from Sark, and the purple-bubbled wine of Corsica. But he could not deny that so far Mr Huggins had been successful in securing vicarious deference from proud menials.

It was not long after midday when Donald arrived and the house-party was walking in the grounds, except those who were upstairs writing letters. The butler sent the fourteen suitcases upstairs, by the hands of the wondering footmen, and indicated to Donald that he could hardly do better than examine the illustrated papers in the gigantic entrance-hall, and drink a bottle of iced lager. Donald timidly agreed and sat down in a discreet corner and gazed round. Though it was the first time he had actually been in one of these superb lounge-halls with their sofas and divans and pouffes and cigarette-boxes and gramophones and wireless sets and tantaluses and tennis racquets and golf clubs, nevertheless he had had the opportunity of studying their appurtenances from the stalls on nineteen out of the twenty-one occasions on which he had visited the theatre during the war, and therefore was thoroughly familiar with them. The only feature which was lacking at Ormerode Towers, but which had not been lacking in the nineteen scenes, was the long French windows without which no English dramatist dares to face his audience.

The house-party returned just before 1 o'clock, and Lady Ormerode was delighted to see him. She introduced him to the crowd of guests, who all looked exactly like each other to Donald's confused glances, and then took him aside for a moment. 'The Duke of Devonshire has been on the telephone,' she whispered confidentially, and with a subtle bending from her massive hips that conveyed even more deference than the butler's more unreserved obeisance. 'You are on no account to telephone him, but you are to go to Chatsworth in time for luncheon on Monday, and to say nothing to anyone.' She laid a beringed finger on her lips and nodded wisely, as if to convey that she too knew what was what, and all that sort of thing.

By tea-time a good deal of Donald's shyness had worn off, and he had been able to disentangle the identities of his fellow-guests from one another. For his particular purpose – the first-hand study of the English people – no set of guests could have been more suitably chosen. Lady Ormerode's catholicity of taste extended to her week-end parties, and her friends had practically nothing in common with each other except their genuine affection for their hostess.

As that Saturday afternoon was extremely wet, Donald had a heaven-sent opportunity for collecting material of the utmost value for his book. And, for a time at least, it would be quite true to say that Mr Huggins' diabolical activities on the telephone were of definite assistance to him. For instance, after lunch, an elderly man whose face with its heavy brown moustache seemed familiar, and who was wearing a grey morning coat that was more beautifully built than any coat Donald had ever seen or imagined, with a superb orchid in one buttonhole and a foreign decoration in the other, slipped an arm through his with a bluff, jovial 'You're the boy I want to see', and led him off to a distant drawing-room down many corridors, talking heartily as he went about greyhound-racing. But as soon as he had got Donald into the distant drawing-room his jolly manner changed into a confidential knowingness.

'Boy,' he said, 'you know me. Everyone knows me. That's my ticket. Now, can you tell me anything?'

He looked at Donald as a kindly uncle might look who was taking a small nephew round the Zoo – an uncle who obviously knows everything that there is to know. Donald, who had lunched well and who did not know that Lady Ormerode's whisky was of pre-war strength, found that he was able to reply to this mysterious opening, 'Surely there's nothing I can tell you about anything.'

'Ah!' replied the man thoughtfully, 'so that's how it stands, does it? Nothing has moved since Tuesday?'

This rather shook Donald.

'What do you mean by nothing?' he asked. The man tapped his waistcoat with a roguish air, as of one man of the world to another.

'That's it,' he said. 'That's what I keep on telling 'em, the blasted monkeys. But they won't see it. Can you beat it?'

'Er – no,' Donald replied hesitatingly but truthfully. It was an intriguing conversation, but somewhat cryptic; and although he longed to know who the monkeys were and why they were blasted and by whom, he longed even more to escape. But the beautifully dressed man pushed a thick forefinger into his buttonhole, and, lowering his voice, whispered, 'Will it go?'

'Go? Go where?'

'I see,' replied the other, which was a great deal more than Donald did, and again, 'I see'; and then, 'Well, I never really thought it would,' and then, to Donald's intense relief, he burst into joviality again, clapped Donald heartily on the back with the words, 'I won't deny I'm sick about it, but there, are we down-hearted? That's my ticket,' and went out of the room quickly.

Donald, completely bewildered, made his way back to the central hall where a lot of bridge was in progress. In one corner the mysterious man with the orchid was talking in eager whispers to a younger man with a beautifully silky moustache and an Old Etonian tie.

It was when Donald discovered, later on in the evening, that his *tête-à-tête* in the distant drawing-room had been with one of the most famous of England's Labour leaders, that he realized for the first time what a unique chance of studying England Lady Ormerode's invitation was giving him. For the Right Honourable Robert Bloomer, M.P., was not only a former President of the Trades Union Congress and for thirty-five years Secretary of the Amalgamated Union of West End Journeymen Tailors, Hem-stitchers, and Cutters, but he was also an ex-Secretary of State. Donald hastily got out his note-book and jotted down his impressions of this famous man, but he was bound to admit that he still did not know what on earth the famous man had been talking about.

He had hardly finished his notes when a young lady of remarkable beauty and elegance came swinging into the hall and came straight across to the sofa, on the edge of which he was perched, and coiled herself down beside him. If Bob Bloomer's homely face was known to thousands, the loveliness of Esmeralda d'Avenant was an inspiration to millions. Theatre-goers adored her at Daly's, the Winter Garden, Drury Lane. Film-fans worshipped her from Pole to Pole. She had the most dazzling smile and the best publicity man in the English-speaking world, and her legs, which, though excellently shaped, were not more noticeably alluring than the legs of many a humble shop-girl or typist, were always insured for ten per cent more than Mistinguett's. Again Donald thanked his stars that he had been invited to Ormerode Towers, for Esmeralda d'Avenant was as typical of a branch of English art as Bob Bloomer of a branch of English labour. And here she was, this exquisite lady, snuggling down between a lot of black satin cushions beside him, actually beside him, on a sofa. Donald was thrilled. Shy and modest though he was, he felt a warm glow steal over him at the flattering thought that this miracle of beauty had selected him, Donald Cameron, out of all that brilliant house-party to honour with her fragrant presence and her radiant smile.

He even began to wonder, so subtle, so irresistible is the flattery of a beautiful woman to every man who ever lived except that superlative boob, St Anthony, which was the particular quality that he possessed that had first attracted the attention of this dragonfly. He wondered what he had said or done. He soon found out. Nothing. It was that infernal Mr Huggins who had been saying and doing. For as soon as Esmeralda had snuggled herself into a graceful attitude, had shaken her long Spanish earrings clear of her short English hair, had drawn up her quite-well-shaped and million-pound legs into a position that complied with the rules of decorum and yet at the same time wrecked the peace of mind and concentration of an Anglo-Indian Major-General across the hall who was desperately trying to create three no-trumps where God had only created two, she looked up at him and said murmurously, 'You are Donald, aren't you? I've got a message for you. Ivor Novello has just telephoned from Hollywood to say that he quite agrees with you, but you're to say nothing now.'

'Is that all he said?' exclaimed Donald, mixing up realities and Mr Huggins for a moment.

'You were expecting more?' purred the siren admiringly. She adored film magnates.

'Oh well, perhaps not,' he conceded, and he relapsed into a state of complete vacuity.

Esmeralda thought she had never seen a film magnate assume so cleverly an expression of innocence. Most of the ones she had had anything to do with were far from innocent. They had, indeed, prided themselves upon their cunning. 'You can't get past me' had been the slogan of Mr Sonnenschein. 'You get up early, but I'm up all night' was emblazoned in letters of gold on the ancestral scutcheon of the Brothers Zinzembaumer, while the senior partner in the firm of Snigglefritz, Snigglefritz, Maclehose & Snigglefritz, specialists in high-art films about Joachim du Bellay, Ronsard, Villon, and Pico della Mirandola, used as his favourite expression, 'Hot Ziggety Dam! I'm sure the hot dog'. This assumption of nervous *naïveté* by one who received telephone calls from Ivor Novello in Hollywood as if they were calls from ordinary people, baffled and piqued and allured Esmeralda. She shot a dark glance from under her lashes at Donald. He paid no attention. She raised her head a little upon its alabaster column and opened her great eyes upon him for a moment. He neither wilted nor blushed. Esmeralda was not accustomed to this sort of thing. She called up her reserves, regardless of the bitter glances of the Major-General's wife – for the Major-General had twice led out of the wrong hand, had revoked once, and had gone down 650 points above the line whereas he ought to have made two no-trumps without the slightest difficulty, and the Major-General's wife, who had not lived in Indian hill stations for nothing, knew exactly why all this had happened – Esmeralda called up her reserves, gave an unconscious hitch to her skirt, and exhibited another seventy-five pounds' worth of leg, and leant forward seductively, turning her full battery of dark eyes upon the doomed youth. No one had ever made the faintest show of resistance against her on the rare occasions on which she had brought that particular attitude into action. She had tried it on old Sonnenschein and he had raised her salary twenty thousand dollars a month on the spot and asked her to be his mistress. As soon as he had signed the contract for the former she had naturally, being a decent English girl – the daughter of a parson, too, called Jukes, who had a cure of souls near Daventry – refused the latter. She had also tried it upon the old Duke of Dorchester, at his house in Grosvenor Square, and the old Duchess of Dorchester, who had been watching through a moth-hole in a thirteenth-century tapestry, had been carried, screaming, to a private nursing-home behind Cavendish Street. Esmeralda once told an intimate friend of hers – Cristal Arlington of Daly's, the Winter Garden, and Drury Lane – that if she had only had a chance to try it on the Crown Prince of Germany there would not have been a war. It was, in effect, her *chef-d'œuvre*, and it brought into action simultaneously her dark liquid eyes, her legs, her slender hands, her graceful arms, her Spanish earrings, and a suggestion of a white and soft bosom. 'Poor young man,' she thought, as she blew the metaphorical whistle and the metaphorical troops went over the top, for Esmeralda was a kind-hearted soul and hated using unnecessary violence, 'Poor young man.'

But to her astonishment the object of her attack and her commiseration paid no attention to her dark liquid eyes, her slender hands, and graceful arms; he did not look at her legs (the Major-General, gallant as ever, had upset the card-table and was making no pretence at picking up the cards); he did not throw so much as a glance at the suggestion of white and soft bosom. Instead, he looked straight in front of him, rose to his feet and exclaimed, 'Blast that bloody Huggins! ' and walked out of the lounge into the rain.

Esmeralda was thrilled. Never had she met such an unusual film magnate. Never had she met such an iron man, such devastating sex appeal. 'If he had been the Crown Prince of Germany,' she said to herself as she watched Donald marching out, 'there would have been a war,' and she could have paid him no higher compliment.

Donald hid in his room for the rest of the afternoon, and his self-confidence was only restored by the extraordinary respect shown him by the footman who had been detailed to look after him. At 6.30 that functionary knocked at his door and came in with a very large cocktail-shaker and a glass upon a tray, and coughed once or twice unobtrusively.

'I beg your pardon, sir,' he said timidly, when Donald looked up, equally timidly, from his book, 'but I've brought you a cocktail, sir, if it won't interfere with your training, sir.'

'My what?' said Donald, his brain beginning to reel.

'Your training, sir,' repeated the flunkey, looking like a priest who has suddenly been ushered into the presence of his Deity. 'They rang up, sir,' he added, and then broke off under the stress of Donald's fearful scowl.

'Who rang up?' Donald asked in a voice that was as near a bark as he had ever got in the course of his mild and gentle life.

'The Chelsea Football Club,' sir,' replied the lackey, and then, the Man triumphing over the Livery, he went on with a rush, 'Oh Mr Wilson, sir, I'm proud to be looking after you, sir,' and then he lowered his voice to a reverent whisper and concluded, 'The finest centre-forward in the world! ' and backed out of the room.

*

The company sat down seventeen to dinner, one chair being vacant. There was Lady Ormerode at one end of the table and Sir Ethelred, looking like a rather subdued and worried Regency buck, a Corinthian who has accidentally swallowed a bodkin, at the other. The guests were, beginning on Sir Ethelred's left, and going round with the port:

Miss Perugia Gaukrodger, the lady novelist of Mr Davies' dinner-party. Miss Gaukrodger's novels were mostly about suppressed desires, and were written in a style that made even the simplest of actions seem perfect monstrosities of abnormality. Her sales were much larger in Paris, where the police are notoriously lax in their moral outlook, than in London, but her fame in both capitals was immense. Sir Ethelred hated her because he knew she had been placed on his left in order to prevent him getting Esmeralda.

Next was Porson W. M. Jebb, a young man whose father had cherished the ambition of seeing his son become one of the great classical scholars of the age. Filled with a love of the classics himself, and inspired by the happy coincidence that had given him the same surname as one of the immortals of scholarship, Mr Jebb, senior, had christened his son Porson after another of the immortals. It was some consolation, as Mr Jebb, senior, often used to say with a sigh, that even if Porson did fail at the Winchester entrance examination, even if he was superannuated from Eton after four successive failures in 'Trials', even if he was ploughed six times in Smalls, nevertheless no one could deny that he was the finest amateur batsman in the world, and that his hundred and sixty-one before lunch in the Sheffield Test Match against Australia was a masterpiece of classic batsmanship. 'Only I had hoped for a different sort of classics,' he used to add mournfully. As for Porson, much of his time and energy was spent in concealing from the world that the initials W. M. in his name stood, lamentably, for Wilamowitz Möllendorff, so intense an admiration had the misguided Mr Jebb, senior, for the mighty Prussian scholar; although, had Mr Jebb, junior, only known it, it was only by the narrowest squeak that he did not get Hermann and Schliemann as well. His only topic of conversation was cricket.

Next to Mr Porson Jebb was a niece of the host, Patience

Ormerode. She was about twenty years of age, and had ivory-coloured cheeks, orange lips, thin, blackened eyebrows, close-cut hair, pale pink ears and purple finger-nails. She smoked all through dinner what are sometimes even now called Russian cigarettes because they are rolled in brown paper and stamped with the two-headed eagle of Tsardom. She was wearing a black frock which terminated in a sheaf of whispy, petal-shaped flounces, and was in no way disconcerted when, half-way through dinner, she deduced from a gleam of pale pink above her stocking that she had forgotten to put on any knickers. She had no topic of conversation and only one adjective at a time. At the moment the adjective was 'grisly'.

Beyond her was the man with the silky moustache. His name was Captain de Wilton-ffallow and he was Conservative member for a South of England constituency. Just before dinner he had taken Donald aside and said, 'Bloomer told me your news.' 'What news?' muttered Donald, looking wildly round for a means of escape. Captain de Wilton-ffallow had nodded approvingly and said, 'You can keep your mouth shut. Good man.' The gallant captain – his military rank was one of those which had mysteriously survived into the days of peace; some have survived, others have not, and no one knows the reason – obviously regarded discretion as a cardinal virtue, for he hardly said a word all through dinner, greatly to the disappointment of the enchanting Esmeralda, who sat on his other side and vastly admired his silky moustache. In fact she found the dinner rather dull, for her left-hand neighbour was the Major-General, and he, poor veteran, was ill at ease. He was also a Conservative Member of Parliament, and he had soldiered on veld and kopje, on Himalayan hill-sides, on Chinese rivers, on burning plains and deserts, and had even, once or twice, visited front-line trenches, or at any rate got as far as battalion headquarters. He knew how to deal with Boers and Pathans and Waziris and Afridis and Chinks and Bolshies and hecklers, and, in fact, with every sort of nigger and dago. And, for he had not neglected the recreational side of a warrior's life, he knew how to flirt with a pretty girl. But he did not know how to flirt with a pretty girl under the eyes of Mrs Major-General who was sitting opposite. For Mrs Major-General knew a thing or two about her warrior's character and she did not trust him an inch. So the Major-General fidgeted, and Esmeralda yawned, and laid plans for vamping Donald into giving her the lead in his new film, and longed to put Patience Ormerode across her knee and give her a quick six with the back of a hair-brush.

On the other side of the hero of Spion Kop, the Khyber, and the Yang-tse-Kiang was a very rich and very plain woman of about thirty-five, whose three specialities were motor-racing, lovers, and giggling. She screamed with shrill laughter at the extremely dubious conversation of the Right Hon. Bob Bloomer, thus causing at least one oasis of sound in the silent desert on that side of the table. Lady Ormerode had the ex-Secretary of State on her right, and on her left, on the strength of the invitation to Chatsworth, Donald.

Next to Donald was the portly wife of the warrior. She drank whisky and soda and, with a vigilant eye upon her spouse, told Donald a good many times that no one could really understand the Indian problem unless they had actually lived there, and that the only solution of the difficulty, now that the initial blunder of not hanging Mr Montagu and Lord Chelmsford years ago had been irrevocably committed, was to let the natives try another Mutiny and then show them what was what. 'A few soldiers like my Horace,' she said quite a number of times, 'ought to be given a free hand. That is what they want,' and she looked across at her Horace in a way that implied that if ever he tried the free-hand business he would get such a fearful clip across the ear. 'Blast them from the guns,' she said, glaring at the superb Esmeralda, and then she went on to describe station life at Landi-Kotal, Quetta, Peshawur, Secunderabad, Amritsar, and Amballa.

Beyond her was a very handsome Polish count who did not speak English, and he had been placed beside a beautiful Russian princess who also did not speak English (greatly to Esmeralda's relief, for the Russian really was lovely) so that they could talk to each other. Unfortunately, the Russian lady's grandfather had, shortly after the regrettable incidents of 1863, caused the Polish count's grandfather to walk all the way to Siberia, an exercise in pedestrianism which the latter had bitterly resented; and furthermore, the Polish count knew, and the

Russian princess knew that he knew, that she was not a princess at all but only a baroness, and had attained the higher rank by the quaint old custom of self-promotion that has always been common among aristocrats in exile. The result was that, although they could have conversed with equal fluency in Polish, Russian, German, or French, they preferred not to recognize each other's existence, and the Major-General told Bob Bloomer that Slavs were always very reserved people.

Next to the princess was an empty chair and beyond that again an American lady called Mrs Poop, whose husband was the senior partner in the well-known stockbroking firm of O. K. Poop and Artaxerxes Tintinfass, Inc. Patience Ormerode's brother, Charles, sat next to her. He was at Trinity College, Cambridge, and he had no topic of conversation and only one adjective at a time. At present it was 'grisly'.

And finally, on Sir Ethelred's right was a Miss Prudence Pott, a Labour M.P.; a woman of painstaking industry, of sterling worth, and of extreme dullness. Sir Ethelred hated her, for he knew that she had only been placed on his right in order to prevent him getting Esmeralda.

These were the people who sat down to dinner at Ormerode Towers that Saturday evening, and Donald reflected that all over England similar parties were sitting down to similar meals in the Week-End Cottages, the Houses, the Mansions, the Manors, Granges, Towers, Courts, Halls, and Abbeys of England.

Lady Ormerode was very worried about the empty chair. She kept on saying plaintively, 'It's just like Rupert. Now I ask you, isn't it just like Rupert?' but as no one knew which Rupert it was out of all the Ruperts that it might have been, no one was able to answer the question for her.

It was not until the woodcock and the *Nuits St Georges* were being simultaneously served that the missing Rupert arrived. He was not in the least disconcerted at being late; not in the least disconcerted by the glittering scene of cut crystal, diamonds, white waistcoats, and feminine loveliness; not in the least disconcerted by the fact that he was wearing old army field-boots, riding-breeches, and a corduroy jacket. But then, as Donald reflected, that was not at all surprising, for the missing Rupert was none other than his friend of the Fleet Street pubs – Mr Harcourt, the poet. Furthermore, Mr Harcourt the poet had been, even to the most charitable eye, drinking. His eye was glittering and roving; his face wore a healthy flush; his manner was assured; and there was a devilish look of mischief about his whole jaunty demeanour. Donald, who was only just beginning to recover from the impact of Mr Huggins, felt a little dizzy. The Major-General glared at the newcomer's costume and muttered something about the Willingdon Club in Bombay.

Lady Ormerode was delighted, Sir Ethelred cold; Miss Perugia Gaukrodger smiled effusively, for Mr Harcourt did a good deal of influential reviewing; Captain de Wilton-ffallow gazed disapprovingly and shut his lips tightly, and was extremely put out when Mr Harcourt saw him and called out genially, 'Hallow, ffallow, how's the coffee swindle?' and Bob Bloomer, tactless as ever, shouted, 'Why, de Wilt, are you in the coffee ramp?' and Captain de Wilton-ffallow, who actually was concerned in the prospective coffee merger but did not know that anyone knew it, blushed furiously.

The Polish count and the Russian princess looked at the corduroy coat and simultaneously said 'Mon Dieu!' and then scowled at each other. Miss Patience Ormerode lit a brown-paper cigarette and murmured 'Grisly!' As it turned out, it was rather an unfortunate remark, for Mr Harcourt with an ineffably sweet smile replied, 'If I'm grisly, you're bare, so we're well matched,' and then turned to talk to his hostess. The Right Honourable Bob Bloomer laughed till he choked, and Esmeralda though that Mr Harcourt was rather sweet.

Mr Harcourt drank a glass of burgundy and looked round the table. There was a lull in a conversation that had never been very brisk. 'What a damned dull party,' he observed blandly. 'How are the lovers, Esmeralda? Going strong?'

The Major-General coughed ferociously and muttered something about the Byculla Club in Bombay. Again it was an unfortunate remark, for Mr Harcourt's quicksilver wits grasped the implication. He leant back and addressed the Right Honourable Mr Bloomer:

'Well, Bloomer, I hear we're going to clear out of India at last.'

Mr Bloomer was surprised. He hadn't heard about it.

'Oh yes, it's quite true,' went on Mr Harcourt, 'though of course it hasn't been officially announced yet. The Indian Civil is going to be abolished and no Englishman is to hold higher rank in the Army than colour-sergeant. And the word Sahib is to be forbidden,' he added, seeing that the Major-General's eyes were already bulging out of their sockets.

'Dear me!' said Esmeralda, with a yawn. Patience Ormerode started to give it as her considered opinion that it was all very grisly, but remembered in time and stopped.

Sir Ethelred said that the trouble about the English was that they were too modest. After all, they were admittedly the finest governors in the world, so why didn't they just go on governing? The Major-General exclaimed 'Hear, hear!' very loudly at this and Mr Bloomer added that the English were too reserved. Captain de Wilton-ffallow stated that in his view if a white man was going to be a white man, he meant, he had to be reserved, and Esmeralda said she thought reserve was all right for women, and Mrs Major-General said that it was the sporting spirit that made the Englishman beloved wherever he went, and cited as an instance the worship accorded by the Waziris to Bongleton Sahib after he had killed a hundred and eleven of the most beautiful ibexes you ever saw in a single week's *shikari* near Landi-Kotal.

'I don't know about shooting,' said Porson Jebb, 'but our Test Match sides are Britain's best ambassadors.' It was his favourite, indeed almost his only, remark.

'The Portuguese are good governors, and so are the Egyptians too,' said Mr Harcourt, peering pointedly into his empty glass as he spoke, and sighing deeply.

This was more than the Major-General could stand. He banged the table with his fist and exclaimed, 'The Portuguese are damned bad governors! And as for the Egyptians—'

'Just as you like,' interrupted Mr Harcourt pleasantly.

After the ladies had left the table, Esmeralda with ill-concealed reluctance, the talk turned to politics. Donald listened attentively and wished that he could openly produce his note-book. For he knew that it was at just such week-end parties as this, and at just this precise moment when cigars and port and old brandy are going round that the affairs of England are very largely settled. And here were four Members of Parliament, three Conservative, and a Coalition Socialist, pushing their chairs back, lighting their cigars, and sipping their brandies.

But the absence of the note-book did not matter very much, for, after all, nothing of importance was settled. The conversation ran on simple and unimpressive lines.

'Well, Bob,' began Sir Ethelred, 'and when are we going to get a really decent tariff instead of this footling ten per cent?'

'As soon as we've drowned all those poisonous Liberals,' replied Mr Bloomer. 'It won't be so long now.'

'Poisonous crew of traitors,' said the Major-General, 'I wish I'd had them in my company in the old days at Abbotabad!'

'Do you think that this Free Trade stuff is lunacy or criminal?' inquired Captain de Wilton-ffallow.

'Definitely criminal,' replied his senior officer. 'They're all in the pay of Moscow.'

'I wouldn't go so far as that,' said Sir Ethelred, who was a kindly man. 'I don't think they actually accept money.'

'Then what on earth is the explanation of it?' asked the Captain.

'Oh, I think it's just a form of insanity,' exclaimed Sir Ethelred amiably. 'You've got to be unhinged to argue that we gain anything by getting cheap wheat from Russia. A man who sees any sort of good in imports must be mad.'

'I hope you're right,' said the Major-General gloomily. 'I'd sooner have to deal with loonies than with traitors. But all the same, a man whose judgement I rely on, a sound man, mind you, told me that he knows for a fact that every Liberal candidate at the last election was sent a thousand roubles in gold to help with his expenses.'

'Whew!' the Captain whistled.

'The trouble with Russia is that there's no cricket there,' said Mr Jebb.

'Grisly,' said young Mr Ormerode, yawning.

'Furthermore,' said the Major-General, 'I myself heard a Liberal say the other day that he would sooner see the people of this country pay a shilling a pound for Russian cocoa than three shillings a pound for Sierra Leone cocoa.'

'Whew! ' the Captain whistled again.

'Why Sierra Leone?' inquired young Mr Ormerode, yawning.

'Because Sierra Leone is in the Empire, sir,' cried the Major-General indignantly, 'and if that isn't either downright, stark, staring insanity or slow, cold-blooded treachery, I don't know what is! '

'I agree,' said Sir Ethelred; 'I agree profoundly that Liberals are insane, but it will need more than that to persuade me that they are treacherous as well.'

'I'm a Liberal,' said Mr Harcourt, suddenly waking up out of a trance, and there was an awkward pause filled up by Mr Jebb, who observed:

'They play quite a good game on the Gold Coast. Matting wickets, of course.'

'I am in favour,' said Mr Harcourt, with painful clarity of diction and a pleasing smile, 'of selling the Gold Coast to the United States as part payment of the War Debt, and the Slave Coast and the Pepper Coast and the Salt Coast and the Mustard Coast,' his voice went off into a sort of croon, 'and the Nutmeg Coast and the Cinnamon Coast and the Vinegar Coast and the Oil Coast, and Northern Nigeria and Southern Nigeria and old Uncle Sierra Leone and all.' His voice had fallen to a murmur; his chin drooped upon his corduroy chest and his head nodded. Then with a last effort he raised his head and, in a silvery-clear voice, wound up his statement of Imperial policy with the words, 'And I would use the British Fleet to coerce Japan into accepting Australia—' and, adding as a final afterthought, 'with all the Australians,' he lay back and fell instantly asleep.

'Let us join the ladies,' exclaimed Sir Ethelred hastily. The cigars were only a quarter smoked, the brandy had only been round once, but at all costs bloodshed had to be averted.

The ladies, who had, as usual upon these occasions, resigned themselves with the traditional submissiveness of their sex to a period of dullness, were startled by the unexpected termination of their dreary vigil, and at the same time alarmed by the appalling look of savagely upon the bloodshot face of the Major-General. It was easy to understand at that moment why the North-West Frontier had enjoyed a period of tranquillity during the years of his command at Peshawur.

It was not a very serene evening. Patience Ormerode, having learnt from the butler of Donald's gigantic film interests, backed him into a corner and described in staccato sentences, often containing words of as many as three syllables, her extraordinary acting in the part of Monna Vanna at her school festival near Cheltenham, puffing bogus Russian smoke into his face all the time and shooting devastating glances at him from her kohl-fringed eyes. Esmeralda, furiously angry, and longing more than ever for a hair-brush and the chance to catch the little swine in a suitable posture, had to fall back upon Porson Jebb, who immediately began to describe, stroke by stroke, his famous innings at the Adelaide Oval against South Australia during the last M.C.C. tour. Esmeralda, bored to the verge of insanity, gazed across at the handsome Polish count and sighed and wished that she had paid more attention to her French governess, or even to her German governess, in the dear old days in the Vicarage near Daventry when she had been simple little Jane Jukes.

Sir Ethelred, the Major-General, de Wilton-ffallow, and Mrs O. K. Poop played bridge under the eye of Mrs Major-General. The Russian princess offered, in very broken English, to give a lesson in French or German to Mr Bloomer – an invitation which was accepted with vast alacrity – and the pair retired to the billiard-room. Young Ormerode looked at the *Play Pictorial* and yawned. Miss Pott, M.P., put on a pair of horn-rimmed glasses and settled down with Lady Ormerode to discuss the proposed amendments to the first two clauses of the Government's Housing Bill, while Miss Perugia Gaukrodger described, with a wealth of painful detail, the plot of her forthcoming novel to Mr Harcourt. It was a moving tale, 877 pages, all about the remorse of a young man for having admitted to himself, while standing beside a soda-fountain in a tea-shop, in Chancery Lane, that if his maternal grandmother, who had died twenty-eight years before, had been as beautiful as Helen of Troy and as seductive as Cleopatra, he would probably have fallen in love with her and married her. But – moving, painful, harrowingly true to life though it undoubtedly was – it left Mr Harcourt cold, for he slept peacefully through it all, from page one to page eight hundred and seventy-seven, including even the four chapters, afterwards so famous as the symbolical key to the whole book, in which the hero watches a cockroach climb up an egg-stained wall in a Bloomsbury bed-sitting-room.

Mr Harcourt woke up with mysterious suddenness at twenty-seven minutes past 10, and, by a curious coincidence, it was at that very instant that the butler came in with two footmen laden with trays of whisky, brandy, syphons, glasses, and biscuits. Mr Harcourt stifled a yawn, mixed a little soda into a glass of whisky, blinked heavily, and stared with an air of extreme puzzlement round the room.

'Good God!' he observed with dismay, 'I've forgotten where I am.'

'You're in Ormerode Towers,' snapped Miss Perugia Gaukrodger, who was beginning to suspect that the famous reviewer had missed one or two of her best bits of description.

'Yes, I know that, my good woman,' replied Mr Harcourt. 'What I mean is, I've forgotten what sort of a party it is. Are we up-to-date moderns, mixing gin and beer and wallowing in T. S. Eliot? Or are we straight-living chaps who sing the Eton Boating Song a good deal? Or are we all just simple boys and girls together, darting in and out of each other's bedrooms from time to time? Strike me pink if I know what to make of it!'

'You're at an ordinary English week-end party, sir,' thundered the Major-General.

'Come, come, General,' said Mr Harcourt severely, 'we want none of your barrack-room licentiousness here. I shall have to sleep on the mat outside Esmeralda's door if this sort of thing is to be allowed.'

'What the devil do you mean?' shouted the exasperated soldier.

'I don't know what sort of chivalry they teach at Sandhurst or Coalville Secondary School or Borstal or Woolwich,' replied Mr Harcourt, with immense dignity, 'but to an old Giggleswickian a woman is sacred.'

'Whatever for?' inquired Esmeralda.

'I've forgottten now,' said Mr Harcourt, 'but they used to tell us.'

'I never see the point,' said Captain de Wilton-ffallow, the rubber now over, 'of sneering at the public-school system. It has its drawbacks, like everything else, but its advantages are so overwhelming that people who attack it are merely stamping themselves as fools.'

'The public school,' agreed Sir Ethelred, 'is the breeding-ground of great men.'

'Not necessarily the public school,' amended the Major-General, who had, like many another successful soldier before him, gone straight from the preparatory school to the crammer and from the crammer, after one or two shots, into Sandhurst. 'Not necessarily the public school, but the public school type.'

'Hear, hear!' said Mr Porson Jebb approvingly.

'Damned good show, the public school,' said young Mr Ormerode. 'Those privately educated oicks are a pretty grisly set of oicks. Grocers' sons and oicks and what not.'

'My father was a grocer,' said Mr Harcourt.

Young Mr Ormerode tried to stammer an apology, while the Major-General muttered, perfectly audibly, 'I'm not surprised to hear it.' Lady Ormerode hastened to cover up this gaucherie by saying, 'But, Rupert, I thought all your family were soldiers?'

'Only the ones who weren't clever enough to be taken into the grocery business,' replied Mr Harcourt sweetly.

'In America,' said Mrs O. K. Poop languidly, 'everyone is clever enough to get into the grocery business.'

'That's why you've got no army,' said the poet.

'The United States Army won the War,' replied Mrs Poop, showing faint traces of animation for the first time that evening.

'Madam!' exclaimed the Major-General, bristling up, but Mr Harcourt interrupted deftly:

'Mrs Boob means the Civil War of 1861.'

'I do not, and my name is Poop,' replied the American lady with sudden vivacity.

'The United States Army—' began the Major-General with impressive slowness.

'Is the best in the world,' said Mrs Poop, leaning back on the sofa, 'and the United States Navy is the best in the world.'

'And the trees in California,' said Mr Harcourt, 'are the tallest in the world.'

'That is so,' said Mrs Poop.

'And the climate is the best in the world.'

'That is so,' said Mrs Poop.

'And the public lavatories are the biggest in the world.'

At this point Esmeralda sighed one of the biggest sighs on record and yawned one of the biggest yawns, and said she was going to bed.

'I wish,' said Mr Harcourt plaintively, 'that someone would tell me if this is the sort of week-end party where I offer to come with you.'

'Really, Rupert!' exclaimed Lady Ormerode, scandalized, 'I won't allow you to say such things.'

'No, but will Esmeralda? That's the point.'

The lady in question smiled and kicked up an elegant heel and waved an elegant hand and said, 'Good night, everyone,' and went out.

One by one the house-party went to bed. The lights were extinguished by a tired-looking footman. The fires were raked out, the shutters bolted, the windows locked. Another Saturday was finished. Another typical week-end had been successfully launched at Ormerode Towers.

Sunday was just the same as the Saturday had been, and Donald went back to Royal Avenue on Monday morning with a note-book full of notes. Mr Harcourt travelled up with him in the same carriage, and, before the train had reached London, he had made great havoc with a pint flask of neat whisky.

chapter 7

'Don't forget Saturday morning Charing Cross Underground Station,' ran the telegram which arrived at Royal Avenue during the week, 'at ten fifteen sharp whatever you do don't be late Hodge.'

Saturday morning was bright and sunny, and at ten minutes past 10 Donald arrived at the Embankment entrance of Charing Cross Underground Station, carrying a small suitcase full of clothes suitable for outdoor sports and pastimes. He was glad that he had arrived too early, for it would have been a dreadful thing for a stranger and a foreigner to have kept such a distinguished man, and his presumably distinguished colleagues, even for an instant from their national game. Laying his bag down on the pavement and putting one foot upon it carefully – for Donald had heard stories of the surpassing dexterity of metropolitan thieves – he waited eagerly for the hands of a neighbouring clock to mark the quarter-past. At twenty minutes to 11 an effeminate-looking young man, carrying a cricketing bag and wearing a pale-blue silk jumper up to his ears, sauntered up, remarked casually, 'You playing?' and, on receiving an answer in the affirmative, dumped his bag at Donald's feet and said, 'Keep an eye on that like a good fellow. I'm going to get a shave,' and sauntered off round the corner.

At five minutes to 11 there was a respectable muster, six of the team having assembled. But at five minutes past, a disintegrating element was introduced by the arrival of Mr Harcourt with the news, which he announced with the air of a shipwrecked mariner who has, after twenty-five years of vigilance, seen a sail, that in the neighbourhood of Charing Cross the pubs opened at 11. So that when Mr Hodge himself turned up at twenty-five minutes past 11, resplendent in flannels, a red-and-white football shirt with a lace-up collar, and a blazer of purple-and-yellow stripes, each stripe being at least two inches across, and surmounted by a purple-and-yellow cap that made him somehow reminiscent of one of the Michelin twins, if not both, he was justly indignant at the slackness of his team.

'They've no sense of time,' he told Donald repeatedly. 'We're late as it is. The match is due to begin at half-past 11, and it's fifty miles from here. I should have been here myself two hours ago but I had my Sunday article to do. It really is too bad.'

When the team, now numbering nine men, had been extricated from the tavern and had been marshalled on the pavement, counted, recounted, and the missing pair identified, it was pointed out by the casual youth who had returned, shining and pomaded from the barber, that the char-à-banc had not yet arrived.

Mr Hodge's indignation became positively alarming and he covered the twenty yards to the public telephone box almost as quickly as Mr Harcourt covered the forty yards back to the door of the pub. Donald remained on the pavement to guard the heap of suitcases, cricket-bags, and stray equipment – one player had arrived with a pair of flannels rolled in a tight ball under his arm and a left-hand batting glove, while another had contributed a cardboard box which he had bought at Hamley's on the way down, and which contained six composite cricket-balls, boys' size, and a pair of bails. It was just as well that Donald did remain on guard, partly because no one else seemed to care whether the luggage was stolen or not, partly because Mr Hodge emerged in a perfect frenzy a minute or two later from the telephone box to borrow two pennies to put in the slot, and partly because by the time the telephone call was at last in full swing and Mr Hodge's command over the byways of British invective was enjoying complete freedom of action, the char-à-banc rolled up beside the kerb.

At 12.30 it was decided not to wait for the missing pair, and the nine cricketers started off. At 2.30, after halts at Catford, the White Hart at Sevenoaks, the Angel at Tunbridge Wells, and three smaller inns at tiny villages, the char-à-banc drew up triumphantly beside the cricket ground of the Kentish village of Fordenden.

Donald was enchanted at his first sight of rural England. And rural England is the real England, unspoilt by factories and financiers and tourists and hustle. He sprang out of the char-à-banc, in which he had been tightly wedged between a very stout publisher who had laughed all the way down and had quivered at each laugh like the needle of seismograph during one of

Japan's larger earthquakes, and a youngish and extremely learned professor of ballistics, and gazed eagerly round. The sight was worth an eager gaze or two. It was a hot summer's afternoon. There was no wind, and the smoke from the red-roofed cottages curled slowly up into the golden haze. The clock on the flint tower of the church struck the half-hour, and the vibrations spread slowly across the shimmering hedgerows, spangled with white blossom of the convolvulus, and lost themselves tremulously among the orchards. Bees lazily drifted. White butterflies flapped their aimless way among the gardens. Delphiniums, larkspur, tiger-lilies, evening-primrose, monk's-hood, sweet-peas, swaggered billiantly above the box hedges, the wooden palings, and the rickety gates. The cricket field itself was a mass of daisies and buttercups and dandelions, tall grasses and purple vetches and thistle-down, and great clumps of dark-red sorrel, except, of course, for the oblong patch in the centre – mown, rolled, watered – a smooth, shining emerald of grass, the Pride of Fordenden, the Wicket.

The entire scene was perfect to the last detail. It was as if Mr Cochran had, with his spectacular genius, brought Ye Olde Englyshe Village straight down by special train from the London Pavilion, complete with synthetic cobwebs (from the Wigan factory), hand-made socks for ye gaffers (called in the cabaret scenes and the North-West Mounted Police scenes, the Gentlemen of the Singing Ensemble), and aluminium Eezi-Milk stools for the dairymaids (or Ladies of the Dancing Ensemble). For there stood the Vicar, beaming absent-mindedly at everyone. There was the forge, with the blacksmith, his hammer discarded, tightening his snake-buckled belt for the fray and loosening his braces to enable his terrific bowling-arm to swing freely in its socket. There on a long bench outside the Three Horseshoes sat a row of elderly men, facing a row of pint tankards, and wearing either long beards or clean-shaven chins and long whiskers. Near them, holding pint tankards in their hands, was another group of men, clustered together and talking with intense animation. Donald thought that one or two of them seemed familiar, but it was not until he turned back to the char-à-banc to ask if he could help with the luggage that he realized that they were Mr Hodge and his team already sampling the proprietor's wares. (A notice above the door of the inn stated that the proprietor's name was A. Bason and that he was licensed to sell wines, spirits, beers, and tobacco.)

All round the cricket field small parties of villagers were patiently waiting for the great match to begin – a match against gentlemen from London is an event in a village – and some of them looked as if they had been waiting for a good long time. But they were not impatient. Village folk are very seldom impatient. Those whose lives are occupied in combating the eccentricities of God regard as very small beer the eccentricities of Man.

Blue-and-green dragonflies played at hide-and-seek among the thistle-down and a pair of swans flew overhead. An ancient man leaned upon a scythe, his sharpening-stone sticking out of a pocket in his velveteen waistcoat. A magpie flapped lazily across the meadows. The parson shook hands with the squire. Doves cooed. The haze flickered. The world stood still.

At twenty minutes to 3, Mr Hodge had completed his rather tricky negotiations with the Fordenden captain, and had arranged that two substitutes should be lent by Fordenden in order that the visitors should field eleven men, and that nine men on each side should bat. But just as the two men on the Fordenden side, who had been detailed for the unpleasant duty of fielding for both sides and batting for neither, had gone off home in high dudgeon, a motor-car arrived containing not only Mr Hodge's two defaulters but a third gentleman in flannels as well, who swore stoutly that he had been invited by Mr Hodge to play and affirmed that he was jolly well going to play. Whoever stood down, it wasn't going to be him. Negotiations therefore had to be reopened, the pair of local Achilles had to be recalled, and at ten minutes to 3 the match began upon a twelve-a-side basis.

Mr Hodge, having won the toss by a system of his own founded upon the differential calculus and the Copernican theory, sent in his opening pair to bat. One was James Livingstone, a very sound club cricketer, and the other one was called, simply, Boone. Boone was a huge, awe-inspiring colossus of a man, weighing at least eighteen stone and wearing all the majestic trappings of a Cambridge Blue. Donald felt that it was hardly fair to loose such cracks upon a humble English village until he fortunately remembered that he, of all people, a foreigner, admitted by courtesy to the National Game, ought not to set himself up to be a judge of what is, and what is not, cricket.

The Fordenden team ranged themselves at the bidding of their captain, the Fordenden baker, in various spots of vantage amid the daisies, buttercups, dandelions, vetches, thistle-down, and clumps of dark-red sorrel; and the blacksmith having taken in, just for luck as it were, yet another reef in his snake-buckle belt, prepared to open the attack. It so happened that, at the end at which he was to bowl, the ground behind the wicket was level for a few yards and then sloped away rather abruptly, so that it was only during the last three or four intensive, galvanic yards of his run that the blacksmith, who took a long run, was visible to the batsman or indeed to anyone on the field of play except the man stationed in the deep field behind him. This man saw nothing of the game except the blacksmith walking back dourly and the blacksmith running up ferociously, and occasionally a ball driven smartly over the brow of the hill in his direction.

The sound club player having taken guard, having twiddled his bat round several times in a nonchalant manner, and having stared arrogantly at each fieldsman in turn, was somewhat surprised to find that, although the field was ready, no bowler was visible. His doubts, however, were resolved a second or two later, when the blacksmith came up, breasting the slope superbly like a mettlesome combination of Vulcan and Venus Anadyomene. The first ball which he delivered was a high full-pitch to leg, of appalling velocity. It must have lighted upon a bare patch among the long grass near long-leg, for it rocketed, first bounce, into the hedge and four byes were reluctantly signalled by the village umpire. The row of gaffers on the rustic bench shook their heads, agreed that it was many years since four byes had been signalled on that ground, and called for more pints of old-and-mild. The other members of Mr Hodge's team blanched visibly and called for more pints of bitter. The youngish professor of ballistics, who was in next, muttered something about muzzle velocities and started to do a sum on the back of an envelope.

The second ball went full-pitch into the wicket-keeper's stomach and there was a delay while the deputy wicket-keeper was invested with the pads and gloves of office. The third ball, making a noise like a partridge, would have hummed past Mr Livingstone's left ear had he not dexterously struck it out of the ground for six, and the fourth took his leg bail with a bullet-like full-pitch. Ten runs for one wicket, last man six. The professor got the fifth ball on the left ear and went back to the Three Horseshoes, while Mr Harcourt had the singular misfortune to hit his wicket before the sixth ball was even delivered. Ten runs for two wickets and one man retired hurt. A slow left-hand bowler was on at the other end, the local rate-collector, a man whose whole life was one of infinite patience and guile. Off his first ball the massive Cambridge Blue was easily stumped, having executed a movement that aroused the professional admiration of the Ancient who was leaning upon his scythe. Donald was puzzled that so famous a player should play so execrable a stroke until it transpired, later on, that a wrong impression had been created and that the portentous Boone had gained his Blue at Cambridge for rowing and not for cricket. Ten runs for three wickets and one man hurt.

The next player was a singular young man. He was small and quiet, and he wore perfectly creased white flannels, white silk socks, a pale-pink silk shirt, and a white cap. On the way down in the char-à-banc he had taken little part in the conversation and even less in the beer-drinking. There was a retiring modesty about him that made him conspicuous in that cricket eleven, and there was a gentleness, an almost finicky gentleness about his movements which hardly seemed virile and athletic. He looked as if a fast ball would knock the bat out of his hands. Donald asked someone what his name was, and was astonished to learn that he was the famous novelist, Robert Southcott himself.

Just as this celebrity, holding his bat as delicately as if it was a flute or a fan, was picking his way through the daisies and thistle-down towards the wicket, Mr Hodge rushed anxiously, tankard in hand, from the Three Horseshoes and bellowed in a most unpoetical voice: 'Play carefully, Bobby. Keep your end up. Runs don't matter.'

'Very well, Bill,' replied Mr Southcott sedately. Donald was interested by this little exchange. It was the Team Spirit at work – the captain instructing his man to play a type of game that was demanded by the state of the team's fortunes, and the individual loyally suppressing his instincts to play a different type of game.

Mr Southcott took guard modestly, glanced furtively round the field as if it was an impertinence to suggest that he would survive long enough to make a study of the fieldsmen's positions worth while, and hit the rate-collector's first ball over the Three Horseshoes into a hay-field. The ball was retrieved by a mob of screaming urchins, handed back to the rate-collector, who scratched his head and then bowled his fast yorker, which Mr Southcott hit into the saloon bar of the Shoes, giving Mr Harcourt such a fright that he required several pints before he fully recovered his nerve. The next ball was very slow and crafty, endowed as it was with every iota of fingerspin and brain-power which a long-service rate-collector could muster. In addition, it was delivered at the extreme end of the crease so as to secure a background of dark laurels instead of a dazzling white screen, and it swung a little in the air; a few moments later the urchins, by this time delirious with ecstasy, were fishing it out of the squire's trout stream with a bamboo pole and an old bucket.

The rate-collector was bewildered. He had never known such a travesty of the game. It was not cricket. It was slogging; it was wild, unscientific bashing; and furthermore, his reputation was in grave danger. The instalments would be harder than ever to collect, and Heaven knew they were hard enough to collect as it was, what with bad times and all. His three famous deliveries had been treated with contempt – the leg-break, the fast yorker, and the slow, swinging off-break out of the laurel bushes. What on earth was he to try now? Another six and he would be laughed out of the parish. Fortunately the village umpire came out of a trance of consternation to the rescue. Thirty-eight years of umpiring for the Fordenden Cricket Club had taught him a thing or two and he called 'Over' firmly and marched off to square-leg. The rate-collector was glad to give way to a Free Forester, who had been specially imported for this match. He was only a moderate bowler, but it was felt that it was worth while giving him a trial, if only for the sake of the scarf round his waist and his cap. At the other end the fast bowler pounded away grimly until an unfortunate accident occurred. Mr South-cott had been treating with apologetic contempt those of his deliveries which came within reach, and the blacksmith's temper had been rising for some time. An urchin had shouted, 'Take him orf! ' and the other urchins, for whom Mr Southcott was by now a firmly established deity, had screamed with delight. The captain had held one or two ominous consultations with the wicket-keeper and other advisers, and the blacksmith knew that his dismissal was at hand unless he produced a supreme effort.

It was the last ball of the over. He halted at the wicket before going back for his run, glared at Mr Harcourt, who had been driven out to umpire by his colleagues – greatly to the regret of Mr Bason, the landlord of the Shoes – glared at Mr Southcott, took another reef in his belt, shook out another inch in his braces, spat on his hand, swung his arm three or four times in a meditative sort of way, grasped the ball tightly in his colossal palm, and then turned smartly about and marched off like a Pomeranian grenadier and vanished over the brow of the hill. Mr Southcott, during these proceedings, leant elegantly upon his bat and admired the view. At last, after a long stillness, the ground shook, the grasses waved violently, small birds arose with shrill clamours, a loud puffing sound alarmed the butter-flies, and the blacksmith, looking more like Venus Anadyo-mene than ever, came thundering over the crest. The world held its breath. Among the spectators, conversation was sud-denly hushed. Even the urchins, understanding somehow that they were assisting at a crisis in affairs, were silent for a moment as the mighty figure swept up to the crease. It was the charge of Von Bredow's Dragoons at Gravelotte over again.

But alas for human ambitions! Mr Harcourt, swaying slightly from leg to leg, had understood the menacing glare of the bow-ler, had marked the preparation for a titanic effort, and – for he was not a poet for nothing – knew exactly what was going on. And Mr Harcourt sober had a very pleasant sense of humour, but Mr Harcourt rather drunk was a perfect demon of impish-ness. Sober, he occasionally resisted a temptation to try to be funny. Rather drunk, never. As the giant whirlwind of vulcanic energy rushed past him to the crease, Mr Harcourt, quivering with excitement and internal laughter, and wobbling uncertainly upon his pins, took a deep breath and bellowed, 'No ball!'

It was too late for the unfortunate bowler to stop himself. The ball flew out of his hand like a bullet and hit third-slip, who was not looking, full pitch on the knee-cap. With a yell of agony third-slip began hopping about like a stork until he tripped over a tussock of grass and fell on his face in a bed of nettles, from which he sprang up again with another drum-splitting yell. The blacksmith himself was flung forward by his own irresistible momentum, startled out of his wits by Mr Harcourt's bellow in his ear, and thrown off his balance by his desperate effort to prevent himself from delivering the ball, and the result was that his gigantic feet got mixed up among each other and he fell heavily in the centre of the wicket, knocking up a cloud of dust and dandelion-seed and twisting his ankle. Rooks by hundreds arose in protest from the vicarage cedars. The urchins howled like intoxicated banshees. The gaffers gaped. Mr Southcott gazed modestly at the ground. Mr Harcourt gazed at the heavens. Mr Harcourt did not think the world had ever been, or could ever be again, quite such a capital place, even though he had laughed internally so much that he had got hiccups.

Mr Hodge, emerging at that moment from the Three Horseshoes, surveyed the scene and then the scoreboard with an imperial air. Then he roared in the same rustic voice as before:

'You needn't play safe any more, Bob. Play your own game.'

'Thank you, Bill,' replied Mr Southcott as sedately as ever, and, on the resumption of the game, he fell into a kind of cricketing trance, defending his wicket skilfully from straight balls, ignoring crooked ones, and scoring one more run in a quarter of an hour before he inadvertently allowed, for the first time during his innings, a ball to strike his person.

'Out!' shrieked the venerable umpire before anyone had time to appeal.

The score at this point was sixty-nine for six, last man fifty-two.

The only other incident in the innings was provided by an American journalist, by name Shakespeare Pollock – an intensely active, alert, on-the-spot young man. Mr Pollock had been roped in at the last moment to make up the eleven, and Mr Hodge and Mr Harcourt had spent quite a lot of time on the way down trying to teach him the fundamental principles of the game. Donald had listened attentively and had been surprised that they made no reference to the Team Spirit. He decided in the end that the reason must have been simply that everyone knows all about it already, and that it is therefore taken for granted.

Mr Pollock stepped up to the wicket in the lively manner of his native mustang, refused to take guard, on the ground that he wouldn't know what to do with it when he had got it, and, striking the first ball he received towards square leg, threw down his bat, and himself set off at a great rate in the direction of coverpoint. There was a paralysed silence. The rustics on the bench rubbed their eyes. On the field no one moved. Mr Pollock stopped suddenly, looked round, and broke into a genial laugh.

'Darn me—' he began, and then he pulled himself up and went on in refined English, 'Well, well! I thought I was playing baseball.' He smiled disarmingly round.

'Baseball is a kind of rounders, isn't it, sir?' said cover-point sympathetically.

Donald thought he had never seen an expression change so suddenly as Mr Pollock's did at this harmless, and true, statement. A look of concentrated, ferocious venom obliterated the disarming smile. Cover-point, simple soul, noticed nothing, however, and Mr Pollock walked back to the wicket in silence and was out next ball.

The next two batsmen, Major Hawker, the team's fast bowler, and Mr Hodge himself, did not score, and the innings closed at sixty-nine, Donald not-out nought. Opinion on the gaffers' bench, which corresponded in years and connoisseurship very closely with the Pavilion at Lord's, was sharply divided on the question whether sixty-nine was, or was not, a winning score.

After a suitable interval for refreshment, Mr Hodge led his men, except Mr Harcourt who was missing, out into the field and placed them at suitable positions in the hay.

The batsmen came in. The redoubtable Major Hawker, the fast bowler, thrust out his chin and prepared to bowl. In a quarter of an hour he had terrified seven batsmen, clean bowled six of them, and broken a stump. Eleven runs, six wickets, last man two.

After the fall of the sixth wicket there was a slight delay. The new batsman, the local rate-collector, had arrived at the crease and was ready. But nothing happened. Suddenly the large publisher, who was acting as wicket-keeper, called out, 'Hi! Where's Hawker?'

The words galvanized Mr Hodge into portentous activity.

'Quick!' he shouted. 'Hurry, run, for God's sake! Bob, George, Percy, to the Shoes!' and he set off at a sort of gallop towards the inn, followed at intervals by the rest of the side except the pretty youth in the blue jumper, who lay down; the wicket-keeper, who did not move; and Mr Shakespeare Pollock, who had shot off the mark and was well ahead of the field.

But they were all too late, even Mr Pollock. The gallant Major, admitted by Mr Bason through the back door, had already lowered a quart and a half of mild-and-bitter, and his subsequent bowling was perfectly innocuous, consisting, as it did, mainly of slow, gentle full-pitches to leg which the village baker and even, occasionally, the rate-collector hit hard and high into the long grass. The score mounted steadily.

Disaster followed disaster. Mr Pollock, presented with an easy chance of a run-out, instead of lobbing the ball back to the wicket-keeper, had another reversion to his college days and flung it with appalling velocity at the unfortunate rate-collector and hit him in the small of the back, shouting triumphantly as he did so, 'Rah, rah, rah!' Mr Livingstone, good club player, missed two easy catches off successive balls. Mr Hodge allowed another easy catch to fall at his feet without attempting to catch it, and explained afterwards that he had been all the time admiring a particularly fine specimen of oak in the squire's garden. He seemed to think that this was a complete justification of his failure to attempt, let alone bring off, the catch. A black spot happened to cross the eye of the ancient umpire just as the baker put all his feet and legs and pads in front of a perfectly straight ball, and, as he plaintively remarked over and over again, he had to give the batsman the benefit of the doubt, hadn't he? It wasn't as if it was his fault that a black spot had crossed his eye just at that moment. And the stout publisher seemed to be suffering from the delusion that the way to make a catch at the wicket was to raise both hands high in the air, utter a piercing yell, and trust to an immense pair of pads to secure the ball. Repeated experiments proved that he was wrong.

The baker lashed away vigorously and the rate-collector dabbed the ball hither and thither until the score – having once been eleven runs for six wickets – was marked up on the board at fifty runs for six wickets. Things were desperate. Twenty to win and five wickets – assuming that the blacksmith's ankle and third-slip's knee-cap would stand the strain – to fall. If the lines on Mr Hodge's face were deep, the lines on the faces of his team when he put himself on to bowl were like plasticine models of the Colorado Canyon. Mr Southcott, without any orders from his captain, discarded his silk sweater from the Rue de la Paix, and went away into the deep field, about a hundred and twenty yards from the wicket. His beautifully brushed head was hardly visible above the daisies. The professor of ballistics sighed deeply. Major Hawker grinned a colossal grin, right across his jolly red face, and edged off in the direction of the Shoes. Livingstone, loyal to his captain, crouched alertly. Mr Shakespeare Pollock rushed about enthusiastically. The remainder of the team drooped.

But the remainder of the team was wrong. For a wicket, a crucial wicket, was secured off Mr Hodge's very first ball. It happened like this. Mr Hodge was a poet, and therefore a theorist, and an idealist. If he was to win a victory at anything, he preferred to win by brains and not by muscle. He would far sooner have his best leg-spinner miss the wicket by an eighth of an inch than dismiss a batsman with a fast, clumsy full-toss. Every ball that he bowled had brain behind it, if not exactness of pitch. And it so happened that he had recently watched a county cricket match between Lancashire, a county that he detested in theory, and Worcestershire, a county that he adored in fact. On the one side were factories and the late Mr Jimmy

83

White; on the other, English apples and Mr Stanley Baldwin. And at this particular match, a Worcestershire bowler, by name Root, a deliciously agricultural name, had outed the tough nuts of the County Palatine by placing all his fieldsmen on the legside and bowling what are technically known as 'in-swingers'.

Mr Hodge, at heart an agrarian, for all his book-learning and his cadences, was determined to do the same. The first part of the performance was easy. He placed all his men upon the legside. The second part – the bowling of the 'in-swingers' – was more complicated, and Mr Hodge's first ball was a slow long-hop on the off-side. The rate-collector, metaphorically rubbing his eyes, felt that this was too good to be true, and he struck the ball sharply into the untenanted off-side and ambled down the wicket with as near an approach to gaiety as a man can achieve who is cut off by the very nature of his profession from the companionship and goodwill of his fellows. He had hardly gone a yard or two when he was paralysed by a hideous yell from the long grass into which the ball had vanished, and still more by the sight of Mr Harcourt, who, aroused from a deep slumber amid a comfortable couch of grasses and daisies, sprang to his feet and, pulling himself together with miraculous rapidity after a lightning if somewhat bleary glance round the field, seized the ball and unerringly threw down the wicket. Fifty for seven, last man twenty-two. Twenty to win: four wickets to fall.

Mr Hodge's next ball was his top-spinner, and it would have, or might have, come very quickly off the ground had it ever hit the ground: as it was, one of the short-legs caught it dexterously and threw it back while the umpire signalled a wide. Mr Hodge then tried some more of Mr Root's stuff and was promptly hit for two sixes and a single. This brought the redoubtable baker to the batting end. Six runs to win and four wickets to fall.

Mr Hodge's fifth ball was not a good one, due mainly to the fact that it slipped out of his hand before he was ready, and it went up and came down in a slow, lazy parabola, about seven feet wide of the wicket on the leg-side. The baker had plenty of time to make up his mind. He could either leave it alone and let it count one run as a wide; or he could spring upon it like a panther and, with a terrific six, finish the match sensationally. He could play the part either of a Quintus Fabius Maximus Cunctator, or of a sort of Tarzan. The baker concealed beneath a modest and floury exterior a mounting ambition. Here was his chance to show the village. He chose the sort of Tarzan, sprang like a panther, whirled his bat cyclonically, and missed the ball by about a foot and a half. The wicket-keeping publisher had also had time in which to think and to move, and he also had covered the seven feet. True, his movements were less like the spring of a panther than the sideways waddle of an aldermanic penguin. But nevertheless he got there, and when the ball had passed the flashing blade of the baker, he launched a mighty kick at it – stooping to grab it was out of the question – and by an amazing fluke kicked it on to the wicket. Even the ancient umpire had to give the baker out, for the baker was still lying flat on his face outside the crease.

'I was bowling for that,' observed Mr Hodge modestly, strolling up the pitch.

'I had plenty of time to use my hands,' remarked the wicket-keeper to the world at large, 'but I preferred to kick it.'

Donald was impressed by the extraordinary subtlety of the game.

Six to win and three wickets to fall.

The next batsman was a schoolboy of about sixteen, an ingenuous youth with pink cheeks and a nervous smile, who quickly fell a victim to Mr Harcourt, now wide awake and beaming upon everyone. For Mr Harcourt, poet that he was, understood exactly what the poor, pink child was feeling, and he knew that if he played the ancient dodge and pretended to lose the ball in the long grass, it was a hundred to one that the lad would lose his head. The batsman at the other end played the fourth ball of Mr Livingstone's next over hard in the direction of Mr Harcourt. Mr Harcourt rushed towards the spot where it had vanished in the jungle. He groped wildly for it, shouting as he did so, 'Come and help. It's lost.' The pink child scuttered nimbly down the pitch. Six runs to win and two wickets to fall. Mr Harcourt smiled demoniacally.

The crisis was now desperate. The fieldsmen drew nearer and nearer to the batsmen, excepting the youth in the blue jumper.

Livingstone balanced himself on his toes. Mr Shakespeare Pollock hopped about almost on top of the batsmen, and breathed excitedly and audibly. Even the imperturbable Mr Southcott discarded the piece of grass which he had been chewing so steadily. Mr Hodge took himself off and put on the Major, who had by now somewhat lived down the quart and a half.

The batsmen crouched down upon their bats and defended stubbornly. A snick through the slips brought a single. A ball which eluded the publisher's gigantic pads brought a bye. A desperate sweep at a straight half-volley sent the ball off the edge of the bat over third-man's head and in normal circumstances would have certainly scored one, and possibly two. But Mr Harcourt was on guard at third-man, and the batsmen, by nature cautious men, one being old and the sexton, the other the postman and therefore a Government official, were taking no risks. Then came another single off a miss-hit, and then an interminable period in which no wicket fell and no run was scored. It was broken at last disastrously, for the postman struck the ball sharply at Mr Pollock, and Mr Pollock picked it up and, in an ecstasy of zeal, flung it madly at the wicket. Two overthrows resulted.

The scores were level and there were two wickets to fall. Silence fell. The gaffers, victims simultaneously of excitement and senility, could hardly raise their pint pots – for it was past 6 o'clock, and the front door of the Three Horseshoes was now as wide open officially as the back door had been unofficially all afternoon.

The Major, his face redder than ever and his chin sticking out almost as far as the Napoleonic Mr Ogilvy's, bowled a fast half-volley on the leg-stump. The sexton, a man of iron muscle from much digging, hit it fair and square in the middle of the bat, and it flashed like a thunderbolt, waist-high, straight at the youth in the blue jumper. With a shrill scream the youth sprang backwards out of its way and fell over on his back. Immediately behind him, so close were the fieldsmen clustered, stood the mighty Boone. There was no chance of escape for him. Even if he had possessed the figure and the agility to perform back-somersaults, he would have lacked the time. He had been unsighted by the youth in the jumper. The thunderbolt struck him in the midriff like a red-hot cannon-ball upon a Spanish galleon, and with the sound of a drumstick upon an insufficiently stretched drum. With a fearful oath, Boone clapped his hands to his outraged stomach and found that the ball was in the way. He looked at it for a moment in astonishment and then threw it down angrily and started to massage the injured spot while the field rang with applause at the brilliance of the catch.

Donald walked up and shyly added his congratulations. Boone scowled at him.

'I didn't want to catch the bloody thing,' he said sourly, massaging away like mad.

'But it may save the side,' ventured Donald.

'Blast the bloody side,' said Boone.

Donald went back to his place.

The scores were level and there was one wicket to fall. The last man in was the blacksmith, leaning heavily upon the shoulder of the baker, who was going to run for him, and limping as if in great pain. He took guard and looked round savagely. He was clearly still in a great rage.

The first ball he received he lashed at wildly and hit straight up in the air to an enormous height. It went up and up, until it became difficult to focus it properly against the deep, cloudless blue of the sky, and it carried with it the hopes and fears of an English village. Up and up it went and then at the top it seemed to hang motionless in the air, poised like a hawk, fighting, as it were, a heroic but forlorn battle against the chief invention of Sir Isaac Newton, and then it began its slow descent.

In the meanwhile things were happening below, on the terrestrial sphere. Indeed, the situation was rapidly becoming what the French call *mouvementé*. In the first place, the blacksmith forgot his sprained ankle and set out at a capital rate for the other end, roaring in a great voice as he went, 'Come on, Joe!' The baker, who was running on behalf of the invalid, also set out, and he also roared 'Come on, Joe!' and side by side, like a pair of high-stepping hackneys, the pair cantered along. From the other end Joe set out on his mission, and he roared 'Come on Bill!' So all three came on. And everything would have been all right, so far as the running was concerned, had it not been for the fact that Joe, very naturally, ran with his head thrown back and his eyes goggling at the hawk-like cricket-ball. And this in itself would not have mattered if it had not been for the fact that the blacksmith and the baker, also very naturally, ran with their heads turned not only upwards but also backwards as well, so that they too gazed at the ball, with an alarming sort of squint and a truly terrific kink in their necks. Half-way down the pitch the three met with a magnificent clang, reminiscent of early, happy days in the tournament-ring at Ashby-de-la-Zouche, and the hopes of the village fell with the resounding fall of their three champions.

But what of the fielding side? Things were not so well with them. If there was doubt and confusion among the warriors of Fordenden, there was also uncertainty and disorganization among the ranks of the invaders. Their main trouble was the excessive concentration of their forces in the neighbourhood of the wicket. Napoleon laid it down that it was impossible to have too many men upon a battlefield, and he used to do everything in his power to call up every available man for a battle. Mr Hodge, after a swift glance at the ascending ball and a swift glance at the disposition of his troops, disagreed profoundly with the Emperor's dictum. He had too many men, far too many. And all except the youth in the blue silk jumper, and the mighty Boone, were moving towards strategical positions underneath the ball, and not one of them appeared to be aware that any of the others existed. Boone had not moved because he was more or less in the right place, but then Boone was not likely to bring off the catch, especially after the episode of the last ball. Major Hawker, shouting 'Mine, mine!' in a magnificently self-confident voice, was coming up from the bowler's end like a battle-cruiser. Mr Harcourt had obviously lost sight of the ball altogether, if indeed he had ever seen it, for he was running round and round Boone and giggling foolishly. Livingstone and Southcott, the two cracks, were approaching competently. Either of them would catch it easily. Mr Hodge had only to choose between them and, coming to a swift decision, he yelled above the din, 'Yours, Livingstone!' Southcott, disciplined cricketer, stopped dead. Then Mr Hodge made a fatal mistake. He remembered Livingstone's two missed sitters, and

he reversed his decision and roared 'Yours Bobby!' Mr Southcott obediently started again, while Livingstone, who had not
heard the second order, went straight on. Captain Hodge had
restored the *status quo*.

In the meantime the professor of ballistics had made a lightning calculation of angles, velocities, density of the air, baro-
meter-readings and temperatures, and had arrived at the conclusion that the critical point, the spot which ought to be marked in the photographs with an X, was one yard to the north-
east of Boone, and he proceeded to take up station there, collid-
ing on the way with Donald and knocking him over. A moment
later Bobby Southcott came racing up and tripped over the
recumbent Donald and was shot head first into the Abra-
ham-like bosom of Boone. Boone stepped back a yard under
the impact and came down with his spiked boot, surmounted by
a good eighteen stone of flesh and blood, upon the professor's
toe. Almost simultaneously, the portly wicket-keeper, whose
movements were a positive triumph of the spirit over the body,
bumped the professor from behind. The learned man was thus
neatly sandwiched between Tweedledum and Tweedledee, and
the sandwich was instantly converted into a ragout by Livingstone, who made up for his lack of extra weight – for he was
always in perfect training – by his extra momentum. And all
the time Mr Shakespeare Pollock hovered alertly upon the outskirts like a Rugby scrum-half, screaming American University
cries in a piercingly high tenor voice.

At last the ball came down. To Mr Hodge it seemed a long
time before the invention of Sir Isaac Newton finally triumph-
ed. And it was a striking testimony to the mathematical and
ballistical skill of the professor that the ball landed with a sharp
report upon the top of his head. Thence it leapt up into the air
a foot or so, cannoned on to Boone's head, and then trickled
slowly down the colossal expanse of the wicket-keeper's back,
bouncing slightly as it reached the massive lower portions. It
was only a foot from the ground when Mr Shakespeare Pollock
sprang into the vortex with a last ear-splitting howl of victory
and grabbed it off the seat of the wicket-keeper's trousers. The
match was a tie. And hardly anyone on the field knew it except
Mr Hodge, the youth in the blue jumper, and Mr Pollock him-

self. For the two batsmen and the runner, undaunted to the last, had picked themselves up and were bent on completing the single that was to give Fordenden the crown of victory. Unfortunately, dazed with their falls, with excitement, and with the noise, they all three ran for the same wicket, simultaneously realized their error, and all three turned and ran for the other – the blacksmith, ankle and all, in the centre and leadiﾑg by a yard, so that they looked like pictures of the Russian *troika*. But their effort was in vain, for Mr Pollock had grabbed the ball and the match was a tie.

And both teams spent the evening at the Three Horseshoes, and Mr Harcourt made a speech in Italian about the glories of England and afterwards fell asleep in a corner, and Donald got home to Royal Avenue at 1 o'clock in the morning, feeling that he had not learnt very much about the English from his experience of their national game.

chapter 8

A few days after this curious experience on the cricket field, Donald's attention was drawn away from the problem of the Englishman's attitude towards his national game by a chance paragraph in a leading newspaper on the subject of Golf. And golf was a matter of grave temptation to Donald at this period of his life.

Both Sir Ethelred Ormerode, M.P., and Sir Ludovic Phibbs, M.P., had invited him to a day's golf at one or other of the large clubs near London to which they belonged; but Donald had made excuses to avoid acceptance, for the following reason. He had played no golf since he had been a lad of eighteen at Aberdeen, and as he had not enough money to join a club in the south and play regularly, he was unwilling to resurrect an ancient passion which he had no means of gratifying. Up to the age of eighteen golf had been a religion to him far more inspiring and appealing than the dry dogmatics of the various sections of the Presbyterian Church which wrangled in those days so enthusiastically in the North-East of Scotland. Since that time, of course, there has been a notable reunion of the sections and public wrangling has perforce come to an end, an end regretted so passionately that the phrase 'a peace-maker' in that part of the world is rapidly acquiring the sense of a busy-body or a spoil-sport. As one ancient soldier of the Faith, whose enthusiasm for the Word was greater than his knowledge of it, was recently heard to observe bitterly into the depths of his patriarchal beard, 'Isn't it enough for them to have been promised the Kingdom of Heaven, without they must poke their disjaskit nebs into Buchan and the Mearns?'

But whatever the rights and wrongs of the once indignant and now cooing Churches, it is a fact that Donald before the War was more interested in golf than in religion, and a handicap of plus one when he was seventeen had marked him out as a coming man. But first the War and then the work of farming the Mains of Balspindie had put an end to all that, and Donald was reluctant to awaken the dragon.

But one day he happened to read in one of the most famous newspapers in the world the following paragraph in a column written by 'Our Golf Correspondent':

'Our recent defeat at the hands of the stern and wild Caledonians was, no doubt, demnition horrid, as our old friend would have said, and had it not been for the amazing series of flukes by which the veteran Bernardo, now well advanced in decreptitude, not only managed to hang on to the metaphorical coat-tails of his slashing young adversary, but even to push his nose in front on the last green, the score of the Sassenachs would have been as blank as their faces. For their majestic leader was snodded on the fourteenth green, and even the Dumkins and the Podder of the team, usually safe cards, met their Bannockburn. And that was that. The only consolation for this unexpected "rewersal" lies in the fact that the Northerners consisted almost entirely of what are called Anglo-Scots, domiciled in England and products of English golf. For there is no doubt that the balance of golfing power has shifted to the south, and

England is now the real custodian of the ancient traditions of the game. Which, as a consolation prize, is all wery capital.'

Donald read this through carefully several times, for it seemed to be a matter of importance to him and his work. He had seen, at very close quarters, the English engaged upon their own ancient, indigenous national pastime, and he had been unable to make head or tail of it.

But it was worth while going out of his way to see how they treated another nation's national game which, according to the golf correspondent, they had mastered perfectly and had, as it were, adopted and nationalized.

The matter was easily arranged, and, on the following Sunday, he was picked up at the corner of Royal Avenue and King's Road by Sir Ludovic Phibbs in a Rolls-Royce limousine car. Sir Ludovic was wearing a superb fur coat and was wrapped in a superb fur rug. On the way down to Cedar Park, the venue of the day's golf, Sir Ludovic talked a good deal about the scandal of the dole. It appeared to be his view that everyone who took the dole ought to be shot in order to teach them not to slack. The solution of the whole trouble was the abolition of Trades Unionism and harder work all round, including Saturday afternoons and a half-day on Sundays. This theme lasted most of the journey, and Donald was not called upon to contribute more than an occasional monosyllable.

Cedar Park is one of the newest of the great golf clubs which are ringed round the north, west, and south of London in such profusion, and what is now the club-house had been in earlier centuries the mansion of a venerable line of marquesses. High taxation had completed the havoc in the venerable finances which had been begun in the Georgian and Victorian generations by high gambling, and the entire estate was sold shortly after the War by the eleventh marquess to a man who had, during it, made an enormous fortune by a most ingenious dodge. For, alone with the late Lord Kitchener, he had realized in August and September of 1914 that the War was going to be a very long business, thus providing ample opportunities for very big business, and that before it was over it would require a

British Army of millions and millions of soldiers. Having first of all taken the precaution of getting himself registered as a man who was indispensable to the civil life of the nation during the great Armageddon, for at the outbreak of hostilities he was only thirty-one years of age, and, in order to be on the safe side, having had himself certified by a medical man as suffering from short sight, varicose veins, a weak heart, and incipient lung trouble, he set himself upon his great task of cornering the world's supply of rum. By the middle of 1917 he had succeeded, and in 1920 he paid ninety-three thousand pounds for Cedar Park, and purchased in addition a house in Upper Brook Street, a hunting-box near Melton, a two-thousand-ton motor-yacht, Lochtarig Castle, Inverness-shire, and the long leases of three luxurious flats in Mayfair in which to entertain, without his wife knowing, by day or night, his numerous lady friends. He was, of course, knighted for his public services during the War. It was not until 1925 that the rum-knight shot himself to avoid an absolutely certain fourteen years for fraudulent conversion, and Cedar Park was acquired by a syndicate of Armenian sportsmen for the purpose of converting it into a country club.

An enormous man in a pale-blue uniform tricked out with thick silver cords and studded with cartwheel silver buttons, opened the door of the car and bowed Sir Ludovic, and a little less impressively, Donald Cameron into the club-house. Donald was painfully conscious that his grey flannel trousers bagged at the knee and that his old blue 1914 golfing-coat had a shine at one elbow and a hole at the other.

The moment he entered the club-house a superb spectacle met his dazzled gaze. It was not the parquet floor, on which his nail-studded shoes squeaked loudly, or the marble columns, or the voluptuous paintings on the ceiling, or the gilt-framed mirrors on the walls, or the chandeliers of a thousand crystals, or even the palms in their gilt pots and synthetic earth, that knocked him all of a heap. It was the group of golfers that was standing in front of the huge fire-place. There were purple jumpers and green jumpers and yellow jumpers and tartan jumpers; there were the biggest, the baggiest, the brightest plus-fours that ever dulled the lustre of a peacock's tail; there were the rosiest of lips, the gayest of cheeks, the flimsiest of silk stockings, and the orangest of finger-nails and probably, if the truth were known, of toe-nails too; there were waves of an unbelievable permanence and lustre; there were jewels, on the men as well as on the women, and foot-long jade and amber cigarette-holders and foot-long cigars with glistening cummerbunds; and there was laughter and gaiety and much bending, courtier-like, from the waist, and much raising of girlish, kohl-fringed eyes, and a great chattering. Donald felt like a navvy, and when, in his agitation, he dropped his clubs with a resounding clash upon the floor and everyone stopped talking and looked at him, he wished he was dead. Another pale-blue-and-silver giant picked up the clubs, held them out at arm's length and examined them in disdainful astonishment – for after years of disuse they were very rusty – and said coldly, 'Clubs go into the locker-room, sir,' and Donald squeaked his way across the parquet after him amid a profound silence.

The locker-room was full of young gentlemen who were discarding their jumpers – which certainly competed with Mr Shelley's idea of Life Staining the White Radiance of Eternity – in favour of brown leather jerkins fastened up the front with that singular arrangement which is called a zipper. Donald edged in furtively, hazily watched the flunkey lay the clubs down upon a bench, and then fled in panic through the nearest open door and found himself suddenly in a wire-netted enclosure which was packed with a dense throng of caddies. The caddies were just as surprised by his appearance in their midst as the elegant ladies and gentlemen in the lounge had been by the fall of the clubs, and a deathly stillness once again paralysed Donald.

He backed awkwardly out of the enclosure, bouncing off caddy after caddy like a cork coming over a rock-studded sluice, and was brought up short at last by what seemed to be a caddy rooted immovably in the ground. Two desperate backward lunges failed to dislodge the obstacle and Donald turned and found it was the wall of the professional's shop. The caddies, and worse still, an exquisitely beautiful young lady with a cupid's-bow mouth and practically no skirt on at all, who had just emerged from the shop, watched him with profound interest. Scarlet in the face, he rushed past the radiant beauty, and hid himself in the darkest corner of the shop and pretended to be utterly absorbed in a driver which he picked out at random from the rack. Rather to his surprise, and greatly to his relief, no one molested him with up-to-date, go-getting salesmanship, and in a few minutes he had pulled himself together and was able to look round and face the world.

Suddenly he gave a start. Something queer was going on inside him. He sniffed the air once, and then again, and then the half-forgotten past came rushing to him across the wasted years. The shining rows of clubs, the boxes of balls, the scent of leather and rubber and gripwax and pitch, the club-makers filing away over the vices and polishing and varnishing and splicing and binding, the casual members waggling a club here and there, the professional listening courteously to tales of apocryphal feats, all the old familiar scenes of his youth came back to him. It was eleven years since he had played a game of golf, thirteen years since he had bought a club. Thirteen wasted years. Dash it, thought Donald, damn it, blast it, I can't afford a new club – I don't want a new club, but I'm going to buy a new club. He spoke diffidently to one of the assistants who was passing behind him, and inquired the price of the drivers.

'It's a new lot just finished, sir,' said the assistant, 'and I'm not sure of the price. I'll ask Mr Glennie.'

Mr Glennie was the professional himself. The great man, who was talking to a member, or rather was listening to a member's grievances against his luck, a ritual which occupied a large part of a professional's working day, happened to overhear the assistant, and he said over his shoulder in the broadest of broad Scottish accents, 'They're fufty-twa shullin' and cheap at that.'

Donald started back. Two pounds twelve for a driver! Things had changed indeed since the days when the great Archie Simpson had sold him a brassy, brand-new, bright yellow, refulgent, with a lovely whippy shaft, for five shillings and ninepence.

His movement of Aberdonian horror brought him out of the dark corner into the sunlight which was streaming through the window, and it was the professional's turn to jump.

'It's Master Donald!' he exclaimed. 'Ye mind me, Master Donald – Jim Glennie, assistant that was at Glenavie to Tommy Anderson that went to the States?'

'Glennie!' cried Donald, a subtle warm feeling suddenly invading his body, and he grasped the professional's huge red hand.

'Man!' cried the latter, 'but I'm glad to see ye. How lang is't sin' we used to ding awa at each other roon' Glenavie? Man, it must be years and years. And fit's aye deein' wi' yer game? Are ye plus sax or seeven?'

'Glennie,' said Donald sadly, 'I haven't touched a club since those old days. This is the first time I've set foot in a professional's shop since you took me that time to see Alec Marling at Balgownie the day before the War broke out.'

'Eh, man, but you're a champion lost,' and the professional shook his head mournfully.

'But, Glennie,' went on Donald, 'where did you learn that fine Buchan accent? You never used to talk like that. Is it since you came south that you've picked it up?'

The big professional looked a little shamefaced and drew Donald back into the dark corner.

'It's good for trade,' he whispered in the pure English of Inverness. 'They like a Scot to be real Scottish. They think it makes a man what they call "a character". God knows why, but there it is. So I just humour them by talking like a Guild Street carter who's having a bit of back-chat with an Aberdeen fishwife. It makes the profits something extraordinary.'

'Hi! Glennie, you old swindler,' shouted a stoutish red-faced man who was smoking a big cigar and wearing a spectroscopic suit of tweeds. 'How much do you want to sting me for this putter?'

'Thirty-twa shullin' and saxpence, Sir Walter,' replied Glennie over his shoulder, 'but ye'll be wastin' yer siller, for neither that club nor any ither wull bring ye doon below eighteen.'

A delighted laugh from a group of men behind Sir Walter greeted this sally.

'You see,' whispered Glennie, 'he'll buy it and he'll tell his friends that I tried to dissuade him, and they'll all agree that I'm a rare old character, and they'll all come and buy too.'

'But fifty-two shillings for a driver!' said Donald. 'Do you mean to say they'll pay that?'

'Yes, of course they will. They'll pay anything so long as it's more than any other professional at any other club charges them. That's the whole secret. Those drivers there aren't a new set at all. They're the same set as I was asking forty-eight shillings for last weekend, but I heard during the week from a friend who keeps an eye open for me, that young Jock Robbie over at Addingdale Manor had put his drivers and brassies up from forty-six shillings to fifty, the dirty young dog. Not that I blame him. It's a new form of commercial competition, Master Donald, a sort of inverted price-cutting. Na, na, Muster Hennessey,' he broke into his trade voice again, 'ye dinna want ony new clubs. Ye're playin' brawly with yer auld yins. Still, if ye want to try yon spoon, tak it oot and play a couple of roons wi' it, and if ye dinna like it put it back.'

He turned to Donald again.

'That's a sure card down here. They always fall for it. They take the club and tell their friends that I've given it to them on trial because I'm not absolutely certain that it will suit their game, and they never bring it back. Not once. Did you say you wanted a driver, Master Donald?'

'Not at fifty-two shillings,' said Donald with a smile.

Glennie indignantly waved away the suggestion.

'You shall have your pick of the shop at cost price,' he said, and then, looking furtively round and lowering his voice until it was almost inaudible, he breathed in Donald's ear, 'Fifteen and six.'

Donald chose a beautiful driver, treading on air all the while and feeling eighteen years of age, and then Sir Ludovic Phibbs came into the shop.

'Ah! There you are, Cameron,' he said genially; 'there are only two couples in front of us now. Are you ready? Good morning, Glennie, you old shark. There's no use trying to swing the lead over Mr Cameron. He's an Aberdonian himself.'

As Donald went out, Glennie thrust a box of balls under his arm and whispered, 'For old times' sake!'

On the first tee Sir Ludovic introduced him to the other two players who were going to make up the match. One was a Mr Wollaston, a clean-shaven, intelligent, large, prosperous-looking man of about forty, and the other was a Mr Gyles, a very dark man, with a toothbrush moustache and a most impressive silence. Both were stockbrokers.

'Now,' said Sir Ludovic heartily, 'I suggest that we play a four-ball foursome, Wollaston and I against you two, on handicap, taking our strokes from the course, five bob corners, half a crown for each birdie, a dollar an eagle, a bob best ball and a bob aggregate and a bob a putt. What about that?'

'Good!' said Mr Wollaston. Mr Gyles nodded, while Donald, who had not understood a single word except the phrase 'four-ball foursome' – and that was incorrect – mumbled a feeble affirmative. The stakes sounded enormous, and the reference to birds of the air sounded mysterious, but he obviously could not raise any objections.

When it was his turn to drive at the first tee, he selected a spot for his tee and tapped it with the toe of his driver. Nothing happened. He looked at his elderly caddy and tapped the ground again. Again nothing happened.

'Want a peg, Cameron?' called out Sir Ludovic.

'Oh no, it's much too early,' protested Donald, under the impression that he was being offered a drink. Everyone laughed ecstatically at this typically Scottish flash of wit, and the elderly caddy lurched forward with a loathsome little contrivance of blue and white celluloid which he offered to his employer. Donald shuddered. They'd be giving him a rubber tee with a tassel in a minute, or lending him a golf-bag with tripod legs. He teed his ball on a pinch of sand with a dexterous twist of his fingers and thumb amid an incredulous silence.

Donald played the round in a sort of daze. After a few holes of uncertainty, much of his old skill came back, and he reeled off fairly good figures. He had a little difficulty with his elderly caddy at the beginning of the round, for, on asking that functionary to hand him 'the iron', he received the reply, 'Which number, sir?' and the following dialogue ensued:

'Which number what?' faltered Donald.

'Which number iron?'

'Er – just the iron.'

'But it must have a number, sir.'

'Why must it?'

'All irons have numbers.'

'But I've only one.'

'Only a number one?'

'No. Only one.'

'Only one what, sir?'

'One iron!' exclaimed Donald, feeling that this music-hall turn might go on for a long time and must be already holding up the entire course.

The elderly caddy at last appreciated the deplorable state of affairs. He looked grievously shocked and said in a reverent tone:

'Mr Fumbledon has eleven.'

'Eleven what?' inquired the startled Donald.

'Eleven irons.'

After this revelation of Mr Fumbledon's greatness, Donald took 'the iron' and topped the ball hard along the ground. The caddy sighed deeply.

Throughout the game Donald never knew what the state of the match was, for the other three, who kept complicated tables upon the backs of envelopes, reckoned solely in cash. Thus, when Donald once timidly asked his partner how they stood, the taciturn Mr Gyles consulted his envelope and replied shortly, after a brief calculation, 'You're up three dollars and a tanner.'

Donald did not venture to ask again, and he knew nothing more about the match until they were ranged in front of the bar in the club-room, when Sir Ludovic and Mr Wollaston put down the empty glasses which had, a moment ago, contained double pink gins, ordered a refill of the four glasses, and then handed over to the bewildered Donald the sum of one pound sixteen and six.

Lunch was an impressive affair. It was served in a large room, panelled in white and gold with a good deal of artificial marble scattered about the walls, by a staff of bewitching young ladies in black frocks, white aprons and caps, and black silk stockings. Bland wine-stewards drifted hither and thither, answering to Christian names and accepting orders and passing them on to subordinates. Corks popped, the scent of the famous club fish-pie mingled itself with all the perfumes of Arabia and Mr Coty, smoke arose from rose-tipped cigarettes, and the rattle of knives and forks played an orchestral accompaniment to the sound of many voices, mostly silvery, like April rain, and full of girlish gaiety.

Sir Ludovic insisted on being host, and ordered Donald's half-pint of beer and double whiskies for himself and Mr Gyles. Mr Wollaston, pleading a diet and the strict orders of Carlsbad medicos, produced a bottle of Berncastler out of a small brown handbag, and polished it off in capital style.

The meal itself consisted of soup, the famous fish-pie, a fricassee of chicken, saddle of mutton or sirloin of roast beef, sweet, savoury, and cheese, topped off with four of the biggest glasses of hunting port that Donald had ever seen. Conversation at lunch was almost entirely about the dole. The party then went back to the main club-room where Mr Wollaston firmly but humorously pushed Sir Ludovic into a very deep chair, and insisted upon taking up the running with four coffees and four double kümmels. Then after a couple of rubbers of bridge, at which Donald managed to win a few shillings, they sallied out to play a second round. The golf was only indifferent in the afternoon. Sir Ludovic complained that, owing to the recrudescence of what he mysteriously called 'the old trouble', he was finding it very difficult to focus the ball clearly, and Mr Wollaston kept on over-swinging so violently that he fell over once and only just saved himself on several other occasions, and Mr Gyles developed a fit of socketing that soon became a menace to the course, causing, as it did, acute nervous shocks to a retired major-general whose sunlit nose only escaped by a miracle, and a bevy of beauty that was admiring, for some reason, the play of a well-known actor-manager.

So after eight holes the afternoon round was abandoned by common consent, and they walked back to the club-house for more bridge and much-needed refreshment. Donald was handed seventeen shillings as his inexplicable winnings over the eight holes. Later on, Sir Ludovic drove, or rather Sir Ludovic's chauffeur drove, Donald back to the corner of King's Road and Royal Avenue. On the way back, Sir Ludovic talked mainly about the dole.

*

Seated in front of the empty grate in his bed-sitting-room, Donald counted his winnings and reflected that golf had changed a great deal since he had last played it.

chapter 9

In the middle of August, Davies telephoned to Donald and asked him to come round to the office in Henrietta Street and report progress.

Donald was frankly depressed, and he said so. 'I'm out of my depth,' he said. 'My feet aren't on the ground.'

Davies laughed. He found his young friend's perplexities amusing.

'I didn't imagine you'd find it very easy,' he said. 'But don't forget what I told you in that infernal pill-box, years ago. I've got a sort of instinctive notion that the English character—'

'There's no such thing,' interrupted Donald. 'They're all different.'

'That the English character,' went on Davies firmly, 'is based fundamentally upon kindliness and poetry. Just keep that notion in mind, whether you agree with it or not. And now listen to me, I've got a job for you.'

'What sort of a job?' inquired Donald suspiciously.

'A private-secretaryship.'

Donald's face fell. 'But I want to write things. I don't think I want—'

'Of course you want to write things, you young donkey. And I'm trying to help you. What I'm offering to you is the private-secretaryship to an English politician – English, mind you – and it's only temporary. The man in question is a very old friend of mine, and his permanent fellow has gone down with scarlet fever.'

'But Parliament isn't sitting,' began Donald.

'There's a little Mr Know-all,' replied Davies pleasantly. 'It hadn't escaped my notice that Parliament isn't sitting. But my friend has just been appointed to the British delegation that is going to the Assembly of the League of Nations at Geneva in a fortnight, and he wants someone to go with him, and hold his hat and coat. Would you care to take it on? All expenses and a fiver a week.'

'For how long?'

'For a month. He might give you a very good notion of the Englishman as an internationalist.'

Donald sprang to his feet.

'Of course!' he exclaimed. 'What a fool I am! And how kind you are! You really are most awfully kind,' he added naïvely.

Mr Davies was pleased.

'That's capital,' he said. 'My friend's name is Sir Henry Wootton, and he's the Conservative member for East Something-or-Other. You'll find him in Vacher's. I'll give you a card to him and I'll ring him up and tell him you're coming to see him. He's a very decent fellow. Apart from that, I won't say another word about him so as not to prejudice you one way or the other. Good-bye and good luck. Come and see me when you get back.'

Sir Henry Wootton was a nice, cheerful, elderly buck of about seventy, and he lived in a large house in Queen's Gate. He had a rosy face, a large white moustache, and blue eyes, and his manners were old-fashioned in their perfection. He received Donald in a rather impressive library, lined with books on all sides. But the impressiveness wore off after a bit, for the books were not the books of a reader, but more like the reference section of a public library or a dusty corridor in a West End Club. *The Dictionary of National Biography* stretched out its interminable array; above it was an old edition of the *Encyclopaedia Britannica*. The *Annual Register* occupied shelf after shelf. Bailey's *Guide to the Turf*, Hansard's *Parliamentary Debates*, the *Gentleman's Magazine*, huge bound volumes of the *Illustrated London News*, the *Field*, *Country Life*, *Horse and Hound*, and other periodicals of bygone ages stood massively, leathery, shoulder to shoulder, rather like the massive, prosperous years of Victorianism which they recorded in their pages. They belonged to a period of the life of England in which there was time not only to read the five-hour speeches of long-dead

Chancellors, but to re-read them in after-years out of leather-bound collections, a period in which a gentleman had leisure for the pursuit of the gentlemanly pastimes.

Sir Henry belonged to that period. He had driven his coach-and-six to the Derby. He had been taken, as a boy, to see Lord Frederick Beauclerk play a single-wicket match at Lord's; he had seen Jem Mace box; he had damned Oscar Wilde's eyes on the steps of the Athenaeum; he had borrowed money from Sam Lewis to back Ormonde with; he had worshipped the Jersey Lily from afar, and the lesser ladies of *Florodora* and *The Geisha* from a little nearer, and a lot of ladies in Paris and Venice from much closer still. And, on inheriting the baronetcy, he had given up all these things and gone into politics. It was the traditional finish to the life of a traditional English gentleman, and Sir Henry was in the tradition.

The beginning of his political life was a welter of right-minded hatred of Mr Lloyd George and his anarchistic theories about land and money. The middle period was a glow of right-minded adoration of Mr Lloyd George and his magnificence as organizer of victory; while the closing phase of Sir Henry's career at St Stephen's was untinged with hatreds or adorations. He had outlived the passions and had glided into a serene tranquillity. He did not understand in the least what had happened to the world or was likely to happen, but he was perfectly happy and perfectly willing to play any part that might be allotted to him. He was an admirable Chairman of Commissions to inquire into things of which he had not known the existence; he did not approve in theory of such things as the Irish Treaty, or votes for young ladies of twenty-one, or supertax, but as they had come and were obviously going to stay, he was quite willing to support them in practice. He liked the older members of the Conservative Party because at least ninety per cent of them were lifelong friends; he liked the 'young chaps' because they were the type that would have ridden straight, if hunting hadn't become so damned prohibitive, and would have chased the girls of *Florodora* and *The Geisha* if they weren't buckling down so damned well to the business of running the country; he liked the handful of Radicals in the House, because they were mostly brainy chaps and he admired brains; he liked the Socialists because they got so angry, and that made him laugh. In fact, he liked everyone except 'those damned turncoats' who jumped about from Party to Party like cats in search of jobs. Sir Henry could not stand them at any price, and said so repeatedly and, for his voice was naturally a rather loud one, loudly.

This, then, was the gentleman who welcomed Donald with old-fashioned politeness into his musty, dusty, leathery library:

'I'll tell you what it is, Cameron,' he said, after the usual courtesies had been exchanged, and a butler had brought in a couple of glasses of sherry and a biscuit-jar (in Sir Henry's life ceremonial 'Misters' played as small a part as Christian names); 'I don't really want a secretary in the proper sense of the word. I'm not going to make speeches with figures and facts and all that sort of rubbish in them. I'm just going to stick to generalities. The truth of the matter is that I don't know much about this League, and I don't know why the P.M. wants me to go. But he's asked me, and so, of course, I'm going. I'm all in favour of peace myself, as every sane man is, but I've got a sort of notion that the best way to keep the peace is the good old British way of building a thumping great fleet and letting the dagoes do what they damned well like, eh? After all, it worked in the past, so why not now? However, I'm told that's all wrong in these modern times, and so I expect it is. They tell me that this League is the dodge now, and if that's so, I'm all in favour of it. Do you see what I mean?'

'Yes, sir,' replied Donald. So far he had found little difficulty in following the thread of Sir Henry's discourse.

'I don't run down the League just because it's new,' went on Sir Henry. 'If we've got to love the black man like a brother, I'm quite prepared to do it. At present I draw the line at loving him like a brother-in-law, but I expect that'll come later. Now your job at Geneva, if you agree to take it on, will be more like a cross between a valet and a friend. I mean you'll have to find my hat for me, and you'll have to keep me posted up with the sporting news from home, and you'll have to see that there's a taxi for me when I want one, and that I don't run out of whisky in the evenings, and all that sort of thing. Do you feel like taking it on for a month?'

'I should be delighted,' replied Donald.

'Splendid. We leave on Friday morning. You'd better run round to the Foreign Office and fix up about passports and so on. And you'd better see if you can find out what this League does, and how it works, and all that sort of thing.'

Donald found it very difficult at Geneva to keep his mind concenrated upon his task. There was so much that was new to be seen, heard, tasted, drunk, and done. With delegates of more than fifty nations concentrated into one town, or worse, into one small quarter of one town, it was almost impossible to remember that he was engaged upon a specific job – the study, at close quarters and at first hand, of the Representatives of England, at work upon international politics. They were, after all, well worth studying. For the English, whatever may be said against their home politics, or their climate, or their cooking, or their love-making, or their art, or their sport, have proved themselves over and over again through the centuries the masters of international diplomacy and foreign affairs. A glance at the history of the world shows how the enemies of England have always collapsed unexpectedly and mysteriously whether owing to the sudden uprising of a southerly gale to drive invading galleons from Gravelines to the Pentland Firth, or owing to a trivial miscalculation which isolated the wing of an army in the obscure Danubian village of Blindheim, or owing to a Spanish ulcer, or to the sinking of a *Lusitania*, and it cannot be supposed that these incidents were all fortuitous. In the same way a glance at the geography of the world shows that in the days of sailing-ships every convenient port somehow or other fell into the hands of the English, except Walfish Bay and Pondicherry; that in the days of coal, every coaling-station was English; that in the days of oil, the only oil-wells that did not already belong to people who wanted selfishly to keep them for themselves, became English; that in 1920 even Walfish Bay, useless as it had become, went the same way as all the rest for the sake of the principle, leaving only Pondicherry as a sort of joke; and that the last scramble, the scramble for aerodromes, fell flat because every reasonably smooth island was already in English hands, except one a good deal north of Siberia, called Wrangel Island, and another in the South Seas called Johnson Island. These two alone were left out by English diplomacy: the first because it is so cold that petrol, oil, and water immediately freeze on arriving there, thus rendering it comparatively unfit for aeronautical manoeuvres; and the other, Johnson Island, because, after a volley of notes and threats to the Norwegian Government – which also laid claim to it – the English Intelligence Service somehow ferreted out the fact that the disputed island had not been sighted since its first discovery, sixty-eight years earlier, by a dipsomaniacal Australian skipper, who had noted it down in his log as appearing on the horizon between two pale-pink lizards in yellow breeches and deer-stalkers; and that no one knew in the least where it was. The English Foreign Office immediately dispatched a most cordial Note to the Norwegian Government relinquishing all claims on Johnson Island, not as a matter of international right and wrong, but as a graceful compliment to the King of Norway, whose birthday was due in a few weeks' time. Meanwhile the English Admiralty marked Johnson Island on its charts as 'disappeared in unrecorded land-subsidence', and two years later, the Air Force, hearing the news, provisionally deleted it from its official list of aerodromes.

Donald ought, therefore, to have found no difficulty in concentrating upon the most fascinating of human spectacles, Experts at Work. The English had proved themselves for hundreds of years the Heads of the Profession, and here they were again, at the very centre of the international world, using all their unrivalled skill for the still further betterment of their Empire.

But there were many distractions. The streets were crowded with strange sights. Abyssinians in great blue robes and wearing great black beards swung proudly along the boulevards; Chinese and Japanese and Siamese and Cochinese and Cingalese and Tonkinese and Annamese moved inscrutably hither and thither. Frenchmen chattered. Australians in big hats strode. Sinn Fein ex-gunmen, now Ministers of State, sat in cafés and told witty stories. Albanians, ill at ease without their habitual arsenal of firearms, scowled at Yugo-Slavs. South Americans abounded, dark men with roving eyes and a passion for kissing typists in lifts. Maharajahs who were descended from ten thousand gods walked as if they were conscious of their ancestry. Newsboys, usually well over eighty years of age, sold papers written in every conceivable language but mainly in the language of the Middle-Western States of the United States; and everywhere pattered private secretaries, racing hither and thither, always in a hurry, always laden with papers, and always just managing to snatch a moment to exchange the latest gossip with each other as they sped by.

In strange contrast to these active young men was the vast, amorphous mass of American tourists who never had anything to do. They eddied about the streets in aimless shoals, like lost mackerel, pointing out celebrities to each other and always getting them wrong; taking endless photographs of obscure Genevese citizens in mistake for German Chancellors or Soviet Observers, and pretending that they had important luncheon-dates. Geneva during September had become as much a pilgrimage for Wyoming, Nebraska, and Boston, to name only three of the main pilgrim-exporting centres, as the Colosseum, the Venus de Milo, the outside of Mr Beerbohm's villa at Rapallo, or the fields at St Mihiel where the German Imperial Army met its first, its only, and its final defeat.

Nor was life in the streets the only distraction. There was the International Club, for instance, where a gentleman in a white coat, called Victor, performed prodigies of activity in the mixing of Bronxes, Gin-Slings, John Collinses, and Brandy St Johns, leaping to and fro, like a demented preacher, for bottles, sugar, lemons, cherries, and straws. His clients were mostly journalists, and very swagger journalists at that. They were not the type which runs round feverishly trying to pick up news. They did not carry note-books in their hip pockets. They did not pester statesmen for interviews. What they did was to play billiards all day in the Club, calling upon the services of Mr Victor from time to time, until a message arrived giving the hour at which the French Foreign Minister, or the German Foreign Minister, was ready to receive them and answer questions. Occasionally the British Foreign Minister received them, but his receptions were not nearly so popular as those of his two colleagues, for the Frenchman could usually be relied upon for several calculated indiscretions, while the German could always be relied upon for free Munich beer. The Englishman, on the other hand, was both discreet and temperate.

There was also the great building of the Secretariat itself, in which the permanent officials were always ready to welcome visitors at any hour during the day. There was the lake, blue, clear, like a polished aquamarine, translucent, exquisite, studded with far-off brick-red sails of barges and white butterfly yachts, and defended by the everlasting snows of Mont Blanc and the Dent du Midi. Boats could be hired for sailing on the lake, the bathing was warm and luxurious, and on the far side were restaurants, where a man might dine with a lovely lady and see what could·be done in the way of wooing by the light of Orion upon dark waters and the sound of little murmurous waves. And anyone who failed to advance his suit in those little lake-side restaurants might just as well reconcile himself at once to a long life of dreary celibacy.

In addition to all these attractions there were the dancing-halls and the cabarets and the cafés in the Old Town, especially the one that wasn't actually the one that Lenin and Trotsky used to frequent in the old days and is now demolished, but wasn't far off, and the Kursaal, and the lounges of the big hotels and the cinemas.

Yes, Geneva was full of distractions for even the keenest of students of international affairs and English policy, and, after the first week of preliminaries, Donald had to make a stern resolution to attend to business and eschew frivolities.

Sir Henry Wootton was thoroughly enjoying himself, and had already devoted several evenings to the discussion of a lot of urgent international business at one of the lake-side restaurants with the permanent deputy-chief of the Exchange-of-Municipal-Experience Section of the Secretariat. The permanent deputy-chief looked very fetching in black velvet and a picture hat, and Sir Henry was as sorry as his secretary when the time came for the application of noses to grindstones.

The normal procedure of the Assembly was as follows. The first week was devoted to speech-making on any subject under the sun by any delegate who wanted to get his name into print in the newspapers of his native country. Nobody listened to them, not even the reporters of the native newspapers, for they had received typewritten copies of the speech which affected them, six or seven hours before it was delivered.

After this week of oratory had been completed, the Assembly split itself up into six Committees, three of which were presided over by an English, French, and German president, two by South Americans, and one by an Asiatic. On this occasion the two South Americans were Panama and Paraguay; the Asiatic was Caspia. But the procedure had to be somewhat modified, as at first no South American delegates were available, for the following rather singular and quite exceptional reason. The second week of the Assembly happened to coincide with the fourth session of the Permanent Committee for the Suppression of Obscene Photographs, Post Cards, Magazines, Advertisements, and Publications in General, and by a curious coincidence all the South Americans, including Cuba, San Domingo, and Haiti – indeed, headed by San Domingo and Haiti, with Cuba well in the running for a place – decided to attend the meetings of the Committee. Fortunately for the work of the Assembly, the sessions of the Permanent Committee for the Suppression of Obscene Photographs, Post Cards, Magazines, Advertisements, and Publications in General came to an abrupt halt on the second day, the entire collection of specimens of the literature in question, so laboriously collected over a long period by the Secretariat, having been pinched by the delegates.

Sir Henry was assigned by the Earl of Osbaldestone, Britain's senior delegate, to the Committee for the Abolition of Social Abuses, and he dispatched Donald first to the Secretariat for documents, which would tell him what exactly the Abuses were, and then to the Staff of Foreign Office experts for information about the British Official Policy which Sir Henry was to expound and advocate.

Donald had no difficulty about the documents. There were sheaves of them, printed and typed, records of past Conferences, verbatim minutes of Committees, draft resolutions, amendments to draft resolutions, alterations to amendments of draft resolutions, cancellations of alterations, copies of speeches, and Press reports from publications as far divided, geographically and politically, as the *Singapore Hardware and Allied Trades Independent*, the *Santiago de Chile Indigo Ex-*

porters' Quarterly, *The Times, Der Wienerwurst und Schnitzeller Tages-Zeitung* of Rothenburg-am-Tauber, a matrimonial journal called *The Link*, the *Manchester Guardian, Who's Who in Cochin-China*, and the *Irish Free State Union of Sewage-Inspectors' Annual Report*.

Donald hired two taxis and filled one up to the roof with the necessary documents and directed the man to drive to Sir Henry's hotel, while he himself went in the other.

After a couple of hours spent in sorting, sifting, and arranging, Donald discovered the crucial sheet of paper on which was printed the agenda of the Commission. It appeared that the two main Abuses at which Sir Henry was due to launch himself were the Illicit Traffic in Synthetic Beer, and the existence in certain countries of Houses of Ill-Repute, discreetly called Licensed Establishments, and Donald set off on his second mission – to obtain the Official Policy on these two matters.

The Foreign Office experts occupied the whole of the second floor of the hotel, and Donald doubtfully entered a sitting-room from which issued a rattle of typewriters, and on the door of which was pinned a label which said, rather surprisingly, 'Chancery'. He was instantly abashed at finding himself in the midst of a perfect vision of beauty and elegance. On all sides radiant young ladies, obviously straight from the establishments of Poirot, Paquin, or Molyneux, were whacking away with dainty fingers at type-writing machines. The air was full of incense. Blood rushed to Donald's head. His eyes went dim. The room darkened. A golden-haired Aphrodite slid up to him but he could not see her. He wanted to fly but his legs would not move. He perspired vehemently, and longed for the quiet midden at the Mains of Balspindie.

After what seemed five or six hours, a vision of blue eyes and golden hair swam out of the mist before him and he stammered a vague and halting statement of his requirements, dropping his hat twice during the recital and, on the second occasion, clutching wildly at the Aphrodite's silken ankle as he groped for it. The goddess was quite unperturbed by the sudden grasp. Lady secretaries at international conferences which are attended by South Americans quickly get accustomed to almost anything.

Nervous Englishmen, or Scotsmen, are child's-play to those who can, with deftness and dignity, handle a Venezuelan.

As soon as Donald had released his grip upon her ankle, had retrieved his hat, and had embarked upon a flood of apologies, she cut him short with kindly firmness, and led him through the roomful of beauty to an inner sanctum into which she pushed him with the words, 'You want Mr Carteret-Pendragon.'

The inner sanctum was a strange contrast to the outer room. It was very large, being one of the largest sitting-rooms in the hotel and seldom occupied during the other months of the year except by Nebraskans and Maharajahs, and was furnished tastefully in green, gold, and marble. There were probably more than one thousand gold tassels on the curtains alone, a source of legitimate pride to the management.

Three young men were sitting in complete silence at three tables, marble-topped and gilt-edged. None of them looked up as Donald came in, and after the golden Venus had closed the door with a snap, a deep, religious soundlessness fell upon the place, as in a cathedral upon a summer's afternoon.

Donald choked down a nervous cough and waited. At last one of the young men laid down his pen, leant back in his chair and said, 'Well?'

'Mr Carteret-Pendragon?'

'That is my name, sir.'

'I am Sir Henry Wootton's private secretary,' began Donald. 'My name is Cameron—'

'How-do-you-do. My name is Carteret-Pendragon. Let me introduce Mr Carshalton-Stanbury, and this is Mr Woldingham-Uffington.'

The two young men got up and bowed gravely and sat down again and went on with their work. Donald noticed that all three were wearing Old Etonian ties.

'It's about Sir Henry and the Social Abuses Commission,' said Donald.

'Sit down,' said Mr Carteret-Pendragon. He was a young man of about thirty with beautiful fair hair, parted at the side and flat and very shiny, a razor-like crease down his grey trousers, pale-yellow horn-rimmed spectacles, and a dark-red carnation in his buttonhole. Mr Carshalton-Stanbury's hair was black, his horn-rims dappled, and his carnation vermilion. Mr Woldingham-Uffington's hair, horn-rims, and carnation were all yellow.

'Sir Henry wants to know what line he is to take about the traffic in Synthetic Beer,' said Donald.

Mr Carteret-Pendragon wrinkled his snow-white brow.

'I don't think I quite follow,' he said in some perplexity.

'Sir Henry thinks that he will probably have to make a speech about it, you see,' explained Donald.

'In a sense, yes,' replied Mr Carteret-Pendragon, 'and in another sense, no. It will,' he added, as if clarifying the position, 'of course, be expected of him.'

'And he wants to know what to say.'

'Oh! the usual things,' said Mr Carteret-Pendragon easily. He went on, checking off the points on his fingers: 'Devotion of British Commonwealth of Free Nations to ideals of League, nation of peace-lovers, all must cooperate, wonderful work of League, praise of the Secretariat, economy in League expenditure, a word about Woodrow Wilson, and a tribute to the French.'

He picked up a document, and began to study it as if the interview had been brought to a conclusion that was satisfactory to everyone.

'But why a tribute to the French?' asked Donald in surprise.

'It's the usual way to finish off a speech here. It does no harm and the French like it.'

'But what about the Synthetic Beer?'

'What about it?' said Mr Carteret-Pendragon in a rather tired voice.

'I mean, what is our policy?'

At the word 'policy' the other two diplomatists started as if they had suddenly been confronted with a rattlesnake, and all three stared at Donald.

'Policy?' repeated Mr Carteret-Pendragon in bewilderment, and Mr Carshalton-Stanbury and Mr Woldingham-Uffington echoed the word and gazed vaguely round the room, like people who have lost something which might turn up unexpectedly at any moment – a dog, for example, or a small child.

'Policy?' repeated Mr Carteret-Pendragon in a firmer voice.

He had quicker wits than the other two, and had grasped what this queer youth in the lounge-suit and no buttonhole was talking about.

'My dear sir,' he went on indulgently, 'we don't have policies about things. We leave all that to the dagoes. It keeps them out of mischief.'

'But don't we – don't you – doesn't Great Britain take an independent line about anything?'

'Whatever for?' inquired Mr Carteret-Pendragon, and the other two murmured the words 'independent line', like men in a maze.

'We are here to preserve balances,' went on the diplomat. 'Our task is to maintain equilibriums – equilibria, I ought to say,' he corrected himself with a small cough. 'After all, there are the proportions, when all is said and done. One must have a sense of equipoise.'

'Naturally,' murmured the other two, hitching up their beautiful trousers about a centimetre and half in complete unison.

'But how does anything get settled?' inquired Donald, feeling remarkably foolish in the presence of these sophisticated men of the great world.

'Oh, they get settled all right – if not now, at some other time, and if not at Geneva, then in London. It's all a matter of fact. When in doubt agree with the Frenchman. Or if you prefer it, disagree with the Italian. It's all one.'

'And what about brothels? What do we say about them?'

'At the last six Assemblies we've simply said that we don't know what they are. All you have to do is to say it again.'

Mr Carteret-Pendragon pondered a moment and then added, 'Broadly speaking, you are fairly safe to take as a generalization, that so far as Organized Vice is concerned, we might, as an Empire, be reasonably described as being more or less against it.'

The interview was now definitely at an end, and Donald went out, feeling that he had gained some sort of insight, at first hand into the subtle diplomacy which had spread the Union Jack upon all the potential aerodromes of the world. He could see that the genius was there, though he could not have explained for the life of him how it worked. But, of course, that was the genius of it.

The outer room was a dull and drab place as he passed through it. For it was by now past 12 o'clock and Beauty had gone off to lunch, leaving only a memory and a fragrance.

The President of the Committee for the Suppression of Social Abuses was the senior Caspian delegate, and he was enabled to carry through the sections on the agenda which dealt with the traffic in dangerous drugs with great expedition, being himself a lifelong addict to heroin, which he injected subcutaneously into his arm, just as Sherlock did, with a silver hypodermic syringe, encrusted with carved turquoises. His expert knowledge enabled him to correct several of the delegates when their rhetoric about the dismal after-effects of drugging carried them out of the sphere of reality into the sphere of imagination. It was the President also who threw a great deal of cold water upon the fervour of the Swiss representative, when that gentleman was affirming with a vast amount of eloquence that Switzerland had entirely extirpated the villainous crew of drug-traffickers from her free and snowy soil. For, having only that very morning run out of his indispensable heroin, the President had approached a gendarme, courteously touched his red fez and inquired whether there was a drug-seller in the vicinity. The gendarme, according to the President, had courteously saluted and replied, 'Does your Excellency perceive that house along the street with pink shutters and an advertisement for the Sun Insurance Company above its door? Your Excellency does? Good. That is the only house in this vicinity that I know of, at which drugs are not procurable.'

But when the drug sections of the agenda had been satisfactorily dealt with and the consideration of a number of important resolutions postponed until the following year, the President's efficiency fell off considerably. This was partly owing to his lack of interest in the subjects, and partly that, between injections, he was inclined to drop off for forty winks. This habit led to one very unfortunate incident.

The item on the agenda which was being discussed was the advisability of compiling a register of deaths from bubonic plague in the ports of Macao, Bangkok, Wei-hai-Wei, and one or two fishing harbours at the southern end of the island of

Formosa, and the Yugoslav delegate, having caught the President's eye just before the latter fell into a quiet snooze, delivered a slashing harangue. He stated, with all the emphasis at his command, that while approving in principle of the register of deaths from bubonic plague, for his Government yielded to none in its loyal adherence to all measures for the pacific betterment of humanity, at the same time he felt that he ought to draw the attention of the Committee to the barbarous conduct of the Hungarian Army in Yugo-Slavia during the Great War. The Hungarian delegate protested warmly, but the President, who was dreaming of the Mahometan Paradise, only smiled sweetly, and the Yugo-Slav continued.

'Libraries, often containing as many as sixty or seventy books,' he cried, 'were burnt. Castles were razed to the ground. Pictures were stolen, including a whole set of reproductions of the works of Rubens in the house of a baron; statues were broken; photogravures slashed; trees cut down, gardens destroyed; women raped—'

'What did you say?' exclaimed the Costa Rican delegate, waking up sharply.

'Women raped,' repeated the Yugo-Slav firmly.

'Mr President,' cried the senior Guatemalan, leaping up in great excitement, 'I beg to move the following resolution: that this Commission reaffirms it unshakable loyalty to the League of Nations, expresses its sincere sympathies for the sufferings of the kingdom of the Serb-Croat-Slovenes, and warmly invites the delegate of that kingdom to submit photographs of the atrocities to which he has alluded.'

'Mr President,' cried the delegate of San Salvador, 'I beg to second that resolution.'

'Agreed, agreed!' shouted an enthusiastic chorus of Latin-American voices.

The President, who had just reached the Seventh Heaven, nodded and smiled. The Yugo-Slav burst into tears of emotion. The New Zealander called across to the South African, 'For God's sake, let's go and have one. These swobs make me sick,' and the two stalwart Colonials marched out, followed hastily by the Australian.

It was some moments before the Yugo-Slav, mastering his

manly sobs, was able to thank the honourable delegates of Guatemala and San Salvador. He held up a huge book.

'This book contains photographs,' he said, 'of the ruined castles of my unhappy country.'

'Only the castles?' asked the Venezuelan hopefully.

'Good God!' cried the Yugo-Slav. 'Isn't that enough for you?'

'No!' replied the Latin-Americans in chorus.

The representative of the kingdom of the Serb-Croat-Slovenes was so disgusted by this infidelity that he addressed himself sulkily to the question on the agenda, the bubonic plague in the Far East. Unfortunately the President, awaking at that moment, injected a dose of heroin into his arm and briskly ruled the speaker out of order, and the Commision broke up in confusion.

But the important Commission was the one devoted to Disarmament. All the senior delegates were represented upon it, and Donald stood in a crowd upon the steps of the Secretariat one morning and watched them arrive. The Frenchmen drove up in four magnificent Delage cars with the Tricolor on the radiators; the Spaniards were in Hispano-Suizas, for to the ignorant world the Hispano is even more Spanish than its name; the Italians in Isotta-Fraschinis, with their secretaries in Fiats; the Belgians in Minervas; while the Germans outdid everyone in vast silver Mercédès cars, driven by world-famous racing-drivers. The United States official Observers were mostly in Packards, Chryslers, Graham-Paiges, Willys-Knights, Buicks. Oldsmobiles, and Stutzes, and the Earl of Osbaldestone and his two chief colleagues came in a four-wheel cab, and his secretaries, Mr Carteret-Pandragon, Mr Carshalton-Stanbury, and Mr Woldingham-Uffington, walked.

Fortunately the prestige of British motor manufacturers was well maintained by the eleven Rolls-Royces, with real tortoise-shell bodies and gold bonnets, specially brought over from England by the Right Honourable Lieutenant-General the Maharajah of Hyderadore.

Donald attended several of the debates of the Disarmament Commission and listened to a masterly speech, lasting nearly an hour and three-quarters, in which the Earl of Osbaldestone explained that Great Britain had no special views on the burning question of the reduction and limitation of the output of nails for the horseshoes of cavalry horses, and to the superb oration by the French Foreign Minister which proved, to the complete satisfaction of Poland, Roumania, Czecho-Slovakia, and Yugo-Slavia, that a reduction of cavalry horseshoe-nails would be to France the equivalent of the withdrawal from the, Vosges, the surrender of Metz, and the abandonment of conscription. His peroration, ending with the immortal words, 'The France of Charlemagne, of Gambetta, of Boulanger, the France of the 22nd of October, the France of the 18th of November, and the France of the 4th of March, is built upon the nails of her immortal horses', drew thunders of applause.

He was followed by a Roumanian lady who descanted a good deal upon the beauties of dawn coming over distant mountain-tops, and whose hand was admiringly kissed at the end of her speech by numbers of swarthy delegates, and she was followed by a small Lithuanian who pointed out in a squeaky voice that the whole question of horseshoes, and nails for horseshoes, was inextricably bound up with the act of dastardly brigandage by which Poland had stolen the ancient Lithuanian capital of Vilna. At this point an unseemly commotion was caused by a loud burst of laughter from a group consisting of the South African representative, the second Indian delegate, and a United States Observer, to whom the Foreign Minister of the Irish Free State had just whispered a vulgar story. The Vice-Chairman, a courtly Chinese, saved the situation by springing to his feet and saying, in slow but perfect French, 'Honourable gentlemen and ladies of the Commission, of which I have the honour unworthily to act as Vice-Chairman, I would crave the permission of you all to put the following consideration before you. The hour is now a quarter to 2, and we have laboured long and earnestly this morning in the cause that we all have at heart, and I would put it to you, in all deference and submission, that the time is at hand when we must decide whether to adjourn now for midday refreshment and resume our task, our so important task, with redoubled vigour later in the day, or whether to continue without rest or interval until we have settled this problem while it is fresh in our minds. I submit, most honourable ladies and gentlemen of the Commission, that we should now come to a decision upon this matter. I will ask the most honourable interpreter to render into English the poor observations which I have had the honour to address to you.'

He bowed with old-world grace to right and to left and sat down. The interpreter, a rosy youth whose knowledge of languages was only equalled by the profundity of his thirst, sprang to his feet eagerly and said in a loud voice, 'The Vice-Chairman says that if we don't stop now we'll be late for lunch,' and, snapping an elastic band round his note-book, he thrust it under his arm and walked out of the room. There was a helpless pause for a moment or two, and then the delegates, in ones and twos, headed by the British Dominions, streamed out into the corridor.

The third week of the Assembly was a dull week for Donald and also for Sir Henry Wootton. Sir Henry had made his two speeches and had found no difficulty in keeping to the lines laid down for him by Mr Carteret-Pendragon. Indeed, his two speeches were so very like each other, and were so carefully phrased in order to avoid giving the impression that Great Britain took any very strong interest in anything, that by a secretarial error the speech against the traffic in Synthetic Beer was printed in the section of the official report relating to Houses of Ill-Repute, and vice versa, and no one noticed that anything was wrong.

But after the two speeches had been delivered there was nothing more to be done.

Donald found that the other private secretaries attached to the delegation were in the same position. Their chiefs had each made their two speeches and their work was finished.

The fourth and last week was a little better, as there was a general inclination to return to lunch-parties, bathing, yachting, and discreet little dinners by starlight. Peace-makers, no less than warriors, need relaxation.

During this last week, part of Donald's duties was to entertain Sir Henry Wootton's sister and brother-in-law, Mr and Mrs Fielding, who were visiting Geneva to watch the League at work. Mr Fielding, a man of about sixty, who looked like a farmer and talked almost as charmingly and learnedly as the great Mr Charles Ossory himself, took a great fancy to Donald, and, by some mysterious process of unobtrusive questioning, succeeded in extracting from him the secret of his book about England.

Mr Fielding was both sympathetic and enthusiastic, and insisted that Donald should visit them in their Buckinghamshire home later in the year.

'No foreigner can understand England, Cameron,' he said, 'until he's seen Buckinghamshire.'

The final sessions of the Assembly were held. The last item on the agenda, the election of the Council, was taken, and a six-hour ballot resulted in the re-election of the entire Council with the exception that San Domingo took the place of Haiti. The last speeches were made. The last tributes to the peaceful ideals of France were paid by the Foreign Ministers of Poland, Roumania, Czecho-Slovakia, and Yugo-Slavia, and the delegates slipped away. The tumult and the oratory died.

Donald, sitting in his sleeper in the Paris express as it pulled out of Bellegarde, the Swiss-French frontier station, ran over in his mind the result of the four weeks' entertainment at which he had assisted, and checked off on a sheet of paper the results that had been achieved. He was flabbergasted to discover that there was hardly a man, woman, or child on the surface of the globe whose lives would not be affected for the better by the plans laid, schemes evolved or furthered, and measures taken during those four weeks. But how these results had been achieved, and when, and by whom, he was utterly unable to say. He was also utterly unable to detect how the English had gone about their inscrutable and mysterious paths their wonders to perform. In his complete bafflement he could only fall back upon the old truism, *ars est celare artem*, and conclude, as the world for centuries has concluded, that in the realms of international affairs the English are the supreme artists.

chapter 10

For a week or two, life in Royal Avenue was rather flat after
Geneva. There was a constraint about it, a sort of grey dullness.
London was formal, solid, relentlessly matter-of-fact. No one
sat on wicker chairs on the pavements at 9.30 drinking sticky
drinks, green and orange and purple; there were no public
places to dance in all night and no one danced even until 3
o'clock in the morning, except people who could afford to
patronize the large hotels, or rather who were told over and
over again by their publicity agents that they couldn't afford not
to patronize the large hotels; no one published paper-covered
novels at a shilling; no one sold magazines full of pictures of
lovely ladies in chemises and shoes, or alternatively silk stockings and earrings; no one seemed to enjoy themselves, and the
sun never shone.

The cricket season was over, and the great English sporting
public had settled down to the contemplation of professional
football. Vast crowds poured down the King's Road and the
Fulham Road every Saturday afternoon to see the matches at
the Craven Bridge ground. Donald went once, partly to watch
the mighty, cloth-capped heart of England, sixty thousand
strong, thronging the terraces of the arena, cheering on their
heroes and hurling good-natured abuse at the referee, and
partly because a famous fellow-countryman was due to visit the
Walham Green Wanderers on behalf of the West Riding United
Football Club in the North of England. This was no less a per-
sonage than the great Mr Jock Thompson, captain and centre-
forward of Scotland, possessor of sixteen international caps. Mr
Thompson had for several years captained the West Riding
United, and when that team came to Craven Bridge, Donald
felt that he owed it to a compatriot to spring a bob and attend
the match.

He was well rewarded, for Mr Thompson displayed all the
wizardry which had raised him to the top of the football tree,
and by much swerving, dodging, feinting, and dribbling he
scored three inimitable goals and brought victory to his team.
No captain can do more. It is true that on that very morning

protracted negotiations between the managements of West Riding United and Walham Green Wanderers had been brought to a satisfactory conclusion, and Mr Jock Thompson had left the former and joined the latter, on consideration of a trifle of fourteen thousand pounds paid by the latter to the former; and it is also true that at 1 o'clock on that very day, a special meeting of directors of the Walham Green Wanderers Football Club had unanimously elected Mr Thompson to be captain of the Walham Green eleven. The fact remains that Mr Thompson gave a superb display and won the match for his side, an exhibition of team-spirit and loyalty, felt Donald, that could not have been surpassed even by cricketers.

An incident that enlivened the tedium of those October weeks was the barefaced burglary of the Royal Avenue house. A man had come to the door and had represented himself to be an official of the Gas, Light, and Coke Company. Being young, with curly brown hair and a plausible manner, he had been cordially welcomed by Gwladys, and had requited her feminine trustfulness by marching off with a suitcase full of clothes, boots, hairbrushes, antimacassars, and a number of other valueless knick-knacks, his plausibility being vastly in excess of his artistic taste or his sense of values. The police were very sympathetic and charming. It was Donald's first personal contact with the London policeman, and he was greatly impressed. For civility and intelligence they came up to everything which he had heard about them, and if they did not actually succeed in apprehending the thief, their thoroughness and business-like methods would undoubtedly have caused him grave alarm had he chanced to remain in the vicinity. Indeed there is little doubt that they would have actually caught him red-handed, if it had not been for the extraordinary and unforeseen coincidence by which all the four policemen who were in Royal Avenue at the moment of the burglary happened to be occupied with other matters of importance to the maintenance of order. For one was at the end of the Avenue, where it joins the King's Road, directing the flow of traffic and maintaining His Majesty's highway for His Majesty's lieges. A second, in the Avenue itself, was attempting to discover, by means of a little reference book, the whereabouts of the particular one of London's twenty-three Gloucester

Roads that a venerable and partly-paralysed Frenchman was trying to get to in a mechanical bath-chair. A third, almost opposite the scene of the audacious crime, was tying up with a bit of string, which he had unearthed from among his draperies, an ancient perambulator which had come to pieces under the strain of a load of howling triplets; while the fourth was entering up in a tiny note-book with a stub of blunt pencil, the particulars of the life, parentage, birthplace, age, profession, residence, place of business, religious denomination, number of children, driving-licence number, and other relevant particulars, of a miscreant whose motor-car carried number-plates that were at least three-quarters of an inch larger than the regulation size.

The guardians of the law were thus fully occupied at the moment of the dastardly outrage, and Gwladys was never called upon to testify, coyly, in a witness-box to the identity of the curly-haired young man who had smiled upon her so fetchingly.

Donald's main distraction during this period of stagnation was theatre-going on behalf of Mr Ogilvy. For Mr Ogilvy, the Napoleon-jawed editor, was temporarily lacking the services of his dramatic critic, Mr Rupert Harcourt, who for some quite inscrutable reason had had a fit of artistic tantrums and had thrown a raw tomato at Mr Ogilvy and, being a poet, had fortunately missed him (although the range was only seven feet and a few inches), and had departed in a temper to Capri.

Mr Ogilvy bore no malice. Poets would be poets. There wasn't enough picturesqueness in life nowadays anyway, thought Mr Ogilvy, and even the smallest originality was a godsend in an era of beastly standardization.

So Mr Harcourt retired to Capri and bought five hundred litres of white wine and a two-piece bathing-suit, and Donald visited the theatres of London in his stead. It was a curious experience, and, at first, he found it almost impossible to get any sort of notion about the state of what is usually called the English Drama. For one thing Donald was very unsophisticated about many phases of life, and the stage was one of them. Any sort of theatre gave him a thrill before ever the curtain went up, so that dramatists started with a big advantage so far as he was concerned. His experience of theatre-going was limited to pre-War Christmas visits to Aberdeen of the D'Oyly Carte Opera Company, led by Henry Lytton and the divine Miss Clara Dow; and, during the War, an occasional comedy or revue. So that, at the period when Mr Ogilvy was dodging tomatoes at a range of seven feet and a few inches, a play would have had to be a very bad play indeed to have displeased Donald.

Another thing which made it difficult for him to get his perspective right was the universally acknowledged fact that the English Drama, as acted in London, is the lowest form of theatrical art in the world, because the Public will only go to visit trash and would religiously boycott any of the really first-class plays which are growing dustier and dustier in the cupboards of disillusioned playwrights, even if any manager was so insane as to produce them on the commercial stage. It is left, Donald soon discovered, to Societies, Clubs, Groups of Intelligent Theatre-Lovers, and Private Associations of Patrons of the Drama to produce these first-class plays on Sunday evenings for one performance only. Hardly a Sunday in the year goes by without the appearance of a masterpiece by Pirandello, Kaiser, Toller, Tchehov, Savoir, Lenormand, Martinez Sierra, or Jean Jacques Bernard, dazzling the eyes for a single day and then dying like the may-fly. Sundays have been on which no fewer than three separate Clubs or Societies have been performing Kaiser's *From Morn to Midnight*, while on five Sundays out of eight in February and March of one year it was possible to see Toller's *Hoppla*. Donald, who was conscientious and painstaking, spent a lot of time in the Chelsea Free Library going through the files of *The Times* and the *Manchester Guardian* in order to learn the technique of dramatic criticism from the two heads of the craft, Mr Morgan and Mr Brown, and he was surprised to discover that in the first seven years of the Peace, twenty-eight of these Sunday Producing Societies had been formed, and that of these twenty-eight, no fewer than twenty-three had started their career with Pirandello's *Six Characters in Search of an Author*.

It was to these Sunday performances of dramatic masterpieces that Donald was looking forward with especial eagerness. He was quite ready to put up with any number of adulteries and murders and high-kicks during the week for the sake of the works of genius, and it was with a real thrill that he presented himself one Sunday evening, thirty-three minutes before the scheduled hour, at the theatre in Shaftesbury Avenue where he was to see, for the first time, a dramatic masterpiece.

There was no orchestra, and the audience came filtering into the stalls in a queer silence, broken only by the gay greetings of celebrities. For each member of the Club seemed determined to recognize, and be recognized by, as many fellow-members as possible. It was almost like a competition, so fiercely did the necks twist, the eyes wander, and the lorgnettes focus. Sixteen people, all total strangers, bowed to Donald, and one man, an elderly, baldish bird with an eye-glass, went so far as to rise in his seat in order to bow more impressively. Donald blinked nervously and tried to nod in such a way that, if he really had met the other party somewhere, the movement would pass for a greeting and, if not, for a twinge of rheumatism in the neck. But the strain became too great, and after a bit Donald concentrated passionately upon his programme.

The piece to be given was the translation of a German masterpiece by Herr Rumpel-Stilzchen, the great exponent of the new Illusionist Symbolism, and it appeared from the programme that the scene was laid throughout in a gallery of a salt-mine in Upper Silesia. It was called, simply, *The Perpetuation of Eternity*. The producer was Herr von Pümpernikkel, described on the back of the programme as 'the Rheinhardt of Mecklenburg-Schwerin', and the incidental choreography was by Dripp. Donald was just wondering what part choreography played in life in Upper Silesian salt-mines when a gong was struck somewhere in the theatre and the lights went out. A pause of seven or eight minutes followed, and then the curtain rose, revealing the eagerly awaited gallery and the exquisite lighting effects of von Pümpernikkel, although actually the latter were not easily detectable at first, as the play opened in complete darkness, and for twenty minutes continued in complete darkness. This period of twenty minutes was occupied by a soliloquy by the Spirit of Polish Maternity which, in Rumpel-Stilzchen's original, was written in Polish. The translators, in order to preserve the sense of strangeness, of exoticism, had, rather cleverly, translated this part into Italian, and the delivery of the soliloquy was punctuated by frequent bursts of applause from those of the audience, apparently about one hundred per cent, who understood Italian. This applause grew more and more marked in emphasis and volume as von Pümpernikkel's lighting gradually illumined the stage and it became possible to distinguish, even as far as the back rows of the stalls, between those who did, and those who did not, pick up the finer points of the Italian language. It appeared that Donald alone did not, until a big, burly man with a sardonic look on his face, who was sitting by himself a few seats away, observed loudly, 'Beastly peasant dialect,' whereupon everyone within ear-shot of him stopped applauding and sneered vigorously. At the end of the soliloquy the lights, now flooding the stage with alternate purple and green, lit up the backs of a row of salt-workers who dug and chanted dismally as they worked. The foreman of the gallery then came forward and shot two of the workers, whether for bad chanting or for bad digging was not made clear, and immediately all the lights went out except for an illuminated screen of salt background upon which was thrown a cinemato-graph-picture of New York skyscrapers as observed from a Zeppelin. Then the Chrysler Building and the Woolworth Building and the rest of them vanished suddenly and were fol-lowed by a ten-minute reel from the Oberammergau Passion play, during which a negro with a megaphone, stationed in the wings, sang with great gusto a song that was popular during the War and was called, 'When that Midnight Choo-choo leaves for Alabam'. The curtain came down on the end of the second verse and the middle of The Last Supper. Subdued but sincere clapping greeted the end of the act, and the more senior of the critics went moodily out for drinks.

The second, third, fourth, and fifth and last acts were packed as full as the first with Illusionist Symbolism of the same bril-liance and irony. It need only be said that among the 'effects' was the murder by the salt-workers of a preference-shareholder of Cerebos Salt, Ltd, by throwing him into a quartz-crushing machine; the tragedy of his final screams, as his top-hat and mother-of-pearl-knobbed cane were sucked into the instrument like the last petals of a rose down a drain, was intensified by a most dramatic 'throw-back' to the shareholder's early boyhood with his dear old father, a town councillor of Hesse-Darmstadt, and his dear old mother, the town councillor's wife, who both drank a good deal of light lager and crooned some folk-songs. There was also a long scene of great poignancy between the Spirit of Irony and the Soul of Upper Silesia, during which the League of Nations came in for some nasty knocks, and there was a powerful bit of the most modern sort of Symbolism in which a salt-digger's mistress was confronted with a lot of the Thoughts which she would have thought if she had been, instead, a champion tricyclist. And Dripp's choreography turned out to be the Dance of Mourners at the Funeral of a Demented House-Agent, said to be symbolical of the housing shortage during 1925 and 1926 in the Silesian towns of Kattowitz and Breslau.

In short, *The Perpetuation of Eternity* was, as one of the penny dailies said next morning, the most arresting piece of thought-provoking symbolism that had been produced since Ernst Toller's *Hoppla* had been staged on the previous Sunday, or since Pirandello's *Six Characters in Search of an Author* on the last Sunday but two. *The Times* gave it three-quarters of a column, but Mr Brown, to Donald's amazement, called it 'a turgid Dripp from the village Pümpernikkel', and inquired 'If this is Upper Silesia, what can Lower be like?'

Donald gave it a guarded notice in Mr Ogilvy's paper.

On the Monday evening of the same week he went to the first night of a play which dealt with adultery against a background of Spiritualism, and a pair of youthful lovers who filled up the gaps with some ingenuous love-making. On the Tuesday, the subject of the play was adultery in the Straits Settlements and the successful love-making of two young jolly things, and on the Wednesday it was adultery in Mayfair with a lot of epigrams, and the two young jolly things. On Thursday there was a clash of two first-nights, and Donald had the choice of adultery among vegetarians and adultery among exponents of Simplified Spelling, and chose the latter by tossing for it. There was nothing on the Friday and Saturday, a translation from Lenormand on the Sunday, all about Freud and Jung and Oedipus, and on Monday an Edgar Wallace, full of blue lights and blackmailers and fun.

The petulant poet remained in Capri for five weeks and came back as brown as a berry, in the best of tempers. He had completely forgotten the episode of the tomato, and Mr Ogilvy said nothing about it and welcomed him back to his post. Donald during the five weeks had visited the theatre thirty-one times and come to a rather curious conclusion about what is called 'the English Theatre-Going Public'. It was this: that the T.-G.P. will often flock to see a bad play provided it makes them laugh or makes them frightened – a real comedian or an ambush in Chinatown is always a winner. It will sometimes flock to see a bad play provided it is a mass of sentimentality. The old melodramas of the bad, bold Bart., and the last-minute redemption of the mortgage or discovery of the marriage-lines, had their roots very deep in the simple Teutonic Soul of London, and often survive triumphantly to this day if they are decked out in an up-to-date setting. It – that is, the T.-G.P. – will almost always go to see a good play, by which Donald meant a play that is good as a play and not as a poem, or as a piece of symbolism, or as a cinematograph, or as an essential transference of the plastic arts to histrionics, or as an interpretation of a mood, or as political propaganda, or as divorce propaganda, or as birth-control, pacifist, prohibitionist, nationalist, internationalist, bimetallist, spiritualist, economist, Bolshevist, or Fascist or any other sort of propaganda. But if a play is good as a play, then the T.-G.P. will go to see it.

And finally, Donald concluded that it would have nothing to do with pretentiousness. A low-brow sitting upon a pork pie or falling into a bran-tub would send it into an ecstasy of merriment; a high-brow doing his best would arouse respectful admiration; but a donkey aping the wise man, or a dull man aping the genius, was always detected by some curious working of mass instinct and utterly and crushingly ignored. And that was why, Donald reflected, Kaiser and Toller and the rest of them could only be acted in front of Societies and Clubs consisting of people who wanted to write like Kaiser and Toller and the rest of them. But the men and women who wrote real plays had no fear of presenting them to the Theatre-Going Public.

'What an inscrutable people are these English,' thought Donald, 'for they do not like Lenormand.'

chapter 11

Life in London on four hundred pounds a year was in many ways pleasanter than life on a wind-swept Buchan farm in winter. There was no early rising as in the farming days at Balspindie, when a farm lassie brought the morning cup of tea and bowl of porridge punctually at 5 o'clock. There was no worrying about the absence or the excessiveness of rain, no anxious study of fluctuating prices of corn and turnips and potatoes, no depressing certainty each year that, whatever the weather or the prices, financial ruin was inevitable. Donald still subscribed to the *Aberdeen Press and Journal*, a new amalgamation of the famous old pair, the *Aberdeen Free Press* and the *Aberdeen Daily Journal*, and he read every week the mournful prognostications of the farming industry, which was clearly on its last legs. The tenant of Balspindie, wrote the D.S.O. advocate from Golden Square, had a melancholy tale of woe to tell when he came in on the first of every month to pay the rent. The advocate, however, guardedly advised Donald not to worry too much about it, for he added that the tenant had just bought a new Morris saloon car and had been overheard, in an incautious moment in the bar of the Imperial Hotel, to remark to a crony that, taking everything all round, by and large, it was just conceivably possible that a man of exceptionally powerful brain might be able to imagine a state of things just a fraction worse than they were at present. Anyway, the tenant was safe for the rent, and that was the main thing.

Donald, therefore, had no cares and anxieties. A net income of four hundred pounds, if properly handled, means complete independence for a young man in London. For London can be either the most expensive or the cheapest city in Europe, and four hundred pounds can be made to go a long way. There was also a little money to be made by occasional reviewing for Mr Ogilvy and even for the great Mr William Hodge himself. On one occasion a parcel arrived at Royal Avenue from Mr Hodge, containing a six-volume interpretation of the Buddhist religion by a Burmese professor at the University of Minneapolis, with a pencil scrawl from Mr Hodge asking for a thousand words about it before the following Friday. Donald, who was a conscientious soul, rushed off in a panic to Mr Hodge's office and protested that he was totally unfit to undertake such a task.

'Why?' demanded Mr Hodge.

'Because—I—I—know nothing about the Buddhist religion,' faltered Donald.

'You will by the time you've read those six volumes,' replied Mr Hodge grimly, putting on a grey top-hat and going out.

But Mr Hodge must have liked Donald's conscientiousness, for he sent him fairly frequent parcels after that, on such subjects as the Civilization of the Andes, Rambles in old Perugia, Ten Days in Soviet Russia, Is the Soul Immortal? the Fundamental Principles of Rugby Football, and Some Notes upon Surrey Rock-Gardens.

All of these Donald read carefully and reviewed carefully, resisting with stern determination the immoral advice of Mr Harcourt on the subject of reviewing.

'Read the publisher's jacket first,' said Mr Harcourt, preaching his scandalous gospel. 'That will usually give you the author's name and some sort of idea of what the book is about. If the jacket says that the book is an illuminating, unique, sensational, thought-provoking exposé from within of the political situation in Sub-Carpathian Ruthenia, then the odds are about three to one that the book is about Sub-Carpathian Ruthenia. About once in four times they put the wrong cover on and you find that it's a book of short stories called Tikkity-Tonk, Old Fish! or a reprint of the Epistle to the Romans, but more often than not they get it right. Very well, then. You've got the subject. You then look at the index of chapters. That gives you the scope of the book, shows you whether it covers the religious question, or gives a list of the hotels, or has a bit about peasant costumes, or goes in for trade statistics, or touches upon the proportion of illegitimate to legitimate kids, or sketches the history of the place since Attila, and so on. By this time you've got the whole substance of the book and then all you've got to do is to read the last two paragraphs of the last chapter, to see whether the author thinks the Sub-Carpathian Ruthenians are good eggs or bad eggs, and there you are.'

But Donald refused to subscribe to this pernicious doctrine, and steadily ploughed his way from cover to cover of each book that was sent to him, and his reviews, if not flashy or full of epigrams, at least arrived punctually; which is much more important from the editorial point of view than all the epigrams that ever were stolen by the twentieth-century reviewers from Wilde, and by Wilde from Whistler, and by Whistler from Octave Mirbeau.

Mr Ogilvy usually sent novels for review, and Donald slogged through some pretty fearful stuff during these months. But the titles fascinated him, and he wrote a short article, and got it accepted by a literary weekly, on the trend of fashion in novel-titles. He himself had entered the literary profession just as one fashion was giving way to another. The dying mode had dealt in vigorous, slashing, totally irrelevant names such as *The Charioteers caught Soul*, *Rat-riddles*, *bilge-bestank* (an exquisite long-short story of a modern Aucassin and Nicolette), and *Shame, shame, Belshazzar!* The new fashion was more shadowy and elusive and emasculate, like faded ladies or very modern poets, and Donald had to review a lot of books with names like *And she said so too*, *So they all went on*, *It was rather a Pity, hein?* and *He shrugged*; *he had to*.

On Sundays Donald usually went for long walks in the deserted City of London, that queer centre of the financial world with its week-day population of half a million desperate workers and its week-end population of ten thousand caretakers and ten thousand sleepy cats. It was at about this period that the Church of England, alive at last to the ever-increasing spread of the insidious tenacles of the Church of Rome, was forging the thunderous counter-stroke that was to revivify Anglicanism and startle the world. The Monk of Wittenberg himself could have devised no more tremendous *coup de main,* or in the circumstances, perhaps, the words *plözlicher Anfall* are more suitable, than the proposal to pull down the churches with which Sir Christopher Wren clogged and cluttered the financial heart of the world, to deconsecrate the sites, and to sell them to the Real Estate Corporations which offered the highest bids, and to devote the proceeds to the organization of another crusade against the Scarlet Woman of the Seven Hills.

Donald spent many happy Saturday afternoons – for they are usually closed on Sundays – in visiting these churches before it should be too late. And even after the officious interference of amateur busy-bodies, Architectural Clubs, painters, poets, architects, Societies for Preserving Ancient Buildings, Members of Parliament, Real Estate Corporations which were temporarily embarrassed for ready money, and scores of other individuals and associations, all, obviously, in close touch with the Vatican, had for the time being succeeded in obstructing the demolitions, he did not feel that he had wasted his time.

For nowhere else but in England's capital are there spires like those tapering silver arrows of English stone, shell-incrusted, sea-worn, glitttering in the sunlight with ten thousand sparkles of tiny diamonds. English churches, built of English stone, by an Englishman, a kindly, poetical man, full of laughter, they were raised for the English people to follow their faith, not torn, like the great cathedrals, by violence and theft from Rome.

Another kindly man, a poet, full of laughter, an Englishman, has written somewhere:

Sir Christopher came to the field of the fire,
And graced it with spire
And nave and choir,
Careful column and carven tire,
    That the ships coming up from the sea
Should hail where the Wards from Ludgate fall
A coronal cluster of steeples tall,
All Hallows, Barking, and by the Wall,
St Bride, St Swithin,
St Catherine Coleman,
St Margaret Pattens,

St Mary-le-Bow,
St Nicholas Cole Abbey,
St Alban, Wood Street,
St Magnus the Martyr,
St Edmund the King,
Whose names like a chime so sweetly call,
And high over all
The Cross and the Ball
On the Riding Redoubtable Dome of Paul.

Only one trivial incident marred the pleasant passing of that
first winter in London. One morning at about 9 o'clock, when
he was setting out on one of these solitary excursions, Donald
got a most painful fright – the most painful, in fact, since the
occasion some years before when an eight-inch shell, having
failed either to enter the earth or to explode, skipped and slith-
ered along the surface of the ground and came to rest, like a
huge, silvery, glistening white-hot salmon, a yard in front of
him. To this day Donald swears that it winked at him. On this
second occasion, in London, he felt the same clutch at his heart,
the same dryness of the roof of his mouth, the same cold feeling
all over his body. For in the King's Road stood three newspaper
boys, with long gloomy faces and not even the heart to cry their
wares. The first bore a white placard on which was printed in
red letters and black letters:

Evening News

ENGLAND OVERWHELMED WITH DISASTER

(*Late Special*)

The second bore a yellow placard on which was printed in black
letters:

Star

IS ENGLAND DOOMED?

(*Late Special*)

The third bore a white placard on which was printed in black
and red letters:

Evening Standard

COLLAPSE OF ENGLAND

(*Late Special*)

Queues of men were standing in front of the boys, digging into their pockets for coins, snatching at the papers, and then stumbling away with ashen faces and quivering lips. Donald, almost numb with the cold of sheer panic, took his place in the queue. The man in front of him held out a shilling and would not even wait for the change. He grabbed the *Star*, glanced at it, exclaimed 'Oh, God!' and reeled drunkenly away, cannoning into passers-by and bumping into a shop-window, his eyes devouring the stop-press news as he went. Donald only just succeeded in retaining his native prudence sufficiently to present a penny rather than a shilling, and drew aside with his paper from the jostling crowd.

There was no difficulty about discovering what the *Star* was trying to convey. There was the giant headline – IS ENGLAND DOOMED? – splashed right across the page, and under it the smaller amplifying headlines, and even they were half an inch high:

MAILEY FINDS A SPOT

DEVASTATING ATTACK AT MELBOURNE

HOBBS OUT FIRST BALL: HEARNE 9, WOOLLEY 0

ENGLAND'S APPALLING DEBACLE

CAN HENDREN SAVE US?

In the Underground at Sloane Square Station an elderly man in a top-hat and black, velvet-collared overcoat, with an elegant long white moustache, and carrying a rolled-up silk umbrella, said fiercely to Donald, 'It all comes of treating it as a game. We don't take things seriously enough in this country, sir, damnation take it all,' and he stepped heavily upon the toes of a humble, clerkly-looking person behind him.

Donald slipped away to another part of the train and read the sad story of England's shame in the Second Test Match against Australia at Melbourne.

Another interesting experience of this period was a visit to the Rugby Football Ground at Twickenham to see the Oxford and Cambridge Rugby Football Match. At about midday on a warm, misty, winter's day Donald went to Waterloo Station and secured a place with eleven other passengers in a third-class railway carriage, having bumped and struggled his way through mobs of young men all looking exactly like each other except that no two of them wore the same coloured scarves or ties.

After about three-quarters of an hour, he reached Twickenham and lunched at an inn upon beer and bread and cheese, and at 1.45 found his place in an enormous grandstand and stared down at the bright green turf so far below. The sun was making a last sickly attempt to pierce the gathering mists, and shed a kind of pallid benevolence upon the rapidly filling stands. But the game did not begin for another hour, and by the time that sixty-five thousand spectators, of whom about thirty thousand appeared to be young men, thirty thousand young women, and five thousand parsons, had packed themselves into their places, the sun had long ago given up the unequal struggle, the mists were massing darkly in the north and east, and a slight drizzle was coming down.

The players ran out to the accompaniment of frenzied cheers and counter-cheers, kicked a ball about smartly for a minute or two, sat down for the photographers, stood up for the Prince of Wales, and then set to work.

By half-time the rain was pouring steadily down, the lovely green of the ground was a dark quagmire, the players were indistinguishable from one another, and before the end of the game the gloom of winter twilight had so enveloped the ground that it was impossible for the spectators to see more than twenty or thirty yards.

After the match was over, the sixty-five thousand spectators formed themselves into a single mighty queue, and set off at a slow shuffle through the mud and rain in the direction of the station. Motor-cars, with headlights flaring, crept along with the pedestrians. At the entrance to the station a long delay took place while train after train drew up at the platform, and railway officials with megaphones informed the crowd, correctly, that the next train was a non-stop to Waterloo and, incorrectly, that there was more room in front. Donald at last got into a carriage with twenty-three others and had to stand for an hour and five minutes, including a halt of twenty minutes outside Waterloo. There were two schools of opinion in the carriage. One faction, consisting of eleven young men with bedraggled light-blue favours and one rather passionate urban dean, maintained warmly that Cambridge had won by two goals, two tries, and a penalty goal against two tries, or nineteen points to six. The rival group of partisans were handicapped by internal dissensions, for seven of them were positive that Cambridge had not scored at all, whereas they had definitely seen Oxford score three tries, convert one of them, and also score a dropped goal, thus winning by fifteen points to nil; while four of them knew for an incontrovertible fact that Oxford had scored, in addition, three penalty goals from penalties awarded, and rightly awarded, against Cambridge for dirty play in the scrums.

It was only because they were tightly wedged into the carriage and none of them could move hand or foot that prevented, so it seemed to Donald, actual violence – certainly the urban dean's language was enough to justify manslaughter – and he was astonished when the controversy dissolved into hearty laughter and they all started chaffing the dean. The dean's powers of repartee were quite devastating.

But all doubts were settled when the train at last pulled in to Waterloo at 6.25, for the evening papers were being sold on the platforms with the authoritative statement that the match had been drawn – each side having scored one try, or three points each.

Two days later Donald went to the Chelsea ground at Stamford Bridge to see Oxford play Cambridge at Association Football. The game began in bright sunshine at 2 p.m. and was played throughout in bright sunshine. A brilliantly open and fast match, resulting in a draw of three goals each, was watched by four thousand silent spectators.

It was during the winter also that Donald had a splendid opportunity of studying the way in which the Englishman sets about his home politics. He had watched at Geneva the methods of international diplomacy which have planted the Union Jack upon all really desirable spots on the surface of the globe and upon almost all the really valuable commodities except quinine in Java, nitrates in Chile, and oil in Oklahoma – and the failure to secure the third of these is considerably offset by the corresponding absence from the Empire of the Oklahomans.

He was now able to examine the psychology of the Englishman when engaged upon the task of operating the political machine which is at once the envy and the model of most of the civilized world. For the Government of the day, having been defeated by seven votes on a proposal to include raisins in the sub-section of the Retail Prices (Control) Bill which referred to currants, figs, dates, prunes, and dried apricots, decided very naturally to treat the defeat as a vote of want of confidence in their policy of Imperial Defence and Development, and, dissolving Parliament, appealed to the suffrages of all right-thinking men and women in the country. The Opposition, with a monstrous whoop of official joy and secretly furious because they had never meant to defeat the Government and were not ready for an election, also rushed into the fray with a passionate appeal for the support of all right-thinking men and women.

Donald was just wondering whether he should offer his services to one or other of the headquarters in London as a canvasser or envelope-addresser when he was delighted to receive a letter from his old Geneva chief, Sir Henry Wootton, asking him to come down to East Anglia and help him in a particularly tough fight against a young Socialist, an Independent Labour Party man, who was a brilliant speaker and was already making alarming headway by means of unscrupulous pledges which it would be utterly impossible to redeem on this side of the millennium. Donald packed a bag, called at the headquarters of the Conservative Party for a bundle of leaflets, pamphlets, handbooks, and notes for speakers, and took the next train for Lincolnshire.

Sir Henry's constituency consisted of Eldonborough, a town of about fifty thousand inhabitants, and a tract of village-dotted country round it. There were many votes in the villages, but they were harder to work than the compact town, and both candidates were concentrating upon Eldonborough.

Donald found Sir Henry in the Crown Hotel, opposite his official headquarters which were in the Conservative Club, and after a warm welcome, was handed over to the Conservative agent, Commander Blinker, late R.N., for instructions. Commander Blinker was every inch a sailor. He had a clear eye, a healthy skin, a loud voice, and a breezy manner.

'Joined for duty, eh?' he shouted, as if it was blowing a tidy gale in the lounge of the Crown, at the same time hitting Donald a fearful clap between the shoulders. 'That's fine. We want everyone we can get if we're going to down these damned Reds. What about a spot of talky-talky, eh? Platform stuff. You know – thumping the old soap-box.'

'I'll do anything you like,' said Donald nervously. He was rather alarmed by this nautical gustiness of manner.

'That's great!' roared the mariner. 'First-class bundobust. We'll put you up tomorrow at the ironworks at tiffin-time. Have you got the hang of our dope?'

Donald pulled out his sheaf of literature from his various pockets, but the gallant Commander waved it all aside.

'You needn't worry about that,' he cried. 'You don't need facts or any tommy-rot of that sort. You stick to our three planks. One – the Empire first, foremost, and all the time. Two – down with the Reds. Three – Work for the Unemployed.'

'Have we – I mean – are there—is there any stuff about how we're going to find work for the Unemployed?' ventured Donald.

Commander Blinker looked at him in astonishment.

'By backing up the Empire, of course,' he bawled, and added, 'That and the abolition of the dole. And now I must vamoose, old chap. Are you going to berth down here? Good. Then I'll give you your sailing-orders tomorrow. So long,' and the jolly tar dashed off to continue elsewhere his organization of victory.

That evening, his duties having not yet begun, Donald attended a Conservative meeting in the Eldonborough Corn Exchange. There were about a thousand people present and there were no fewer than forty-two Union Jacks tastefully draped, some the right way up, some upside down, and some sideways, on the platform and the walls. An immense mezzotint of Mr Gladstone hung on the wall behind the chairman, for there was no Liberal candidate and it was of paramount importance to catch the votes of all right-thinking Liberals.

The chairman, a stout, genial man, started the proceedings by stating humorously that the first duty of a chairman was to stand up, shut up, and sit down, but there were just one or two things he wanted to say. After explaining that he was only going to say those one or two things very briefly, and explaining why he was going to be brief, and coining the delightful epigram that, after all, brevity was the soul of wit, and adding that if he wasn't brief a lot of the candidate's valuable time would be wasted and they all knew what a busy man a candidate was, and especially such a good candidate as they had got in their old and trusted Member who was, if the ladies would pardon the expression, damned well going to be their Member again, the chairman then got down to the main body of his brief introductory remarks, and told a story about an Irishman whom he happened to know personally; a story which, he thought, was a very good illustration of the sterling merits of the Conservative Party, which, after all, had always been the true friend of Ireland, and of the affection which it inspired in all sections of the British public. The chairman sat down about twenty minutes later, and then, amid loud applause and the singing of 'For he's a jolly good fellow', led by the stentorian Commander Blinker, Sir Henry got up beaming with benevolence all over his kindly face, and told them a story about an Aberdonian and a Jew, and after that said that he stood for the Empire and the dear old flag, and that he, at any rate, wasn't going to kow-tow to any dirty crew of Bolshies in Moscow who never washed their necks, and said that what he meant to say, and he said it with all the emphasis at his command, frankly and definitely, was that he was in favour of the most stringent economy consistent with the immediate launching of twenty new cruisers to protect the trade routes of our far-flung Empire, that he was in favour of the abolition of the dole which was sapping their British manhood, that he was in favour of work for all, and against the policy of scuttle in India. He then launched upon a denunciation of Free Trade, which he wittily described in rather daring biblical language as an 'outworn shibboleth', but was abruptly pulled up by the vigilant Blinker, who whispered, in a whisper like a steam-riveter at work, that the Liberal and Free-Trade vote was of paramount importance.

Sir Henry stopped at once and sat down amid prolonged cheering, but Donald was in an agony of nervous apprehension. He was sincerely fond of Sir Henry. He liked him and respected him as a kindly gentleman. But never in his life had he listened to such an appallingly bad speech, or one that more pathetically asked to be torn to shreds of ridicule by hecklers. Donald hid his perspiring face in his hands. He simply could not bear to watch the public humiliation of a friend. He cursed himself for having come to the meeting, for having come to Eldonborough at all. Now it was beginning – the chairman was asking for questions – the humiliation was about to start – yes, there was the first one – a snorter too.

'Mr Chairman, when the candidate says he is in favour of work for all, how does he propose to provide it?'

Donald groaned. The very first man had put his finger on one of the vital weaknesses. Sir Henry rose.

'I am very glad indeed that the question has been asked,' he said, 'and I should like to take this opportunity of thanking the gentleman who asked it, and of congratulating him. Our policy, roughly speaking, is to see that jobs, and adequately paid jobs, are provided at once for everyone.' He sat down again amid applause.

Donald gasped. 'Good God!' he thought, 'they'll start throwing things.'

The man who had asked the question rose again.

'Thank you very much,' he said, and sat down. Again Donald gasped.

There was only one other question. A fierce-looking young man, wearing a red-and-white handkerchief round his neck, asked aggressively:

'Mr Chairman, I should like to know what the candidate's policy is about housing.'

Sir Henry rose, thanked the gentleman who had asked the question, and congratulated him, and stated that his policy was to get the maximum number of houses built at the minimum cost in the shortest possible time.

The fierce-looking young man thanked the candidate, and the meeting diffused itself into votes of thanks, resolutions of confidence, and the National Anthem.

Donald walked out into the street in a dream.

For a few minutes he stood, irresolute, bewildered, and at last began to drift aimlessly along the unknown streets of Eldonborough, reflecting, as he went, that he was indeed a stranger in a strange land. After a little, absorbed though he was in his own thoughts, he could not help becoming gradually aware that crowds of people were hastening past him in the same direction as himself, and, increasing his speed, he came round a corner upon a large hall at the doors of which were enormous posters, stating in letters of scarlet fire:

ERNEST DODDS HERE TONIGHT
ERNIE FOR ELDONBOROUGH

A young man on the steps of the hall, almost concealed behind a colossal scarlet rosette, informed him that the great Champion of the People, the Crusader of the Proletariat, was going to address a mass meeting in a few minutes, and that there was still room for a few in the gallery.

Donald went in and secured a good seat in the front row of a sort of organist's loft, for the hall belonged to a Nonconformist church. There were about a thousand people in the building, and the chairman, a very thin, severe-looking man, was just rising to address the meeting. He began by saying that the audience had not come to listen to him, and that, therefore, he was going to say nothing at all. There was just a story he wanted to tell them, because he thought it illustrated very well the criminal proclivities of the Conservative Party and the depths of execration with which it was regarded throughout the country, a story about a personal friend of his, an Irishman. He then proceeded to recount the anecdote which Donald had already heard that evening and which had, moreover, already appeared in that week's Punch. After that he delivered a passionate harangue against Capitalism, and then, later, luckily remembered the presence of Mr Dodds and called upon him to say a few words.

Mr Dodds soon proved himself to be an orator of the fieriest brand. He struck the table resounding blows. He swept the glass of water into the front row of the stalls. He leapt about from side to side as if the platform was red-hot. He shouted and he stormed. He thundered and banged. He compared the Tory Party to Judas Iscariot, and Mr Baldwin, curiously enough, to the Crown Prince of Germany. He compared Mr Arthur Henderson to Mr Standfast and and Lord Parmoor to St Francis of Assisi. He compared the Socialist Party to the Angels of the Lord, and frequently alluded to the Liberals as right-thinking men and women, and he pointed several times with a torrent of eulogy to an old plaster cast of Bismarck which had been produced from somewhere and, as a counterblast to the mezzotint of Gladstone, ostentatiously labelled 'Cobden'.

Ernie was obviously a wizard when it came to figures. He proved in a whirlwind of arithmetic that if there were no rich there would be no poor, that if all the money was taken away from everyone, then everyone would have £317 a year, that if dividends were forbidden industry would be saved, and that the only way to avoid the imminent bankruptcy of the Bank of England was by the abolition of the Stock Exchange and the suppression of Press Syndicates. In conclusion, he pledged himself to advocate the limitation of incomes to £400 a year, the raising of unemployment benefit to £4 a week, and the abolition of the beer-tax. Again Donald was aghast. It seemed impossible that this candidate also should escape being torn to bits by the hecklers. Again he was wrong.

Only two questions were asked.

The first was: 'Where will you put the money above £400 a year that you take from the rich?'

And the answer was: 'Into the pockets of the poor.'

The second was: 'Where will get the money to pay for the raising of the dole?'

And the answer was: 'Out of the pockets of the rich.'

The meeting then dissolved in votes of thanks and much singing of 'The Red Flag', with its stirring descriptions of open Proletarian activities in Chicago's halls in free America, and of secret Proletarian intrigues in the Tsarist vaults of Moscow.

After these two meetings, Donald realized that there was some force in Commander Blinker's sublime contempt for 'facts and tommy-rot of that sort', and he tore up his sheaf of literature and confined himself on the soap-box and at the street-corner to simple eloquence about the Flag, the Throne, and the Commonwealth.

*

After fourteen days of oratory, the free citizens of Eldon-borough and District went to the ballot-boxes, and at noon on the day after polling-day, the returning-officer announced, to a crowd of some ten thousand people, that after three recounts the result of the election was: Mr Ernest Dodds, twenty-one thousand and forty-three votes; Sir Henry Wootton, twenty-one thousand and forty-three votes – and the result was therefore a tie. Both candidates then thanked the returning-officer, both claimed the result as a smashing victory for their respective principles, both emphasized the cleanliness and true British sportsmanship of the contest, and then they shook hands amid deafening cheers.

chapter 12

It is always rather a problem how to spend Christmas. Forced festivities can often be as tedius as forced isolation, and over-eating has definite drawbacks. Donald, a stranger in a strange land, found it very difficult to know what to do. He had no re-lations to visit, and he did not like to thrust himself upon any of the friends who had been so kind to him during the months that he had spent in England. For Christmas is essentially the feast of the Family, and it is the only season of the year in which the Englishman instinctively prefers to be surrounded with his relations rather than with his friends. And Donald had to be very careful about admitting his prospective isolation, for he knew that his English acquaintances would violate even the Yuletide sanctity of the home rather than allow him to be lonely at Christmas. When the Englishman does let himself go, he hates to think that others may not be so fortunately situated.

Donald, therefore, decided that the best thing to do would be to avoid embarrassing these worthy folk either by his presence at their feast or by his absence from any feast, and he saw the solution of the problem in the window of a Haymarket travel-bureau. For the modest sum of ten pounds he could travel in a small steamship from Hull to Danzig, spend one day in Danzig.

and return from Danzig to back to Hull, all in seven days. Impulsively he went in and bought a ticket, and at 5 o'clock on a drizzly, foggy, winter's afternoon he found himself, with spirits rapidly sinking, in the gloomy city of Kingston-upon-Hull. As he stood in the centre of that dismal spread of squalor and shivered in the cold and listened to the screaming trams, he began to regret bitterly his impulse. The only shred of consolation that he could find for the fact that he was standing – cold, wet, and lonely – in the town of Hull, was that he might be standing cold, wet, and lonely in the town of Goole, which, as seen from the train, looked even bloodier than Hull.

The boat was not due to sail until 8 o'clock; the pubs did not open until 6 o'clock. An hour had to be spent in this desperate wilderness of slate and stone and rain before even a drink could be got. Donald's spirits went lower and lower. He cursed that infernal impulse in the Haymarket. He cursed Hull and the North Sea and Danzig and himself and Christmas, and the insane rules for the opening and shutting of public-houses, and the English and England and the weather. At 6 o'clock he entered the smallest, the squalidest, the smelliest public-house he had ever been in and drank a half-pint of abominable beer and fled, almost in tears, to the ship. The ship itself put the finishing touch to his despair. It was very small and very dirty. It looked, to Donald's feverish and distorted vision, as if it was about three times the size of an ordinary rowing-boat. Actually it was about 1800 tons, and very old. The crew was Polish, the officers Russian, except the wireless operator, who was German, and there was to be only one other passenger. Donald stood on the quay and looked at the rusty hen-coop in which he was going to spend three days and three nights upon a wintry North Sea. And, what somehow made it worse, he was going to spend them in the hen-coop voluntarily. He was under no sort of compulsion. He had taken his passage of his own free will. Seventy-two hours there, in the company of a parcel of foreigners and a strange Englishman, and seventy-two hours back in the company of God knew who.

In the depths of despondency, he leant against a warehouse and watched a party of dock labourers helped, or rather hindered, by the Polish sailors, struggling to hoist a queer-shaped engine on to the ship. The operation was superintended by a foreman who was encrusted from head to foot in grit and coal-dust and general grime, and Donald was appalled to learn from the company's agent that this foreman was to be his fellow-passenger in the hen-coop.

At 8 o'clock the tiny ship began to plunge its way laboriously down the Humber, and Donald sat down to a solitary dinner – for the foreman had disappeared with his machine into the hold. Dinner was excellent, and whisky out of bond at five shillings a bottle restored a little of the forlorn traveller's spirits.

By some meteorological caprice the North Sea next day was a sheet of misty steel and, after a large breakfast, Donald leant on the taffrail and watched the distant fishing-fleets and the timber ships from Russia and Finland, and began to enjoy himself.

Just before lunch the foreman appeared, wearing a smart grey suit and a stiff collar and blue tie secured with a ring, spruced up to the nines. The removal of the grit and coal-dust revealed a thin, clean-shaven face, close-cut grey hair, and a general appearance of about sixty years of age. He talked in a broad Yorkshire accent that was sometimes a little difficult to understand.

'I'm real glad to meet you, Mister,' he exclaimed, grasping Donald's hand in a huge, thin, bony grip. 'My name is Rhodes, but I'm mostly called William, or Will, or Bill, but mostly William. Shall we go in to dinner? The bell's gone.'

Mr Rhodes proved to be a great conversationalist. In fact he hardly ever stopped talking. Donald, who spoke French and a certain amount of halting German, wondered if he would have to interpret for Mr Rhodes on the ship. He also wondered how Mr Rhodes was going to manage when he reached Poland. He also wondered why on earth the engineering firm, which had made the queer-looking machine, had not sent a more educated caretaker with it. For whatever William's technical efficiency might be, it jumped to the eyes that he had not been educated at Eton.

'I'm taking a machine to Warsaw,' said William, tucking away at the garlic sausages and cold tunny-fish and onions; 'a machine for pumping out sewers. Oh! it's lovely. It'll pump out a five-thousand-gallon sewer in eighty-five seconds, all by steam

144

vacuum. I'm going to teach the fellows how to use it. Our folk built it in the shops, and I had the assembling of it. I drove it down from Leeds yesterday – first time it's ever been on the road. But do you know what, Mister?' He leant across the table earnestly. 'Have you ever seen the crest of the Corporation of Warsaw? You haven't? Well, you mightn't believe me, but it's the upper half of a woman without any clothes on. Can you beat it? And there it is, painted on both sides of that sewer-pump, and me, William Rhodes, that's known throughout the length and breadth of the East Riding, sitting atop of that machine and driving her to Hull yesterday. I tell you I fair blushed with shame as I came through some of those villages where I'm known. It's indecent, Mister, that's what it is. Down-right indecent.'

Mr Rhodes made hay of an omelette and ordered a small bottle of beer and went on.

'Have you ever been in Hungary, Mister?'

'No,' replied Donald, 'but I've got a friend out there who says—'

'I would like right well to hear about him,' said William sincerely. 'I spent two years in Hungary once with a machine for weeding between the rows of fruit-trees. It's a lovely country – Hungary, with miles of peaches and apples and cherries, but they were terrible troubled with weeds. Fine chaps, those Hungarians; I liked them. It was a lovely machine. I took it out to show those fellows how to use it, and I stayed two years. Queer, wasn't it?'

Donald agreed that it was extremely queer, and started to tell Mr Rhodes about his friend who had a castle in Transylvania.

'Just one moment, Mister,' interposed Mr Rhodes. 'I want very much to hear about your friend, but before we get on to him, Transylvania's in Roumania, isn't it?'

'Yes,' replied Donald, 'by the Treaty of Trianon—'

'I was in Roumania before the War,' said Mr Rhodes reminiscently, 'with machines for oil-boring. I was teaching those fellows how to use them. Queer folk, the Roumanians. I was there nearly three years. Do you know I got to like those folk quite a lot after a bit. Yes, I liked them quite a lot. Queer, isn't it?'

'Very queer,' said Donald with just a touch of coldness in his voice.

'Russia, now,' pursued Mr Rhodes, 'that is a queer place. I was there before the War, with dredgers. We were to dredge a canal near Petersburg and I went out to show those fellows how to manage the scoops and grapplers. It was mostly grapplers – the canal was full of rocks you see – and some nob or other had got a contract for supplying barges for the machines, a Grand Duke or Heir Apparent as like as not, and the barges were rotten. Yes, Mister, they were rotten. And every time we grappled a rock and hauled, instead of the rock coming up, the barge went over, and the grappler with it. In another month we'd have had to dredge the canal for dredging-machines. We couldn't use our own barges, because this nob, whoever he was, had bribed everyone right and left. It would have been a scream if we hadn't been working on a time-limit – job not done by a certain date, no money. And then this nob would get the contract himself, fish up our grapplers, and make a packet. My word, but it was a business.'

'What happened in the end?' inquired Donald politely.

Mr Rhodes blushed.

'To tell you the truth, Mister, I had to do a thing I didn't like doing. But I had my firm to consider, and I've been with them now for one-and-forty years. I couldn't let them down, now, could I? So what could I do but what I did?'

'And what was that?'

'Well, I bribed the chief engineer to certify that the canal was dredged. It was the only way round that nob. He had bribed everyone except the chief. That's a cardinal rule in life, Mister, and I pass it on to you with pleasure, because I like you. Never bribe if you can possibly help it, but when you do, only bribe the heads. Stick to that and you can't go wrong.'

Donald promised to stick to that, and escaped as soon as possible to the top-deck with a book, and saw no more of William until the evening. By the time the steward was ringing the bell and announcing that dinner was ready, Donald was so bored by his own company, by the unvarying oiliness of the sea, and by the absence of anything to look at except the wintry sun and, once or twice an hour, a timber-ship, that he found himself almost longing for a storm and almost looking forward to William's company at table.

William began to talk even before he had sat down.

'Have you ever travelled in Spain?' he started at once. 'It's a very queer country. I don't know that I've ever been in a queerer; not that Java isn't queer too, but then you expect that from black men. But in Spain they're white and that makes it all the funnier. Bone-lazy, that's the trouble. And when I say bone-lazy, I mean bone-lazy. If a Spaniard doesn't want to work, he won't. Not if you offered him a million pounds. I spent eight months in Spain some years ago, digging irrigation canals. At least I had to do the digging in the end, though it wasn't what I went out for originally. My firm built some canal ploughs, beauties, steam-machines you understand, and fitted with four-foot plough-sheaves, and I went out with them to teach those fellows how to use them. Well, I'd spend a week teaching a fellow, and then, just as I'd got him in good shape, he'd remember that his cousin's aunt had got scarlet fever or something, and off he'd go and I'd have to start again with a new fellow. I stuck it for six weeks and then I ploughed the canals myself and went back to Leeds.'

'How did you manage to make yourself understood to all these people?' asked Donald. 'Do they all talk English?'

'None of them,' said Mr Rhodes, 'until you get up Scandinavia way. But most of them understand a bit of German, and I just talk German to them until I've picked up enough of their lingo to rub along in.'

This unexpected linguistic talent in a working engineer startled Donald.

'Where did you learn your German?' he asked.

'I'm bi-lingual in English and German,' answered the engineer. 'You see, my father was forty years in the same firm and he was their representative in Hamburg when I was born. But I can get along in most languages except French. I never had a job of work to do in France in all my life. But as I was saying, Mister, Demerara is a queer place. Rum's cheaper than water in Demerara. Have you ever drunk rum?'

'During the War—' began Donald.

'I can tell you a curious thing about Demerara rum,' proceeded William.

'Most of ours came from Jamaica during the war.'

147

'I was in Demerara ploughing drainage-ways for getting water out of canals,' said William. 'It was a queer job, because I had to make a machine that would go through the water as well as do the ploughing. It took me a time to do it, I can tell you, but I hit on a lovely notion. I made a special carburettor that would take rum instead of petrol. What do you think of that? Rum, ninety overproof, at a penny a gallon and petrol at one and eleven. But do you know what I hadn't reckoned on?'

'I've no idea,' murmured Donald, overwhelmed by this flow of technical wizardry.

'Why!' exclaimed William triumphantly, 'I hadn't reckoned that rum at ninety overproof would eat into ordinary steel just as I'd eat into that cheese,' and he helped himself to a cut at the Camembert that made the steward jump.

'But I beat that rum,' went on William, sinking his voice to an impressive whisper. 'I beat it, and do you know how? I got some old tank-engines that had been sold for scrap, lovely engines, all specially hardened aluminium, and I coppered those engines and I fitted them into my drainage-ploughs, and by gum, Mister, I ploughed drainage-ways eight and a half per cent faster than they'd ever been ploughed before in those parts. By gum, those fellows were surprised. I was teaching them, do you see? And I taught them another thing, too. Do you know that they were sending out their folks on foot to work – two hours there and two hours back? Did you ever hear such silliness? I made them see it though, and before I left Demerara I built them a light railway, plumb through a greenwood savannah, too. I don't know if you've ever built a light railway through a greenwood savannah, Mister?'

Donald was forced to admit that so far this experience had eluded him. He would have liked very much to have indicated that hardly a week passed in which he did not drive railways through greenwood savannahs. It sounded a romantic sort of undertaking. But his native honesty prevented him, although it did occur to him that William would never find out that he was lying because William would not listen to him in any case.

'I had to make them a machine, first of all, for uprooting the trees,' proceeded the inexorable wizard, 'and then I went to them and said, "Look here, Misters," I said, "there's all that fine greenwood timber lying there and going to waste. It all belongs to you, and there's money in it. All you want is a couple of sixty-foot steel barges to bring the trunks down the canal to the sea, and a steam saw-mill to cut it up.' And then after we'd got the wood cut up, they gave me a hundred pounds to go back to Leeds. They said if I stayed any longer I'd sell them a machine for hoisting them into bed at night and tucking them up; but of course that was just their joke, because I never heard of any such machine or of anybody asking for tenders for one.'

William spent that evening in the wireless operator's cabin – the operator, or 'Sparks' as William invariably called him, was a German-speaking Pole from Poznan who had served in the German Imperial Navy and been sunk at Jutland – discussing the latest developments in wireless and showing the operator one or two small contrivances of his own invention.

Next morning the good ship *Wilno* chugged doggedly up the Elbe, through the lock-gates at Braunebüttel, and into the Kiel Canal, that mighty witness to an overwhelming Imperial ambition. For sixty miles, at ten miles an hour, the *Wilno* steamed between the concrete walls, with flat pasture-land and woods and windmills on each side, passing from time to time reminders of vanished Power, great iron railway bridges raised on vast embankments to allow for the passage of tripod-masts of *Derfflingers* and *Von der Tanns* and *Hindenburgs*; deserted repair-shops on whose crumbling walls was still visible the Black Eagle of Hohenzollern; and ruined quays for the tying-up of small ships to make way for the Hoch See Flotte, now lying derelict, encrusted with seaweed, at the bottom of a far-off Orkney bay.

For mile after mile the *Wilno* met no ship in the Imperial Canal, not even a barge or dredger or skiff, except a single oil-tanker, carrying the Hammer and Sickle upon its great Red Flag, and a string of timber-ships. Ten miles from Kiel the *Wilno* slowed up, and there was a great running to and fro among the officers and much frenzied talk. William hung about the door of the engine-room, listening to the sound of the engines and excitedly maintaining to Donald that something was up with some fearfully technical apparatus that he seemed to know all about. After a little, his expert diagnosis was confirmed by 'Sparks', who had torn himself away from an account on his loud-speaker of a boxing match in Berlin, to find out what was up, and William darted off to his cabin for his overalls. He spent the next four hours on his back in the engine-room, welding or riveting or performing some such mysterious feat, to the vast admiration of the Polish engineers, and the *Wilno* resumed its normal speed. That night at dinner the captain sent William a bottle of champagne, which distressed William a good deal, for he greatly preferred his small bottle of beer, but did not want to hurt the captain's feelings. He insisted upon Donald helping him out with it, and he related during the meal a queer experience he had once had when, after taking a dozen steam-tractors from Vladivostok to Samarcand, he had been asked to survey the camel-route from Samarcand to the Afghan frontiers to see if it could be made practical for motor-buses with caterpillar wheels.

After dinner that night there was an informal concert and William danced a clog-dance and told mildly improper stories in German and sang 'Ilkley Moor'. By this time Wilhelm, or Weely, was the life and soul of the ship.

On the third afternoon the great towers of the Marienkirche rose above the waters of the Bay of Danzig. William pointed them out to Donald.

'Another journey over,' he said, and then he added unexpectedly, 'I'm getting too old for journeys. Thirty-five years I've been travelling the world, and there's only one place I want to see, and that's Leeds. When I was younger it was different. Take my advice, Mister, and travel when you're young. If you get a chance to go to Honolulu when you're twenty-five, take it, like I did. Because you won't be half so keen to go back at fifty-five, like I did.'

Donald asked him if he ever thought of asking the firm to let him stay at home. William shook his head.

'It's the foreign pay,' he explained. 'That, and the travelling allowances. I've got two sons, and until the second one is fair started, I can't afford to give it up.'

'Are they going into the firm too?' Donald asked. 'You said your father was in it before you.'

'Yes, but my sons won't be,' said William. 'I'm only a working engineer, and when I get back to Leeds after the trip abroad, back I go to the bench in the assembling-shop. I've never known anything except machines. But I've saved enough in forty-and-one years to give them a better chance. They've both been to Leeds University, and that's not bad for the sons of a shop-foreman.'

Donald asked him what they were going to be.

'The eldest is a schoolmaster with a fine job near Birmingham, and the youngest is just finishing to be a parson. A parson! That's queer, isn't it? And him mad on cricket, too. They wanted him to play for Yorkshire, but he wouldn't. " 'Tis a great game," he said, "but 'tisn't a life." And I reckon he's right. But I've seen him bat all afternoon for the Chapel, or the Scouts. He doesn't get very many runs, mind you, but there's mighty few in Leeds or Bradford can get him out. And the funny thing is we've called him Parson ever since he was a nipper. Never smoked, never touched a drop. No films or skirts. But put him with Scouts, or Boys' Brigade, or Y.M.C.A., and he's as happy as happy. Ay! when he's settled in a parish, I reckon I'll be able to chuck the travelling and stick to Leeds.'

'And chuck the engineering too?'

'Nay, lad,' said William, breaking into his broadest Yorkshire, 'I'll never chuck the shop till the shop chucks me, and that won't be for many a year yet.' He held out his two great thin hands and went on, with perfect simplicity: 'I can make any machine in the world with these two. I'm a craftsman, lad, as good as any in the North Country. And it isn't only that.' He laid one of his hands upon Donald's sleeve and said with earnestness: 'There's poetry in machines. You'll maybe not understand. But that's how I see it. Some folks like books and music and poems, but I get all that out of machines. I take a lot of steel and I put it into different shapes, and it works. It works. D'you see? It works as true as a hair to the thousandth part of an inch just as I made it and meant it. I'll go on making machines till my dying day, even if it's only toy engines for grandchildren. There now,' he broke off, as a bell clanged vehemently in the depths of the ship, and someone shouted in a loud voice, 'I thought we weren't going to round that buoy. The skipper's drunk, you see, and he told me just now on the bridge that he couldn't see the buoy, but that the ship had done the trip often enough and ought to round the buoy on her own.'

There was more shouting and bell-clanging, the first officer ran up to the bridge, the engines slowed, then reversed, and the good ship *Wilno* managed to slip round the right side of the buoy. The pilot-boat came alongside and the pilot stepped aboard. The ancient city of Danzig came steadily towards them. The voyage was at an end.

Donald felt that he was parting from a lifelong friend when he shook hands on the quay with William, once again in his overalls, ready to land his machine.

He had learnt a good deal about England upon that rusty Polish hen-coop.

chapter 13

The S.S. *Wilno* bucketed laboriously into Hull on the morning of the last day of the year, and Donald reached London that evening. He found a few letters waiting for him, among them one from Sir Henry Wootton's brother-in-law, Mr Fielding, whom he had met at Geneva, inviting him to spend a few days with him at his country cottage in Buckinghamshire. 'It won't be a party,' wrote Mr Fielding, 'but just ourselves. I hope you won't find it too dull.' There was also a book about the Lepidoptera of the Shan States to be reviewed for Mr Hodge. Donald immediately wrote an acceptance to Mr Fielding, and then settled down to the insects. At 10.30 he had mastered the chapters about the flying scorpions (discovered in 1925 by a young Harvard lepidopterist, who had fled to the wilds of Upper Burma in order to try to forget the passionate love which he bore for Miss Norma Talmadge, and officialy named by him in a moment of bitter and unchivalrous irony (so rare in Harvard men, Scorpio normatalmadgensis) and he laid the book down, put on his hat and coat, and set out for St Paul's Cathedral.

Almost all his life he had known that on New Year's Eve, St Paul's Cathedral is, as the evening papers and the penny dailies so wittily describe it, year after year, the Scotchman's Mecca, and he was determined, now that he had the opportunity, to perform this pilgrimage. At 11.15 he had got as far as the Church of St Martin Ludgate, half-way up from Ludgate Circus to St Paul's, and there he stuck, wedged in on all sides by solid masses of Englishmen. On all sides rose hearty English laughter, and the accents of those who 'were born within sound of Bowe Bells and eat buttered tostes', as the old chronicle says, and of those who had come up from Somerset, and of those whose homes had once been in Wiltshire and Yorkshire and Devonshire and Lancashire – especially Lancashire. Donald even thought he could detect once or twice a Middlesex accent amid all the chatter. All around him echoed the words 'haggis' and 'Lauder' and 'whusky' and 'hoots' and 'baw-bee', the traditional patter of the English music-hall, with its strange words and its mysterious pronunciations, and, above it all, there was a steady drone like the hum of a great dynamo, or the fabled recitation of Browning in Boston drawing-rooms, or the murmur of distant waterfalls, the steady drone of many voices saying, 'Do you know the one about the Aberdonian and the Jew?'

Donald went home.

Two days later he was at Marylebone Station, quietest and most dignified of stations, where the porters go on tiptoe, where the barrows are rubber-tyred and the trains sidle mysteriously in and out with only the faintest of toots upon their whistles so as not to disturb the signalmen, and there he bought a ticket to Aylesbury from a man who whispered that the cost was nine-and-six, and that a train would probably start from Number 5 platform as soon as the engine-driver had come back from the pictures, and the guard had been to see his old mother in Baker Street.

Sure enough a train marked Aylesbury was standing at Number 5 platform. According to the timetable it was due to start in ten minutes, but the platform was deserted and there were no passengers in the carriages. The station was silent. The newspaper boy was asleep. A horse, waiting all harnessed beside a loaded van, lay down and yawned. The dust filtered slowly down through the winter sunbeams, gradually obliterating a label upon a wooden crate which said 'Urgent. Perishable.'

Donald took a seat in a third-class smoker and waited. An engine-driver came stealthily up the platform. A stoker, walking like a cat, followed him. After a few minutes a guard appeared at the door of the carriage and seemed rather surprised at seeing Donald.

'Do you wish to travel, sir?' he asked gently, and when Donald had said that he was desirous of going as far as Aylesbury, the guard touched his hat and said in a most respectful manner, 'If you wish it, sir.' He reminded Donald of the immortal butler, Jeeves. Donald fancied, but he was not quite sure, that he heard the guard whisper to the engine-driver, 'I think we might make a start now, Gerald,' and he rather thinks the engine-driver replied in the same undertone, 'Just as you wish, Horace.'

Anyway, a moment or two later the train slipped out of the station and gathered speed in the direction of Aylesbury.

The railway which begins, or ends, according to the way in which you look at it, from or at Marylebone, used to be called the Great Central Railway, but is now merged with lots of other railways into one large concern called the London, Midland and South Coast or some such name. The reason for the merger was that dividends might be raised, or lowered, or something. Anyway, the line used to be called the Great Central and it is like no other of the north-bound lines. For it runs through lovely, magical rural England. It goes to places that you have never heard of before, but when you have heard of them you want to live in them – Great Missenden and Wendover and High Wycombe and Princes Risborough and Quainton Road, and Akeman Street and Blackthorn. It goes to places that do not need a railway, that never use a railway, that probably do not yet know that they have got a railway. It goes to way-side halts where the only passengers are milk-churns. It visits lonely platforms where the only tickets are bought by geese and ducks. It stops in the middle of buttercup meadows to pick up eggs and flowers. It glides past the great pile of willow branches that are maturing to make England's cricket-bats. It is a dreamer among railways, a poet, kindly and absurd and lovely.

You can sit at your carriage window in a Great Central train and gallop your horse from Amersham to Aylesbury without a check for a factory or a detour for a field of corn or a break for a slum. Pasture and hedge, and pasture and hedge, and pasture and hedge, mile after mile after mile, grey-green and brown and russet, and silver where the little rivers tangle themselves among reeds and trodden watering-pools.

There are no mountains or ravines or noisy tunnels or dizzy viaducts. The Great Central is like that old stream of Asia Minor. It meanders and meanders until at last it reaches, loveliest of English names, the Vale of Aylesbury.

Mr Fielding was waiting on the platform. He was a man of about sixty – broad-shouldered, pink-cheeked, white-moustached, who looked as if he spent a good deal of time in the open air and not very much time in the study.

He had an ancient Ford car outside, loaded up with baskets and parcels and paper-bags. 'Been marketing,' he explained. 'It's a fixed rule of the house that anyone who takes a car into Aylesbury has to do the shopping for everyone, though who the deuce fixed the rule I'm blest if I know. It's all very nice for the women, but a fine fool I look matching ribbons.' It was probably thirty years since anyone had asked Mr Fielding to match a ribbon, but it was his stock phrase to cover any feminine commission.

A three-mile clatter in the veteran car – 'I never can get the new car,' explained Mr Fielding. 'I never have been able to get our new cars. That's why I have to hang on to one that my daughters say they wouldn't be seen dead in' – brought them to 'The Golden Hind', which was the name of Mr Fielding's house. It was a long, low building of pale-red brick and unstained timber-beams and ivy and queer-shaped windows with badly-fitting frames, and an ancient iron-studded door of oak that was almost white, and dark-red tiles and lichen and moss and stone-crop. A flagged path led up to the door, and on each side of the path were acres of lawns in their rough, worm-casty, twiggy, shaggy winter coats. Through the deepening twilight Donald could see a pale-red brick wall beyond the lawns and the tops of green-houses peering over it, and beyond that again a cluster of ancient barns and the twisted curl-papers of a monster haystack. A jumble of terrier dogs hurled themselves out of an open window at the sound of the Ford, and lights sprang up in the windows and over the front door. The clock on a square, flinty, Saxon church-tower struck six. From a little further down the road came the clinkety-clink of hammer upon anvil and the jingling sound of harness as the horse that was being shod, by the light of a torch, shifted its feet restlessly. In the distance a dog barked and an owl cried out suddenly from a wood of willow-trees. Sappho's evening star, which brings home everything that the bright dawn has scattered – the sheep, the goat, and the little child to its mother – shone in a frosty sky and the moving moon was softly going up.

'Mind your head in the house,' said Mr Fielding, smacking the dogs affectionately. 'It's a perfect death-trap. One of these days I'm going to pull it down and build a labour-saving affair, all made of concrete and ebony.'

Donald stooped as he went in, but not far enough, and hit his head a shattering blow almost at once upon an oak beam. It was very painful, but at least it broke the ice as well as the skin, and by the time that Mrs Fielding had finished fussing round with iodine and bandages and lint, and Mary Willock, the married daughter, and Winifred, the unmarried daughter, had fetched neat little leather satchels which contained everything that was necessary for the emergency treatment of dogs, cows, goats, and horses, and George Willock, the son-in-law, had uncorked with dazzling rapidity a bottle of Napoleon brandy, and Mr Fielding himself had weighed in with a decanter of Harvey's Bristol Cream Sherry, and the jumble of terriers had licked his face and hands and fought a brisk skirmish across his chest, Donald felt that he had been an intimate friend of the family for years.

As soon as the wound had been dressed and everyone had celebrated the recovery of the patient in Mr Harvey's amazing sherry, Mrs Fielding shooed them all off to get ready for dinner. Dinner was at 7.15, and no one was to dress. Donald crept up to his room amid a jungle of grey oak beams and crept down again at 7.10. His host was already down. Donald asked him if there was any story attached to the naming of the house after Drake's ship.

'Not much of a story,' said Mr Fielding. 'The records show that in 1550 the house was an inn, but no one knows what it was called in those days. All that is known is that it changed its name to celebrate Drake's voyage round the world. When I bought it – thirty years ago – it was a tumble-down farmhouse with water running in through the roof, and it was called Holt's. I got the story out of the parish records, and changed its name back to "The Golden Hind". There's a curious thing about that changing, too. About six months after I'd told everyone – the Post Office and the inn-keeper and the local gossips and so on – about the change, an old man came to see me. He was very, very old. The local people said he was well over a hundred, but there were no records about him. He said he was glad I'd gone back to the old name. I asked him how he knew anything about the old name and he said he didn't, but that his grandfather had told him that the Admiral was a great man. I asked him what Admiral he meant, and he said he couldn't remember, and he wasn't even sure that his grandfather had ever told him, and he wouldn't take his oath that his grandfather had ever known, but anyway the Admiral was a great man. You see, Cameron, it's an old country. Incredibly old. And there aren't many changes. Families go on and on and on. Sometimes a boy goes off to be a soldier, and sometimes a girl goes off to be a parlour-maid, but ninety per cent of them stick to the soil. And have stuck to the soil for centuries. There's a village near here – Eynesbury St Clement – a matter of five or six hundred souls all told. Well, a fellow from London came down last year and ferreted around in the parish records and so on, and he found a list of the bowmen that went from Eynesbury St Clement to Agincourt. There were the names of twenty-four bowmen, and eighteen of their names are on the Eynesbury St Clement war memorial for the Great War.'

Dinner was served punctually at 7.15, and there was no delay between the soup and the roast chicken or between the roast chicken and the baked apples, for Mr Fielding had to take the chair at a Committee of the local Boy Scouts at 8 o'clock, and

Winifred was meeting the vicar at 8.15 to discuss a prospective jumble sale, and at 9 o'clock both Mr and Mrs Fielding were due at the Annual General Meeting of the Lawn Tennis Club. And as Mrs Fielding, who was President of the Lawn Tennis Club, had to retire to prepare her presidential address, and as the married daughter and her husband seized the first opportunity after dinner to rush out to the stables to a horse that had colic, Donald was left with an hour or two upon his hands. He spent it in the best possible way. He strolled across in the starlight to the Crooked Billet, sometimes called the Mary Wells, for no known reason, and sometimes the Donkey, for no known reason, asked for a pint of bitter, which was handed to him in an early-Victorian pewter mug, and sat down in a corner of the bar-parlour. It was a small bar-parlour and the low ceiling was a tangled mass of oak beams. The fire-place stretched almost across one side of the room and the flickering oil-lamp threw queer shadows into its cavernous depths. A jumble of ancient iron cooking appliances – spits, pots, chains, saw-toothed racks, cauldrons – lay in one corner. A bench with a high back, polished by the corduroys of centuries into a shiny pale yellow, jutted out from the wall in a semicircle so that the man at one end would have his back against the wall, and the man at the other would be exactly opposite the centre of the fire-place. On the high, smoke-blackened mantel-shelf were wooden gun-rests and a row of Rochester ware jars, decorated with green and purple flowers and gilt bands, and labelled 'Shrub', 'Whisky', 'Gin', 'Oporto', 'Cinnamon', 'Peach', and 'Lemon'. There was a pock-marked dart-board in one corner, and on an old oak table a shove-ha'penny board and piece of chalk.

The room was full of the smoke of cheap tobacco.

The conversation only faltered for a moment when the strange gentleman came in, for the courtesy of the country-side is universal and there is no inquistiveness. The gentry, of course, are different, for they have little to do except to be inquisitive and to play lawn tennis, and, nowadays, to grapple unsuccessfully with the intricacies of contract bridge. But they are a separate race. As a rule they are only a single remove from one or other of the four great breeding-grounds of the English rural gentry – London's suburbs, Clyde's banks, Boston, and the torrid plains of Hindostan. And each little family group, living each in its eight-bedroomed or ten-bedroomed house, detached from other houses, detached indeed from everything in the world, has its own separate interests. They have no common bond except gossip and lawn tennis and bridge. The soil means nothing to them, nor the seasons and their fruits, nor the nesting of birds, nor the first green budding of elm-trees, nor the sound of the flight of swans. Their desires are thwarted. They have no escape from gentility, no desperate romances, no love-making under the leaf-falling moon, nothing, nothing but bridge and lawn tennis, and lawn tennis and bridge, until Death parts them even from their cards and their racquets.

But it is different with those who live on the earth and for the earth. They have no interest in each other's petty lives. They do not discuss the village. They are concerned with vaster things than fashionable hats and informatory doubles. The tiller of the soil lives his life very close to Nature, and of all men he is the most natural.

So when Donald entered the bar-room of the Crooked Billet, he aroused only the slightest of attention for a moment or two, and in a minute he was almost forgotten, and was able to look round at his ease. There were ten men in the room and all were old. Seven of the ten had beards, and the others had clean-shaven chins and long side-whiskers. Most of them wore corduroys, but one was resplendent in a dark tweed suit and a very dirty dickey, unadorned by a tie. The cheeks of all of them were pink and the eyes of all of them were clear. They were talking about politics.

'Well,' said one, who must have been well over eighty, and whose back was bowed with a lifetime of digging and an old age of rheumatism, 'when Lord Salisbury was in office I voted for Lord Salisbury, and when Mr Gladstone was in office I voted for Mr Gladstone, because there never was a ha'porth of difference between them that ever I could see.'

'Ah! now, Lord Salisbury,' said another, 'there was a man for you. I heard him speak once and I couldn't understand one word he said. Not one word. A fine gentleman, he was.'

'I never rightly understood,' said a third man who had a straw bag of carpentering tools between his feet and a violin tied on his back with a piece of black tape, 'why Mr Gladstone gave the licence to the grocers. Did a lot of harm to the houses, and didn't do any good to the Liberal Party.'

'It didn't do any good to the Liberal Party,' said a wizened little man with a cheerful face, 'when the Earl Rosebery won the Derby when he was Prime Minister, but it did a deal of good to my pocket,' and he winked several times and nodded his head knowingly.

A man who had been dozing in a corner suddenly woke up and lifted an ancient, wrinkled, pink-and-brown countenance to the company. His white beard shone bravely in the beam of the oil-lamp and he thrust it forward as he propped his chin upon a newly cut holly cudgel. 'I remember,' he said in a deep whisper which came as rather a shock to Donald, who from his experience of stage old men had expected a falsetto piping, 'I remember the year when Mr Harry Chaplin won the Derby and there isn't another of you young chaps that can say as much. I was working in his gardens and he gave me a shilling – gave us all a shilling, all of us working in his gardens and stables – and I knocked a hole in it and wore it on my watch-chain for five-and-thirty years, but I lost it afterwards. Mr Harry Chaplin, that was.'

The old man's head drooped and in a few moments he was asleep again.

'Ah! Mr Chaplin,' struck in another ancient, 'there was a gentleman for you.'

'Yes, he was a gentleman all right,' said the man with the violin. 'There aren't too many of them about nowadays.'

'That's right,' nodded the man who voted impartially for Lord Salisbury and Mr Gladstone. 'Why, I can remember the time when old Squire Rushbrooke was up at the Manor, and the Parson at that time, Stoke his name was – you remember Parson Stoke, Mr Davis?'

'I remember Parson Stoke, Mr Stillaway. Remember him clear.'

'Well, Parson Stoke said to me once that in the writings about the parish there had been Rushbrookes at the Manor for hundreds and hundreds of years.'

'I reckon it was the War put a stop to all that.'

'Ay, the War put a stop to a great many things.'

'I reckon,' said the man with the violin, 'that we could do with a bit more of Mr Dickens in this country. A few more Sam Wellers. That's what we want.'

'I saw Mr Dickens once,' said another rheumatism-backed gaffer who had not spoken up to now. 'A fine-looking gentleman with a fine big beard, same as Mr Stillaway's, only bigger. He was a gentleman who liked a good laugh, he was.'

'Ah!' said the man with the violin, 'that's what the trouble is. People don't seem to laugh now like they used to. I don't know why it is.'

The man in the dickey drained off his glass pint-mug and called for another pint of mild-and-bitter.

'Well, has anyone got their antirrhinums in yet?' he inquired, and he looked round with a gleam in his eye which said as clearly as possible that he had got his antirrhinums in that morning and that it was high time that the others did the same. It was equally clear from the shuffling feet and evasive replies that no one else had got their antirrhinums in yet.

There was a pause in the conversation, and Donald plucked up sufficient courage to ask his neighbour when the Hunt was likely to be meeting in the district.

'They meet at Tainton Green tomorrow, sir,' replied the man politely. 'That's a matter of two miles from here.'

'More like two miles and a furlong, Mr Young,' said Mr Stillaway.

'That's right, Mr Stillaway,' agreed Mr Davis. 'It's every bit of a furlong above the two miles.'

'You're working in Tainton, Mr Stovold,' Mr Young appealed to the violinist. 'Would you say it's as much as a furlong above the two miles?'

'Well, I'm not sure that I wouldn't, Mr Young,' replied Mr Stovold. 'I reckon it is maybe a furlong all but a chain or two.'

The ancient with the holly-stick woke up again. He seemed to have an uncanny power of hearing in his sleep, for he observed, 'They'll find near Stacey's tomorrow over to Tainton. There's an outlier there. I saw him today, the old rascal.' He laughed a sudden high laugh, and added, 'I remember finding at Stacey's when I was second horse-man to Mr Selby. Two hours and forty minutes, she gave us, and I never saw a faster run. We killed her at Grendon Church.'

'What year would that be, Mr Darley?' inquired the man in the dickey.

Mr Darley cogitated, and finally said:

'I can't rightly remember, but it was the year that Mr Selby sent us all up to London to see the Great Exhibition. It was a long time ago.'

'Would that be Mr Selby from over Ludgershall way?' asked Mr Stillaway. But Mr Darley was asleep again.

'How old is he?' Donald asked, and several voices answered simultaneously, 'He's ninety-eight come Martinmas, sir.'

Donald asked then if there was likely to be a large muster at the meet, and Mr Stovold, the violinist, shook his head sadly.

'You can't tell, sir. Not nowadays. You see, fox-hunting has changed since I was a young man.'

'Ah, that it has,' the others nodded agreement.

'When I was a young man in these parts,' went on Mr Stovold, 'all the gentry knew each other and we knew all the gentry – their faces, I mean. And you could tell who was going to fox-hunt each day as easy as anything. It was all homely-like, a sort of family as you might say. But now it's all ladies and gentlemen from London. They come down in their motor-cars, and they go back in their motor-cars, and they bring their horses in motor-cars, and it's all changed. They're strangers. When I was a nipper, working over at Mr Binstead's—'

'I remember Mr Binstead,' interrupted old Mr Davis. 'He's dead these five-and-forty years.'

'That's right, Mr Davis. He died in the year of the great frost when young Sam Byles skated from Bovington's water-meadow at Aylesbury to the Bull at Launton for a wager. As I was saying, when I was a nipper over at Mr Binstead's, if I opened a gate or found a gap, as like as not the gentleman would know me by name and say, "Much obliged to you, Bill," or "Thank you, Stovold. Hope your mother's rheumatism is better," But nowadays you're more likely to get a "Hurry up, blast you" for your pains.'

'That's it. That's what you're more likely to get now,' said

Mr Young, and the others nodded and puffed away at their pipes.

Mr Stovold went on.

'And there's another thing. They don't use the inns as they used to. Time was when this very house would serve beer, or maybe cherry-brandy, or sloe-gin to twenty or thirty fox-hunters in a single afternoon. But now it all comes down from London in great silver bottles that they carry in the back pocket of their breeches. And they get their breeches in London, instead of in Bicester as they used to do. And ladies and gentlemen come down in motor-cars to watch, and they keep on heading the fox and blocking up the lanes and frightening the horses. Mr Davis, what would old Mr Holford have said to a gentleman who headed the fox in a motor-car?'

They all, except the ninety-eight-year-old, still asleep, laughed at this, and Mr Davis slapped his corduroy leg and said, 'God Almighty, I don't know what Mr Holford wouldn't have said. He'd have fair killed him.'

'Who was Mr Holford?' asked Donald.

'When did Mr Holford die, Mr Stovold?' Mr Davis passed on the question.

'Mr Holford? It was the year before the war – not the war against the Germans. The war in Africa.'

'That's right. The year after the old Queen had her processions and all.'

Donald looked round the semicircle of wrinkled, wind-worn, ancient, glowing faces, and rather diffidently ventured on another question.

'Why is it,' he said, 'that some of the young men of the village don't come in here for a drink? Is there another inn in the village?'

'No, sir,' said Mr Davis, smoothing his head with a hard thin hand. 'They don't drink here nor anywhere else, the young chaps. They hardly drink at all.'

'Why is that?' asked Donald.

Mr Stovold, the violinist, seemed to be the readiest with his tongue, for it was he who answered.

'There's several reasons for it, sir. For one thing, there isn't the money about that there used to be; and then beer costs twice as much; and then there's picture-houses and sharrabangs and motor-bicycles with girls sitting on behind. And then in this village the Boy Scouts are very strong ,and lots of the young chaps are Rovers and don't drink so as to be an example to the Scouts and the Cubs. And then, you see, there's no one between them and old chaps like us.'

'All the rest were killed, you mean?'

'Most of them, sir. Forty-two were killed from this village and they'd be men of thirty-five and forty by now.'

'Ah! That War didn't do any of us any good,' said Mr Stillaway. 'Nothing's been the same since.'

'Yes, and what did we gain by it?' asked Mr Young.

'Nothing,' said Mr Davis.

Donald made a halting remark about Belgium and national honour and treaties, which the semicircle listened to attentively. Then Mr Stillaway, the impartial voter, replied:

'But can you tell me, sir, what national honour does for me? I've worked on the land all my life, and the least I've ever earned is four-and-six a week and the most is twenty-nine shillings. It isn't a fortune, either of them. In 1914 a man comes down to the green here, and he makes a speech about just that very national honour that you've been talking about. Mind you, sir, in 1914 the nation and all its honour was giving me twenty-two shillings a week and I was working seventy-four hours a week for it. But I had to give three sons and eight grandsons to fight for the national honour. Eleven of them. And three were killed and two lost legs. And what good did that do to them or to me or Mr Davis here, or Mr Darley? Cost of living is higher. Beer is more expensive and so is tobacco. And my grandsons, the ones that weren't killed, can't get work. And all that for what you call national honour.'

'That's right.' 'Mr Stillaway's hit it.' 'That's as true as I'm sitting here,' came as muttered applause.

Ancient Darley raised his venerable head once more.

'We fought on the wrong side,' he whispered strongly. 'Those Frenchies were never any use to us. My father saw the beacons on the downs of Sussex when Boney was on the other side. The Germans never did us any harm. It's all they Frenchies.'

'Ah! That's right,' echoed every antique voice in the parlour.

'My father saw the sails of Lord Nelson's ships many a time,' whispered the ancient, 'and old Boney sitting over there with his army like a squirrel with a nest of nuts. And my father said to me, and I say to you young chaps, 'What's the good of it all? What's the good of all these wars?'

He broke off into an ancient laugh.

'I'm not a scholar, never was, and don't suppose now I ever will be. But one thing my father used to say, and he taught me to say it, was this: "I am a true labourer: I earn that I eat, get that I wear, owe no man hate, envy no man's happiness, glad of other men's good, content with my own harm; and the greatest of my pride is to see my ewes graze and my lambs suck." I don't know where he got it from. Maybe his father taught it to him. Or maybe it was Parson. War! What good is war to us?'

A voice, gently authoritative, came through the eddying smoke-clouds. 'Time, gentlemen, please. If you please, gentlemen. Time. Ten o'clock. Act of Parliament, gentlemen, please.'

Donald walked slowly and thoughtfully home under a clear cold sky. The Great Bear was pointing at the Pole Star and the Pleiades were a golden blur and Cassiopeia was twinkling and Orion was flaunting his old-fashioned military equipment. The black, gaunt hedges were like wrought-iron work against the starlight. Dogs barked in the distance and footfalls clinked in the village street. Another English day was over.

At The Golden Hind, Mr and Mrs Fielding were seated side by side at a desk, poring over a small, dog-eared note-book. The others had gone to bed. Mr Fielding looked up and said, 'Help yourself to whisky, Cameron. We'll be finished in a moment.'

Donald poured himself out a drink and sat down by the blazing log-fire. His host and hostess went on with their work.

'If Mrs Burchett can't pay her rent,' said Mr Fielding decisively, 'we'll just have to go without it, that's all.'

'She can't possibly pay, John. She's had rheumatism so badly all the winter that she's had to give up washing, and that means dropping fifteen shillings a week at least, and both her boys are out of work.'

'All right. Strike off Mrs Burchett. The next is Henry Davis.

Henry's been out of work now twelve weeks—'

'And his wife's had twins.'

'All right. Strike off Henry Davis. We can't worry him for rent just now. And the last is old Mrs Mitchell, and she says will we take two shillings a week next month instead of four and six. What's the trouble there, Florence?'

'Young Mitchell's been in trouble again.'

'Damn that young Mitchell!' exclaimed Mr Fielding. 'Whereabouts is it this time?'

'Down at Bristol, I hear,' replied Mrs Fielding. 'A maid-servant, as usual. She got an order against him and he didn't pay, so now he's in Bristol prison.'

'All right,' said Mr Fielding, 'we'll put down Mrs Mitchell for two shillings instead of four-and-six. I'd like to get that young blackguard up before me at Quarter Sessions; I'd make him jump. Is that all?'

'Mrs Taylor's roof is leaking.'

'I'll send up that carpenter fellow, Stovold, tomorrow.'

'And a gate wants renewing at the lower paddock. I saw it this afternoon when I was out for a walk. And, John, do you think we could find a job for young Butter? His father was killed, you remember, and his mother has a pretty hard time of it.'

'We're employing far more hands already than we ought to,' grumbled Mr Fielding.

'Yes, I know, dear. But Mrs Butter does have such a hard time, and he's such a nice boy. I thought we might put him on to do a little trenching beyond the orchard for a new onion bed.'

'All right, all right,' said Mr Fielding. Donald thought that his tone of grudging concession was very clumsily assumed and that secretly he was delighted at finding a reasonable excuse for employing young Butter.

'Well now, my dear, is that all?' he went on. 'Mr Cameron will think us very rude.'

Mrs Fielding smiled maternally at Donald and said:

'I am sure that Mr Cameron will think nothing of the kind. There's only one thing more. The thatcher is coming up at 9 o'clock tomorrow morning about the end barn. It must be done soon or there'll be no roof left. Will you see him?'

'Oh yes, I'll see him,' said Mr Fielding enthusiastically. 'He's promised to lend me a ferret for clearing out the rats at the stables. I expect he'll bring it along with him.'

They both got up and came over to the fire.

'Well, Cameron,' said Mr Fielding. 'We've been neglecting you scandalously.'

'I've been enjoying myself enormously,' replied Donald. 'You see, I was a farmer myself once. But it was a different sort of farming to all this.'

'You don't look like a farmer, Mr Cameron,' said Mrs Fielding. Mrs Fielding was a gentle, comely woman, with a voice like the purr of a cat, and large, soft, grey eyes.

'I've tried very hard to get rid of the traces.'

'Why, didn't you like farming?' she asked in surprise. 'We all adore living on the land.'

'But what a different sort of land!' cried Donald. 'Where I farmed, the soil was poor and the stones were plentiful. I grew oats and turnips and potatoes. Six months in the year the wind blew from the Arctic Circle straight into my front door. Everything was grey – a granite farmhouse, slate roofs, stone dykes, and grey skies, and in winter it was dark at 3 o'clock in the afternoon. But here—' – he threw his arms out – 'here, what a difference! You've got colour here. Your houses are red, and you have hedges with flowers in them instead of stone dykes. You've got fruit blossom, and it's warm down here – and – and I somehow can't explain – you've been here such a long time. You're settled and cosy. I've been over in the Crooked Billet just now, listening to your old men talking. One of them had seen Dickens and one of them quoted Shakespeare – though he didn't know it was Shakespeare – and I felt – I don't quite know what I did feel – but I wouldn't have been a bit surprised if they'd told me all about their experiences at Crécy or Poitiers. I'd have believed them . . . We haven't anything like that in Scotland.'

'You've got other things to be proud of,' said Mrs Fielding gently.

'Of course we have!' replied Donald patriotically. 'Lots of them. But somehow all this down here makes Scotland seem rather disjointed.'

'You were such blood-thirsty ruffians,' said Mr Fielding

genially. 'That was your trouble. Always scrapping. Look at our wars. We had that local affair at Sedgmoor, and the Cromwell stuff, and the Wars of the Roses, but that's about all in the last six hundred years, except when your Douglases came marauding over the Border. No wonder things have got settled down a bit.'

'Yes, I suppose that's it, partly. But I think it's also that you're such a friendly race. It seems to me that you like things and people so much.'

'Well, there isn't much point in quarrelling all the time, is there?'

'Of course there isn't much point,' answered Donald; 'there isn't any point. But people do it all the same. Especially on the west coast of Scotland. But down here it's different. I think the English have done lots of beastly things in the past – like Cromwell's sack of Drogheda, or the destruction of the Summer Palace in Pekin and the Old Fort at Delhi, or letting Marshal Ney be shot. But I think that every time it was just a fit of bad temper, and as soon as it was over they became as kind and as friendly as ever. I think the longest fit they've ever had was the way they treated Napoleon. But with the Scots, and the French, and lots of other races, there's far too much permanent bad temper.'

'We're too busy money-making,' said Mr Fielding with a laugh. 'Nation of shopkeepers, eh?'

'Oh no, no,' exclaimed Donald earnestly, 'that's a libel. You're the most unpractical race in the world.'

'Oh, come, come, Mr Cameron!' said Mrs Fielding reproachfully. 'You can't possibly defend that statement.'

'Yes, Cameron,' chimed in her husband, 'that's going a bit too far. If there's one thing we are good at, it's money-making and business. I sometimes think we go a bit too far the other way and drive too hard bargains.'

'I couldn't help overhearing,' said Donald drily, 'that you were preparing to drive some pretty hard bargains with your tenants just now.'

Mr Fielding became indignant.

'That's a different story altogether. It so happened that one

168

or two of them have had a bit of hard luck lately, and one can't Shylock the poor devils. But when it comes to a business deal, I flatter myself I'm as good a man as my neighbours.'

'Perhaps that's because they're all English,' said Donald.

Mr Fielding laughed delightedly.

'You mean that if you settled down here as a sort of Farfrae you'd soon turn me into a Mayor of Casterbridge.'

'Talking about that,' said Mrs Fielding, knitting away with a fury that contrasted oddly with her gentle placidity of voice and manner, 'what is that copy of *Tess* that is lying on the hall table? I don't think I've seen it before.'

Mr Fielding looked down and coughed, and then thumped his chest to call attention to the fact that the cough was physical, not nervous.

'It's a first edition, my dear,' he said.

'I saw that it was a first edition,' she replied. 'Where did you find it? Upstairs somewhere?'

'No – er – as a matter of fact, I picked it up today. It's quite valuable.'

'In Aylesbury?'

'Er – no. Not exactly. Er – here.'

'John, the vicar has been at you again. How much did you give him?' Mrs Fielding stopped knitting.

'Well, my dear, he's got seven children and a first edition is no use to him. He can get just as much fun out of a Tauchnitz.'

'How much did you give him?' said Mrs Fielding patiently.

'It's in perfect preservation,' replied her lord and master.

'Three hundred pounds?'

Mr Fielding sighed.

'As a matter of fact—' he began, but she gently interrupted him.

'If you want to conceal that sort of thing from me, John, you shouldn't use my cheque-book.'

Mr Fielding laughed, and then turned to Donald.

'I'm afraid I drove a pretty hard bargain with the poor old vicar, but after all, business is business.'

'Considering that the market value of a *Tess* first edition probably isn't more than fifty pounds—'

'Oh, nonsense!' cried Mr Fielding, jumping up. 'It's a first-class investment. What does it matter anyway? One more drink and then bedtime – eh, chickabiddy. But as for saying that the English are bad businessmen, it's all rubbish! Say when, Cameron.'

chapter 14

Breakfast at 'The Golden Hind' was at 8.30, and at 9 o'clock sharp a maid came into the breakfast-room and announced in an almost unintelligible Buckinghamshire accent:

'Thatcher come, sir.'

Mr Fielding threw down his *Times* and bustled out, and Donald strolled after him unobtrusively. The thatcher was a tall, thin man of an indeterminate age – perhaps forty, perhaps seventy. His cheeks, of course, were a healthy red, like all Buckinghamshire cheeks, and a long brown moustache drooped down past each corner of his mouth almost to the edges of his chin. His eyes were pale blue. He wore corduroys and an old army leather jerkin without sleeves, and a tie without a collar, and he held his old tweed cap in both hands in front of him.

Mr Fielding plunged at once into a complicated conversation, full of technical terms of carpentering and thatching, full of joists and trusses and ties and overhang and twists and pins. Each appeared to understand the other perfectly. Donald could make head or tail of neither.

'There's a fine old trade dying out,' said Mr Fielding, after the man had gone. 'Old Mells is the only thatcher for many miles round and there's not a better craftsman in the land. And yet he can't get enough work to keep him busy all the week. He has to do hedging and ditching and odd-job gardening, and he's the village sexton too. Sad, isn't it? When he's dead there won't be a thacher at all.'

'Hasn't he got any sons?' inquired Donald. 'A lot of these trades are hereditary, aren't they?'

'They were hereditary,' replied Mr Fielding, 'but this is the last generation of it. There has been a thatcher called Mells in this village for centuries, I expect, but the old man you saw just now – he's got two sons and both of them are motor mechanics in Aylesbury. That's the rule nowadays. The stupid sons become farm labourers and the clever ones become mechanics. In the old days both clever sons and stupid sons followed their father's trade, except the occasional enterprising one who joined the army. But garages have spoilt all that.'

Mrs Fielding, a bundle of tradesmen's books under each arm, letters and bills and receipts and circulars and bulb catalogues and newspapers in her hands, and a cheque-book in her mouth, came out of the dining-room. Her husband relieved her of the impediment to speech, and she asked Donald what he would like to do.

Donald said that he had thought of walking over to Tainton Green to see the Meet, and he fancied that a fleeting glimmer of relief was visible on the faces of both host and hostess. A guest in the country who cannot amuse himself is a nuisance to busy people.

'Would you like the car? Or a bicycle?' asked Mr Fielding promptly.

'I think I'd sooner walk,' replied Donald, and again he thought they looked relieved.

'It's about two miles,' said Mrs Fielding. 'If you start a little after 10 you'll be in plenty of time. The Meet's at 11 o'clock.'

It was a warm January morning, sunny and spring-like, and Donald felt that there should have been buttercups in the meadows with larks above them, and swallows fooling about, and cowslips, and great drifts of the flower which the English call bluebells but the Scots wild hyacinths. The air was very still, and far away a bell was tolling. Cows and sheep grazed in the fields, and ploughland chequered the greenness of the pasture with dark, kindly smears of earth. Somewhere near an axe was pecking at a tree, and on the edge of a copse of young oaks a band of small children were happily collecting firewood and putting it into a cart, home-made from a soap-box and a pair of ancient bicycle wheels.

Donald dived into a network of narrow lanes, un-signposted,

untouched by the influence of Mr Macadam, and flanked on each side by strips of grass which were a good deal wider than the lanes themselves. No buildings were visible. There was no sign of human life. Donald was in the heart of rural England.

He was recalled from his day-dreaming about village Hampdens and plodding ploughmen, and the short and simple annals of the poor, by a terrific blast upon an electric motor-horn about two yards behind him. He sprang into the air in alarm and spun round to find himself facing the silver bonnet of a colossal pale-blue-and-silver Rolls-Royce, out of the driver's seat of which was leaning a young man with a red face. It was not the pink of the gaffers' faces in the Crooked Billet, but a mottled red.

'Hey! You!' shouted the young man. 'When you've finished sleeping in the middle of the road, where the devil's Tainton Green?'

'I imagine it's straight on,' replied Donald politely, 'but I'm afraid—'

'Oh God!' interrupted the young man, 'another bloody stranger!' and he released the clutch and the great car slid away.

Tainton Green looked as if a celestial town-planner had scattered Tudor cottages out of a pepper-pot and then, as an afterthought, had flung down a handful of rather larger Queen Anne houses. The newest house in the village must have been about two hundred years old. There was in Tainton Green what house-agents call 'a wealth of old timber', and the cottages which it adorned stood at every conceivable angle to each other in an irregular ring round the Green.

But Donald had no desire at the moment to examine architecture. His whole attention was concentrated upon the most famous of all English sporting spectacles, the Meet of a pack of English foxhounds. As he had expected, there was no detail missing from the scene that has been so often described in books and pictures. Everything was there – dogs, shiny horses, admiring villagers, huntsmen in velvet caps, a horseman with a long whip and a brass horn, sharp-looking grooms in neat leggings and black-and-white check breeches, rows of motor-cars of immense brilliance and beauty (even the pale-blue-and-silver Rolls-Royce which had passed Donald in the lane was not particularly conspicuous), motor horse-boxes, liveried chauffeurs, liveried footmen, each carrying a fur rug over his left arm and looking bored and contemptuous, and here and there an occasional pony-trap. The pony-traps – there were not more than half a dozen of them – roused the chauffeurs a little from their massive stolidity into lofty smiles.

And, of course, there were the ladies and gentlemen who were going to risk their bones, perhaps even their necks, for the sake of sport. The first thing that struck Donald was the drabness of the feminine hunting-kit and the gorgeousness of the masculine. The women mostly wore queer-shaped bowler hats and black habits, with here and there a touch of white. But the men wore shiny toppers and scarlet coats and white or pale-yellow breeches and huge orange-topped boots and high stocks, and they strode about the Green like captains of Spanish galleons, or colonels of Napoleon's light cavalry, seeing no one except each other, but allowing themselves to be seen by everyone, chins out, heads high, superbly disdainful, like the camels of Bactria who alone know the hundredth name of God.

One of them stepped heavily into a puddle beside Donald and splashed him with mud and went on, his eyes fixed on eternal space, as if neither Donald nor the puddle had ever existed. Another, seated upon his charger like Bellerophon upon Pegasus, halted a yard or two away, and addressed a beautiful girl who was curveting round and round upon a mettlesome steed. 'These bloody yokels who clutter up the place ought to be shot,' he said. 'Don't you agree, Pud?'

The beautiful girl persuaded her horse to stand still for a moment and looked at Donald as if he was some kind of slug. 'Bloody bastards,' she agreed, and then was curveted away again.

A colonel of Napoleonic light cavalry came past, perhaps a Hussar of Conflans – Donald could almost hear the clatter of his sabre upon the streets of Vienna or Warsaw or Berlin, and see the swing of the pale-blue, silver-buttoned dolman and the nodding of the horse-hair plume – stopped, put an eyeglass in his eye, and addressed the horseman.

'Hullo, Ted!' said Lasalle.

'Hullo, Squibs,' replied Bellerophon, looking more than ever like a Bactrian camel, 'I say, these bloody yokels who clutter up the place ought to be shot.'

The *beau sabreur* looked quickly round and, seeing that at the moment no one was within ear-shot – for Donald, being only a yokel, was like a stone or a stump or a cow, and could not actually be said to be there at all – he lowered his voice and said urgently, 'Look here, Ted, don't touch Moggeridge Ordinaries till they hit half a dollar. We're doing a wrangle, see? Weinstein's coming in with us, and so's old Potts and old Finkelberg. Get me?'

He winked, and Donald thought that somehow he looked less like a swaggering hussar than before. For some ridiculous reason, Donald found himself thinking of week-ends at Brighton and peroxide.

All this time more cars and more horses and more intrepid sportswomen and sportsmen had been arriving, and punctually at 11 o'clock the whole apparatus of fox-killing, dogs, horses, women, and men moved off sedately towards a wood outside the village. Donald counted a hundred and seven riders and approximately sixty dogs. It was a formidable cavalcade. From a little rising ground he watched them enter a field and gradually spread out into a scattered semi-circle as they approached the wood which was presumed to be the lair of one of the doomed vermin. They rode slowly, in little groups, and halted while the advance guard of scarlet and velvet and horn vanished among the trees. There was a pause of ten minutes, and then came the sound of distant shouting, and the horses sprang into activity. The hunt was up. The riders streamed away along the edges of the wood and vanished over a slope and reappeared on a far-off hill-side, a spectacle of unbelievable picturesqueness and romance. Donald stood and strained his eyes until the last scarlet pin-head had vanished behind the horizon of dark woods, leaving an empty landscape of dull greys and browns and greens. The splendour had gone, and Donald walked slowly homewards.

Half-way home he found that at his rate of walking he would be back at 'The Golden Hind' before 12 o'clock, which would never do. Mr and Mrs Fielding would be busy, and they would abandon their busyness to try and entertain him and everyone would feel embarrassed. It was a warm morning; a tree-stump on the edge of a coppice was dry, and Donald had a book. He sat down in the sunshine and plunged into *The Trail of the Poisoned Carpet*, a work of fiction of which the nature and the absorbing interest can be readily judged when it is stated that Donald had just reached the point when the heroine, slim Miranda Tremayne, drugged, and bound hand and foot, was being lowered in an empty caviar barrel into a disused mineshaft by La Sapphirita, a Bolshevik spy, and Boris Fernandowski, agent of the Ogpu.

Donald was soon completely absorbed. He read the chapter which described the brilliant rescue of slim Miranda by huge, ugly Dick Trelawney, who happened to alight providentially at the mouth of the mine-shaft in a racing balloon. He read the great scenes of Dick's fight with Ah Boo Wu and his gang in the Limehouse main drain, the reappearance of the secret submarine off Valparaiso, the forgery of Sir Dalhousie Canning's signature to the Bungiskhan Treaty, and the theft of the Poisoned Carpet itself from the nunnery in Hull, and he had just reached the point at which La Sapphirita has put cyanide upon the claws of a Siamese cat and, disguised in black satin trousers as a Government window-cleaner, has inserted the animal into the Far Eastern Department of the Foreign Office where huge, ugly Dick Trelawney is at work with an atlas and a manual of geography trying to discover exactly where Bungiskhan is, with which he has negotiated the Treaty. Donald had just reached this point when he became slowly aware that the stillness of the country-side was being broken by distant voices. A faint hallooing came across the fields, and then suddenly, out of the hedge on the other side of the road – tired, muddy, panting, limping, desperate – came the fox. He passed within a yard of Donald without appearing to see him and lolloped slowly into the coppice.

Donald watched him go and wished him good luck, adding aloud, 'And a fat chance you've got! All alone against sixty dogs and a hundred and seven riders and a hundred and seven horses – two hundred and seventy-four against one.'

He moved down the road to get out of the way of the pursuing angels, who were so nobly bent upon saving the countryside from vermin. The shouting and hallooing came nearer, but the human sounds were overwhelmed in the wild, excited, parrot-like, monkey-like yapping and screaming of the hounds, as they came pouring through the hedge in brave pursuit, all sixty of the intrepid heroes. Then came the first of the riders, the men in velvet caps and the men with the horns, taking the hedges with the lovely slow curve of a horse that knows it can jump and knows that its rider can be trusted. Behind them came the mob, galloping like Prince Rupert across the fields, the leaders unerringly finding the gaps and the gates, and the followers forming up into blasphemous queues behind them. Donald was astonished that so few of them made any attempt to jump the hedges. One or two deliberately set their horses at them, and five or six were obviously less keen about it than their mounts, and did their unsuccessful best to dissuade them from the peril-ous leap, but at least eighty per cent disdained such showy tac-tics and preferred the gates and gaps, where a reputation for hard riding could be more easily obtained by a lot of hard swear-ing.

There was a halt at the edge of the coppice, for the fox had gone to ground. He had outrun the whole two hundred and seventy-four of them, and in doing so he had provided an hour and a half of the best sport which the Hunt had seen that season. But though he had outrun them all, and though he had provided such sport, they had the laugh on him in the end. For they got a lot of spades and a couple of terrier dogs and dug him out of his hole and killed him; because, after all, the countryside must be saved from vermin even if ladies and gentlemen have to chase them on horseback for an hour and a half, and furthermore it would be an act of callous cruelty to dumb animals, which no Englishman could be guilty of, to deprive the sixty dogs of the midday meal which they had so bravely earned.

Donald resumed his homeward journey and in ten minutes came upon an animated scene. Just where his winding lane joined the main road, a caravan of gypsies had halted their motley crew of painted wagons. They could only have arrived within the last two hours, because Donald had not seen them on his way to Tainton Green.

The T-head where the lane actually joined the road was almost blocked with horses, and six or eight of the fox-hunters were standing dismounted among the riders, all with their backs to Donald and facing the main road. Beyond this façade of mud-bespattered black and scarlet and horse-flesh, furious voices were being raised, and language that would have startled Nell Gwynne, or brought a blush to the cheeks of Burke and Hare, was being freely used. Donald edged his way between the ditch and one of the horses into the front row of the stalls, and by the time he had reached his place, the flow of words had given way to a fast bout of fisticuffs. One of the antagonists was a six-foot, scarlet-coated, scarlet-faced young man; the other was a lean, dirty, dark gypsy. The muddied Adonis fought with a classical straight left; the smoky *chal* relied upon short-arm punches, low when possible. The bout only lasted a few seconds, for the fighters were dragged apart by other gentlemen in red coats, and the gypsy retired sullenly under the overwhelming force with which he was now faced.

The comments of the ring were so clear, and expressed so forcibly and so repeatedly, that Donald had no difficulty in discovering what it was all about.

'The bloody swine was kicking his horse!' said a girl of about nineteen, with lips like the petals of a rose.

'Bloody swine!' said another girl, the perfection of whose fragile face was a little marred by a diagonal stain of mud about six inches long and three inches broad.

A short, tubby man, who looked very rich, shouted out:

'Bravo, Ralph! Well done, boy!'

Two men on foot discussed the matter in grave undertones.

'Thank God it was a gypsy and not an Englishman,' the first said.

'An Englishman wouldn't do a thing like that,' said the second, rather shocked.

'If there's one thing that gets me mad,' said the first, 'it's cruelty to animals. I don't care whether it's a mouse or an elephant, it simply makes me see red.'

'Absolutely,' said the second. 'One can stand a good deal, but one can't stand that.'

'I never go abroad nowadays,' said the first, 'except to Le Touquet and Monte Carlo and Switzerland and so on, because

I simply cannot stand the way those chaps treat animals.'

'Just like this dago,' assented the other. 'Do you know the first thing I'm going to do when I get back to town tonight? I'm going to invite Ralph out to the best dinner at the Ritz that money can buy.'

'By jove!' cried the second enthusiastically. 'Let me in on that, old chap. We'll share exes.'

They drifted away.

A horseman, pale with passion, and covered with clay from silk hat to orange-topped boots, was staring wildly in front of him and repeating over and over again to the world in general, 'I'll report him to the Society for the Prevention of Cruelty to Animals, I'll report him to the Society for the Prevention of Cruelty to Animals!'

An old lady of about seventy, perched like a sparrow upon an enormous black horse, kept on saying plaintively: 'Why doesn't someone flog him? I can't understand why no one flogs him.'

Donald heard no more, for at that moment the shoulder of a horse took him neatly in the small of the back and knocked him into the hedge. The woman who was riding never even glanced in his direction. She was about fifty years of age and her mouth and jaw were resolute and her eye unwavering, and Donald recognized her at once as one of the nurses in a hospital near Hazebrouck in Flanders in which he had had measles. One pouring wet night when the hospital, which by an unfortunate mischance had been placed immediately beside a large ammunition dump, was being bombed by German aircraft, this hardfaced Diana carried out seven wounded officers from a burning ward into which the stretcher-bearers refused to go, and rigged up a shelter for them from the rain, and boiled tea for them by the light of the blazing huts, to the accompaniment of a full orchestra of machine-guns, anti-aircraft artillery, bombs, pattering splinters, and screams and groans. And on another occasion she held the icy hand of a dying subaltern for twenty-seven hours. And on another she told the Matron what she thought of her.

Donald picked himself out of the hedge and went slowly back to 'The Golden Hind'. Another fox had been found and the hunt had vanished with extraordinary swiftness, leaving nothing behind them save innumerable hoof-marks in the mud, a few gaps in fences for the farmers to repair, and the memory of a gallant panorama.

Donald had just time before lunch to reach the chapter in which Miranda, slimmer than ever, is lured by a false message into the bargain basement of an antique shop in Fez.

On Monday morning he read in *The Times* that the second fox had completely let down the North Bucks Hunt. The wretched creature had nipped off at a great rate and in five minutes had dived into a hole from which not even the valiant terriers could extract him. He was, in fact, as *The Times* said, 'a bad fox'.

The rest of the weekend passed pleasantly in visits to the ducks, turkeys, hens, geese, goats, guinea-fowl, cows, horses, and other livestock which lived in or around the rambling, lichened, mossy old barns at the back of 'The Golden Hind'; in wandering round the village with Mr and Mrs Fielding, which was a slow business because both of them stopped to talk to every man, woman, child, and three-quarters of the horses and dogs, that they met; in exploring with Mr Fielding the Saxon church and listening to him talking learnedly upon architecture; in discussing French novels, and the English Restoration Drama, and the decay of craftsmanship, and the taxation of land values, and the music of Arnold Bax, and Reparations, and fifty other subjects about which Mr and Mrs Fielding obviously knew far more than Donald; in helping the married daughter and her husband with the colic-stricken horse; in holding wool for the unmarried daughter, who was going to knit a jumper for herself in the intervals between dancing and badminton and trips to London and riding and Girl Guides and Women's Institutes and Women's British Legion and Glee-Club rehearsals and amateur theatricals; and in much good eating and drinking and pleasant sleeping.

On Monday morning another meandering train crept stealthily towards Marylebone Station with Donald among its passengers. On the journey, he read in *The Times* that the Bill for the Prevention of the Exportation of Worn-Out English Horses to

Belgium and other countries, which had in the last Parliament passed without a division its first reading, its second reading, and all its Committee stages, and was simply waiting for the formality of the third reading, had been reintroduced into the new Parliament and had every prospect of securing a first reading within the next two years.

chapter 15

During the early spring months of that year Donald was very busy. He had collected enough notes about England and the English to fill fourteen large exercise-books, and he decided that it was high time to start putting them together in some sort of shape before making any more expeditions to collect new material. He would continue, naturally, in his daily round to keep his eyes open for happenings or sayings or sights which would throw further light upon the extraordinary problem in front of him, and to miss no opportunities during his spare time of adding to his notes. But he laid down a schedule of working hours and rigidly adhered to it, giving up the visits to Fleet Street, the week-end parties which cut into Fridays and Mondays and completely annexed Saturday mornings, and the afternoon visits to Museums and Galleries and other sights of London. Only the evenings were kept completely free from work. At 5 o'clock Donald shut his note-books for the day. Sometimes he spent the whole evening strolling about the streets, looking at the people and the shops and the buildings, and trying to asses the quality or qualities in each district that distinguished it from the rest, and seeking for the descriptive adjective or phrase for each. Sometimes he spent evenings in trying to find the exact line which divided one district from another, to delimit, for instance, the frontier between the Preference-Shareholder District of South Kensington and the Faded Refinement of the dwellers in Earls Court; or the boundary that divides the Zionism of West Hampstead from the Pen Club of Well Walk and

Keats Grove; or the exact spot where the influence of Nude Picture Post Cards in Praed Street wanes before the empurpled major-generals of Petersburg Square.

Once Donald went to see greyhound racing, one of the latest of English sports, and one of the kindliest. For there is no tearing to pieces of a tired fox by sixty dogs, nor do the followers of the chase pursue their quarry out to sea in boats as the intrepid stag-hunters of Kent and the West of England are wont to do, thus bringing themselves within the scope of the musical petition for those in peril on the sea. Nor do greyhound racers, when horse and hound and even motor-boats have failed, polish off their animal with a machine-gun, a weapon that stag-hunters handle with all the dexterity of a Chicago gangster and with a good deal less risk of reprisals. But these followers of the nimble greyhound have one little trick in common with the more virile, danger-loving sportsmen of Kent and the western moors. For when the quarry has been captured intact, it is taken back and used again. The only real difference between the mechanical hare of the tracks and the carted deer of the moors is that there is no way of proving for certain that the mechanical hare really enjoys being hunted – which, as everyone knows, is the fact with the carted deer.

Another small piece of evidence of the kindliness of greyhound racing that Donald noticed was a specially equipped amusement park for the children, whose mothers were fully occupied in backing their fancies at the ring-side. A sand-pit, a couple of swings, a see-saw, and some rocking-horses provided occupation for the older children of three or four years of age, while the younger ones were kept happy and amused in their prams by the lovely lights of the so-called stadium, filtering most intriguingly through the smoke of fags and cheap cigars, and by the good-humoured shouting of the bookmakers, with whom their mammas were doing business, and by the clear, loud voice of the announcer, until well past 11 o'clock at night.

On another evening Donald paid a shilling to watch a professional billiards match near Leicester Square, but he found it rather dull. For one of the players never had to play a difficult stroke – each stroke in a break of 1161 was so easy that Donald, whose highest break was 27, made in the hospital in Edinburgh, was quite confident that he could have made it – and the other player had such amazing good luck that after two or three ordinary strokes the balls happened to run together in a heap beside one of the cushions, and he then proceeded to tap them about with such pussy-like velvetiness that he scored 1641 in no time. All the while the audience sat and smoked and stared in impenetrable silence, the professional who was out of action lay back on an uncomfortable chair and gazed at the ceiling, while the only sound was the monotonous Cockney drone of the marker: 'Five hundred and two, five hundred and four, five hundred and six, five hundred and eight, five hundred and ten,' until Donald began to wonder if the words 'five' and 'hundred' existed, and if so, whether they meant anything. The break came to an end unexpectedly with a failure to pot a ball that was lying on the very edge of a pocket, a stroke that Donald could have made blindfolded and using the long rest.

But the two great functions of the winter, so far as Donald was concerned, were the dance at Lady Ormerode's house in Eaton Square, and Esmeralda's party at the Hotel Joséphine. There were about five hundred people at Lady Ormerode's and not much space for dancing, as the room only held three hundred. But nobody minded. The house was packed. The noise of the chatter was deafening. Crowds of people danced. Crowds of people sat on the stairs and smoked cigarettes. Donald, who knew very few of his fellow-guests, leant against the wall near the foot of the main staircase and counted that at one moment the smoke of a hundred and seventeen cigarettes was ascending simultaneously, sixty-five of which were being smoked and fifty-two were unextinguished stubs, lying up the white-painted stairs and burning neat black holes in the red carpet.

In the supper-room he met Esmeralda d'Avenant, all in black except for a pair of scarlet and paste ear-rings, and a white gardenia upon one shoulder, superbly beautiful as ever. She was surrounded by a group of men. The moment she saw Donald come in, she cut ruthlessly through the circle and came straight across to him.

'I must have the next but two and the two after that, Donald,' she cried impetuously. 'I want to talk to you.'

An agitated outcry of protest arose from the abandoned swains. She turned on them in a flash and smiled brilliantly. 'Can't help it, darlings,' she said. 'I adore you all, but business is business.' Donald was too paralysed to do anything. He was caught in the web of the glittering spider. The fatal kindliness of Mr Huggins had overtaken him once more. He felt despairingly that when Esmeralda did discover, as she was bound very soon to discover, that he had no connection of any kind with Hollywood or Elstree or any other film-producing centre in the world, her annoyance would be very great. Donald felt that Esmeralda was just the sort of person who might express very great annoyance with extreme measures, even with physical violence. In the days of Sir Lancelot and the Troubadours it was considered a great compliment if a Lady condescended so far as to inflict a physical injury upon a Knight. But in these sordid days of rationalization and universal suffrage the outlook is different, and Donald was very anxious to avoid the danger of receiving, in public, a quick hook to the button from that white and exquisite, but undeniably muscular, right arm of Esmeralda.

He therefore smiled wanly and muttered something about the delight that he would experience in dancing the next but two and the two after that with her, and fled in anguish to the upper part of the house, where he found a deserted balcony looking out over the square. It was an L-shaped balcony, for it was at a corner of the house, itself a corner-house, and Donald hid himself in the furthest obscurity of the arm of the L that was invisible from the inside. He leant over the iron railing and mopped his brow and watched the traffic swirling up the cross-streets from the direction of Victoria, hooting madly as it neared the square and then skidding all over the place as it met the traffic that came hooting and swirling down the centre of the square. Donald grew quite absorbed in the sight. Over and over again an accident was only averted by inches. Cars waltzed gracefully into safety; lorries slipped sideways out of danger; pedestrians fled screaming; and the air was filled with the squeaking and grinding of brakes, the blaring of electric horns, and the shouting of angry drivers. But it was too good to last, and after twenty minutes of miracles a long, low sports car struck a stately limousine, laden with pearls and diamonds, fair and square at right angles below the water-line, just as the torpedo struck the bullion-carrying S.S. *Egypt* off the coast of Ushant in 1916.

The limousine rose on one side, hovered in the air, and then heeled over and sank upon the pavement. A motor-bicycle which had been taking the natural advantage of its speed and it's rider's skill to pass the limousine at fifty-five miles an hour on the wrong side at a blind corner, swerved on to the pavement to avoid the mighty wreck, touched the top of it and bounced clean over it full-pitch into a coffee-stall, which was being pushed by its owner to its stance in Battersea.

The torpedoing sports car, as if aghast at its unexpected feat, backed suddenly away from its prostrate victim into a lorry and the lorry swung round into a glazier's van. The glazier's van, to judge from the Homeric crashes that immediately followed, seemed to contain most of the Alexandra Palace, and in a second the road was strewn feet deep with splintered glass, cups and saucers, ham sandwiches, sausage rolls, tyres, pieces of twisted metal, packets of cigarettes, coffee-urns, bits of wood, and a great variety of odds and ends such as tweed caps, spanners, buttons, and oil-cans, and the whole was instantly fused into one harmonious broth by a flood of petrol, oil, water, tea, and coffee.

It was an entrancing spectacle. Donald watched the motor-bicyclist emerge with a penny bun so firmly stuck in his eye that it required a pair of pincers to extract it; he saw the face of the coffee-stall keeper, who was standing in complete silence, as if his powers of language were not adequate to do justice to the situation; he listened with admiration to the lorry-driver's theories about the parentage of the young man who was driving the sports car, and to the glazier's theories about the after-life that he would allot to the lorry-driver should the Almighty give him a free hand; and finally he watched the brave souls who volunteered to dive into the sunken limousine in order to rescue the bullion, and, if possible, the passengers. It was not until the crowd, which had sprung up through the paving stones of the deserted streets, completely obscured his view that Donald realized with a gasp and a sort of clutch at his heart, that at least three quarters of an hour had passed since he had taken refuge on the balcony, and that certainly the next dance but two and probably the next two after that were by this time over. But worse was to follow. He was no longer alone upon the balcony. At some time or other during his absorption in the drama below, other people had found his retreat, and the voices of a man and a woman were clearly audible from the other arm of the L. Nor was that all. For the first few words that came round the corner were: 'You see, if we got married.'

Donald's first idea had been to push his way past them and escape from the unpleasant position into which he had got himself. But at those words he shrank back again. It was surely better to eavesdrop a passionate proposal of marriage than to interrupt it. So long as he was undiscovered, the former could do no harm. Heaven only knew how many lives might not be ruined by the latter. This might be the lover's only chance to make his declaration – he might be sailing early next morning to North Borneo. This might be the psychological moment when the strains of the Blue Danube, together with the frosty full moon and Pommery 1919, had just tipped the scale against a life-time of bachelorhood. Another lover might be waiting for the next dance to try his luck with her. A seductive adventuress might even now be hanging about downstairs to try her luck with him. No. Interruption was impossible. Donald shrank back and tried to hold his breath.

'You see if we got married,' went on the man's voice, 'we wouldn't be so badly off. I've got three hundred of my own, and I get four hundred from the shop; that's seven hundred, and you've got two-fifty – do you think you could sting the old man for a bit more than two-fifty?'

'Might squeeze another hundred,' said the girl's voice, cool, precise, steady. 'Not more. He doesn't part easily.'

'That's rather grim,' said the man.

'Yes, and what makes it so damned grim,' said the girl, 'is that Father and Mother are both about a hundred and eighty, and they've got no business to hang on to four or five thousand and dish me out a grim little handful of pence.'

'Yes. That is damned grim. Still it leaves us a thousand.'

'A thousand doesn't go far,' pointed out the girl. 'You can't get a service flat under five hundred.'

'The grim thing is,' said the man, 'that one can't possibly live anywhere else except in a service flat.'

'Good God, no,' replied the girl. 'You can't see me grimly ordering the meals and darning your grim socks, can you?'

'Good God, no.'

'Then for God's sake, be practical. Five hundred for the flat leaves five hundred for everything else.'

'That's a rather grim prospect,' said the man gloomily. 'And I'm damned fond of you, Slick.'

'And I'm damned fond of you, Crabface.'

'But still, five hundred for everything else—'

'No good,' she said decisively. There was a pause, then she went on, 'I tell you what I'll do. I'll put it up to the centenarians that it's high time they cut themselves down a bit. They can't enjoy themselves any more, so they ought to pass it on to those who can. If they shove on another three hundred, I'll take the risk and have a shot at it, Crabface.'

'Good egg,' replied the gentleman.

'But anything under three hundred, nothing doing.'

'That's O.K. by me, Chief.'

'Right. Shall we beat it? I've got the next with Snootles.'

'Right. So long, Slick. All the grimmest.'

'All the grimmest, Crabface.'

Donald was alone on the balcony. He went slowly down the stairs. At the foot Esmeralda was waiting with shining eyes and a radiant smile on her warm, red cupid's-bow.

'Oh, Donald,' she said huskily, 'you are the sweetest pet in the world. Do you know that you've won me two hundred pounds!'

Donald blinked. Esmeralda continued to look at him very much as the older soldiers of the Grande Armée must have looked at the Emperor Napoleon. Donald felt that if he had pinched her ear at that moment she would have fallen upon her colossally insured knees on the stone floor, and thus caused great agitation at Lloyd's.

Instead he murmured, 'How have I done that?'

'Because I bet "Snarks" Muggleston and Tony Spratt and "Becher's" Boldingham that you'd cut my three dances. And they were so sure of my S.A. that they jumped at it, and so I've won all round – a lovely compliment from them, and two hundred pounds, and—' her famous smile vanished and her famous look of wistfulness succeeded it, 'another slap in the eye from you.' She smiled again and added, 'I think you're fascinating.'

Donald was just offering up a short prayer that this might be the end of the conversation, and of the whole episode, for already three or four pretty men were hovering near, waiting to pounce upon the lovely creature the moment she gave the slightest indication of having finished with her film magnate. But who should roll up at that very instant – red, rollicking, and beautifully dressed – but Mr Huggins himself. Mr Huggins had none of the diffidence and tact of the group of pretty men, for he committed the unheard-of atrocity of interrupting Esmeralda at a *tête-à-tête* with a cheery shout of:

'Esmeralda – what ho! Cameron – what ho! Huggins – what ho! As fine a looking trio as there's been seen since the bishop took the two typists to Frinton-on-Sea during Septuagesima. Keep the fun clean, girls and boys, that's all I ask. Cameron, I didn't know you knew Esmeralda – divinest of ladies that ever played the soubrette in the musical version of *Hamlet*.'

'Lunatic!' said Esmeralda graciously. She liked Mr Huggins because he was not the same sort of type as 'Snarks' Muggleston, and Tony Spratt and 'Becher's' Boldingham. 'Of course, I know Mr Cameron. But he's cruel and hard-hearted and he won't give me a job.'

'The low fiend of Hell!' shouted Mr Huggins indignantly. 'Won't give you a job? I'll give you a job myself in my factory at Waterlooville, where I have the State monopoly for the manufacture of left-foot gum-boots for men who have lost their right legs and live in marshy districts. Won't give you a job, indeed, the dirty sweep!'

'Thank you, Tommy,' replied Esmeralda, 'but I'd sooner have a job in Mr Cameron's film.'

Mr Huggins, of course, had entirely forgotten all about the disinterested efforts which he had made to smooth Donald's path at Ormerode Towers, and he stared in amazement. Donald shuffled his feet and felt exceedingly uneasy. Esmeralda flouted was one thing – she seemed to like being flouted; Esmeralda deceived would be a very different affair, he felt.

Tommy Huggins shook a warning forefinger at her.

'Don't, for Heaven's sake, fall for that ancient dodge, darling,' he implored. 'The bogus film magnate is the oldest and most hackneyed of all the tricks. Cameron, I'm ashamed of you! Trying to seduce an innocent girl like this with your old-fashioned methods. Don't stutter at me, sir. I am shocked. If you feel you must seduce Esmeralda, if you owe it to your little old mother, or to the flag we all revere, or to the tradition of your dear old school, to seduce Esmeralda, at least use up-to-date methods. There's nothing annoys me so much as slovenly craftsmanship. Please don't stammer like that. The truth is that you've had too many easy successes and you're getting slipshod. This handsome youth, Esmeralda, has been for years the Lothario of Wolverhampton. His dark name has even extended into the outer suburbs of West Bromwich. Cave-man stuff, you know. A slap across the ear with a wet halibut, catch you by the ankle and the seat of the pants and chuck you into a passing tram-car. That's his style. And before you know where you are, he's offering you cream buns in an A.B.C.'

Esmeralda's eyes twinkled. 'That's all you know, Tommy.'

'But I tell you Cameron's not a film man. Are you, Cameron?'

'Well, I— er—'

'There you are! What did I say? Confirms every word I've spoken. And if you want to know what his profession really is, he is Baccarat Instructor at the Mount Carmel Tabernacle in the Harrow Road.'

'Thank you,' said Esmeralda, and she turned her main batteries upon Donald.

'Are you a film magnate, Donald?' she asked.

'No,' he replied firmly. It was high time to end all this. The group of furious hoverers had increased to nine, and they were beginning to look dangerous.

'Are you quite, quite sure?'

'Yes.'

Esmeralda sighed.

Then, 'Will you come to my party?' she whispered. 'Next Monday at the Joséphine.'

'I'm afraid I—'

'Oh, Donald, you couldn't be as cruel as all that!'

'I don't mean—'

She laid an ivory hand upon his sleeve.

'You will come?' The words were hardly audible.

'All right,' said Donald sulkily.

Esmeralda smiled brilliantly and rejoined the hoverers.

'Come and have a drink,' said Mr Huggins.

'Go to hell,' said Donald.

chapter 16

The Hôtel Joséphine was a new hotel, run up in a few weeks upon the site of Plantagenet House, which had been for so many years the ancestral home of the Silversteins – the Vienna Silversteins, not the Buenos Aires lot. The building of it had been a patriotic undertaking, for it was designed to coordinate with the Come-to-England movement and the Buy British slogan. If foreigners were to be lured away from the pleasures of Montmartre and Montparnasse, if old-fashioned English hospitality was to be substituted for the meretricious professionalism of Cannes, Nice, and Monte Carlo, it was obvious that comfortable English hotels would have to be provided to house the new visitors. Hence the Hôtel Joséphine.

Everything about it was English, including even the staff. The real name of Bordanaro, the manager, was Hirst; Giacomo, the head waiter in the Restaurant, and Benedetto, the head waiter in the Grill, were a pair of brothers from Merthyr Tydfil called Maggs. Signor Alessandro di Betucci, the *chef d'orchestre*, started life in Billericay as Frank Windlesham. And so it was with all the Luigis, the Cosimos, the Pieros, Francescos, Cesares, and Emanueles who served the *côtelettes aux pastè-*

189

ques and the *filets de sole ravigote* and the *royans à la Borde-laise* and the *soufflés glacés aux pistaches,* and all the other *chefs-d'oeuvre* of Monsieur Etienne Bomboudiac (*né* Wilson) who presided over the cusine. All, without exception, were English. For the rest, the hotel was equipped with a *salle de patinage, a salle d'escrime,* half a dozen ballrooms, a thousand bedrooms, a thousand bathrooms, and all the other amenities of modern life.

Esmeralda, in her usual lavish style, had engaged the half-dozen ballrooms for her party. Three were reserved for supping, three for dancing. In the latter, three orchestras of coloured gentlemen performed prodigies of the musical art, and small printed notices, discreetly displayed upon the walls here and there, informed the world that, although these musicians might present a somewhat alien appearance, nevertheless they were of true British strain and were subjects of the great British Empire, being Canadian citizens from Edmonton, Alberta, and Saskatoon, Saskatchewan.

Donald arrived at about 11.30, and was just about to mingle unobtrusively in the crowd and hide in some obscure corner when he suddenly realized that he knew quite a number of his fellow-guests. There was Mr Hodge, for instance, wearing an enormous gardenia in his coat and a large pearl in his shirt, talking to Bob Bloomer, the ex-cabinet minister. Mr Bloomer's evening-coat was a triumph of the cutter's art. Captain de Wilton-ffallow was in a corner with Mr Carteret-Pendragon, Mr Woldingham-Uffingham, and Mr Carshalton-Stanbury. They were standing like statues, in a beautiful and poised immobility, and from time to time their lips moved slightly as if a rose-leaf had been stirred by a zephyr. They bowed gravely to Donald, and the lights gleamed upon the silkiness of their moustaches. Once or twice during the evening Donald found himself near them, and on each occasion he heard one or other of them murmur the same phrase, 'Well, yes and no.'

Patience Ormerode was there, and Donald noticed two differences about her since they had sat down to dinner that evening at Ormerode Towers. Her universal adjective was now 'wan' instead of 'grisly', and she was wearing knickers. As an offset, however, to this unexpected dressiness, the lower joints of her spine shone with an admirable polish. She puffed a blast of cigarette-smoke into Donald's face, nodded to him, and observed, 'Rupert's sober. Wan, isn't it?' and the next instant she was deep in conversation with one of the Imperialists from Edmonton (or Saskatoon). Lady Ormerode herself was sitting in a corner with Mr Huggins and was laughing so much that she was apparently about to have an apoplectic fit. The alleged Channel Islander was talking very fast and very loudly, but fortunately even his voice was drowned by the din.

Miss Perugia Gaukrodger, in a terrific confection of puce and lemon-yellow, with long green gloves and green shoes that did not quite match the gloves, had backed Robert Southcott into an angle between two tables in one of the supper-rooms and was reading aloud to him from a small note-book. In a brief lull of saxophonous prodigies, the words, 'and I get fifteen per cent over five thousand copies and twenty per cent on anything over ten thousand. For colonial editions—' were wafted across the room. Mr Southcott's eye was a little glazed, and from time to time he mopped his brow with a silk handkerchief.

Another group that Donald ran into consisted of the youngish professor of ballistics who had played cricket, the exquisite Vision of blue and gold and silk who had typed so stoutly at Geneva amid the clouds of Latin-Americans, the Polish count who spoke no English, and Mr Charles Ossory. They were listening in French to Mr Ossory.

From time to time Major Hawker's laugh resounded through the rooms like the clang of a gong. He was extremely busy entertaining Mrs O. K. Poop, and his palpable success was obviously very distasteful to young Porson Jebb, who was longing to explain to Mrs Poop the difference between baseball and cricket. Miss Prudence Pott, M.P., upon whom young Porson had had to fall back as an audience, was allowing her mind to wander, and no one can appreciate the finer points of cricket if they allow their minds to wander.

A very silent trio, Sir Ethelred Ormerode, Sir Ludovic Phibbs, and Sir Henry Wootton, had frankly given up conversation for the quails and were tucking away for all they were worth. Shakespeare Pollock, the American, on the other hand, was darting about in great form, chattering of this and that. There was a great stir when the Russian baroness-princess came in; she was looking so lovely that Major Hawker abandoned Mrs O. K. Poop instantly, and raced round the rooms hunting for someone to introduce him.

Esmeralda's heart misgave her for a moment when she saw the Slavonic beauty come sailing in, and she half regretted that she had invited her. But the next moment she was herself again. After all, pretty gentlemen were grouped round her at least ten deep, and had she not received that very morning her new draft contract from Appelbaum & Zedekiah Rose, Inc., and was there not more than a rumour that 'Snarks' Muggleston wanted to fight 'Becher's' Boldingham on the sands at Calais with rapiers, all for the love of her? Let the little beast do her wretched little vamp stuff, thought Esmeralda, sweeping the room with her liquid eyes, and making a mental note to give Major Hawker a clip on the jaw next time the opportunity offered. For the gallant Major was no waster of time, and was already bending low over the princess's slender fingers; his nearest rival and senior officer, the Major-General, had been coldly headed back by Mrs Major-General just as he was beginning to edge towards the Divinity.

The crowd continued to pour in. Esmeralda seemed to have a great many friends, but the six rooms were never entirely packed. For there were other parties in London that evening and lots of guests were 'going on'.

At about 3 o'clock the crowd was thinning and Donald was thinking of strolling home in the moonlight, when Esmeralda came across the room to him and whispered in his ear, 'Sausages and bacon on the roof at 4. Don't tell a soul.'

It was apparently a privileged invitation, for Donald watched her moving slowly about the rooms, whispering here and there to some of the guests, and letting others depart without a pang. The Russian princess was allowed to go, and Major Hawker was allowed to escort her to her taxi, or to her home for all that Esmeralda cared. 'Snarks' and 'Becher's' were glowering too divinely at each other to let Esmeralda worry about trivialities.

The sausage-and-bacon party on the roof-garden started beautifully. The moon was at the full; the faintest dappling of tarnished silver was silhouetting St Paul's away to the east, and the lights of London were dulling the stars. In the Park, a blue haze drifted among the trees. The sausages were real home-made Buckinghamshire. The bacon was done to a crisp. The Munich Löwenbräu beer was so cool and smooth that it might almost have been English. And there had been a moment, a delicious moment, when it almost looked as if 'Becher's' was trying to push 'Snarks' to the edge of the roof in order to chuck him over.

The air was warm, very warm for April, and it rapidly grew warmer.

'Quite like Abbotabad,' said the Major-General, fanning his face with a napkin.

'More like Amritsar,' amended his wife. The warrior hastily agreed. The little episode of the princess was still marked up on the slate against him, and he knew it.

'It is remarkably warm,' said Sir Ethelred, signing to a waiting Lorenzo to refill his glass.

Suddenly Bob Bloomer sniffed loudly once or twice.

'Queer smell,' he observed, and the next moment the tranquillity of the April morning was shattered by a cry of 'Fire!' from the hotel beneath them.

'Ladies and gentlemen!' said the Major-General, rising to his feet and rapping on the table, 'I am the senior officer present. You will kindly regard me as Officer Commanding Joséphine Roof Garden.'

Murmurs of 'Hear, hear', 'Agreed', and some slight applause greeted this announcement.

The Major-General continued:

'Captain de Wilton-ffallow, reconnoitre the main staircase and report to me.'

'Yes, sir.'

'Mr Carteret-Pendragon, reconnoitre the outside fire-escape and report to me.'

'In writing?' inquired the diplomat, and there was a general laugh.

'Mr Cameron, Mr Carshalton-Stanbury, and Mr Woldingham-Uffingham, reconnoitre for other routes of retreat, and report to me. Remainder, sit at ease.'

The noise below had swiftly become pandemoniac, but there

was not, as yet, an audible sound of crackling flames. The fire was not as close as that. But the hotel was full of shouts, screams, the opening of windows, the slamming of doors, and the splintering of glass.

At the supper-table no one moved. The Lorenzo, aided by a Giuliano, went round refilling the tumblers with a new supply of Löwenbräu.

'Has anyone got a camera?' called out Esmeralda from her end of the long table. There was no answer, and she went on, 'Oh, well, we'll just have to go straight to the nearest studio the moment we get out.'

'How about a few rescue scenes?' suggested Mr Harcourt. 'Esmeralda in my arms, and so on?'

'I should adore it,' said Esmeralda, bestowing her loveliest smile on the poet.

'You couldn't carry her,' snarled 'Becher's' Boldingham.

'Come, come!' said Mr Harcourt severely, 'she's not as heavy as all that.'

Poor Mr Boldingham was covered with confusion and started to explain, but was loudly laughed down, especially by 'Snarks' Muggleston, who thought that the infernal poet wasn't such a bad fellow after all.

'I hope there's time to get our names into the Society Jottings,' said Patience Ormerode, pushing her chair back and hitching up her frock in order to adjust the top of a stocking. It was the longest sentence she had uttered all the evening.

'Not a hope!' shouted Mr Huggins jovially. 'The dailies have gone to press ages ago.'

'How wan!' said Patience, relapsing into gloomy silence.

Captain de Wilton-ffallow came back, rubbing his eyes.

'It's not the top floor, sir,' he reported, 'but the one below that. It's blazing.'

'What about the staircase?' rapped out the O.C. Roof Garden.

'Quite impossible, sir. Mass of flames.'

'Very well, sir.' Captain de Wilton-ffallow sat down and went on with a sausage.

Mr Carteret-Pendragon was the next to return.

'Well, sir, is there a fire-escape?' demanded the Major-General.

'Yes, and no,' replied Mr Carteret-Pendragon. 'To the extent that there undoubtedly is a fire-escape, the answer is in the affirmative. But in that the fire-escape stops short four stories below us, the answer, so far as practical politics are concerned, is in the negative.'

Donald was spokesman for the other expedition.

'There's no other way off the roof,' he reported.

'Very well,' said the Major-General, 'there's nothing to be done except wait for the fire-engines. How long do you give us before it reaches us, Captain de Wilton-ffallow?'

The Captain shrugged his shoulders.

'It's hard to say. Perhaps five or ten minutes.'

'That's rather wan,' said Patience.

'Don't let's lose our heads and try to extinguish it with the beer,' said Mr Huggins firmly. 'That would be the last straw.'

Esmeralda sighed. 'It's a bit hard to be asked to face one's Maker without a single flashlight man,' she said.

'Never mind,' said Mr Harcourt, looking over the parapet down into Park Lane, 'you are going to play to capacity in your farewell performance. The house is filling up beautifully.'

'Positively the last appearance,' said Mr Huggins.

'Miss d'Avenant literally finished in a blaze,' said Mr Harcourt.

'The whole thing went with a roar,' suggested Mr Huggins.

'All of us were aflame,' said Mr Harcourt.

'Sweet pets!' said Esmeralda. 'Becher's' and 'Snarks' shuffled uneasily and scowled.

'What annoys me,' exclaimed Bob Bloomer, 'is that my job at the West End Journeyman Tailors will go to Bert Stukeley and he's a dirty little crook.'

Mr Carteret-Pendragon shook his head disapprovingly and murmured, 'A very actionable statement,' and the other two diplomats gravely concurred.

'Any signs of a fire-engine, waiter, what's your name?' barked the Major-General.

'My name, sir, is Giuliano,' replied the waiter.

195

'I didn't ask you your name,' the O.C. roared at him, 'I asked you if there were any signs of a fire-engine.'

'You did ask him his name,' Donald ventured.

'Discipline, by God!' thundered the Major-General, glaring at him. 'Anyway, he's a damned dago!'

'Just like the dear old days at Peshawur,' murmured Mrs Major-General, with an adoring look at her Horace.

'My surname is Ellis,' said Giuliano unexpectedly.

'And a fire-engine has arrived,' added Bob Bloomer.

It was not a moment too soon, for the flames had climbed into the floor immediately beneath the roof-garden, and smoke was already pouring up the staircase. The crackling and roaring of the fire was getting louder and louder, and the air was full of grit and dust and burning smells.

'Dammit,' mutttered de Wilton-ffallow into Donald's ear, 'we're in a tight place.'

'The garrison will form column of route,' shouted the Major-General above the din, 'preparatory to descending by the ladder. Ladies leading.'

'And no camera,' sighed Esmeralda, as she took her place behind Lady Ormerode.

'The ladder's coming up,' reported Bloomer.

'And the floor's going down,' added Mr Harcourt, darting across to an unfinished glass of beer and pouring it hastily down his throat.

'Blast!' exclaimed Mr Huggins. 'I thought I'd finished them all.'

'Very bad form,' said Mr Carteret-Pendragon gravely.

'Deplorable,' agreed Mr Carshalton-Stanbury.

'Not done,' added Mr Woldingham-Uffingham.

'Here it is!' shouted Bloomer, and the top of a scarlet ladder shot up over the parapet. Two firemen in full uniform and a civilian in dungarees leapt one after another on to the roof-garden, and the work of rescue began.

'Hullo, mister!' cried a voice in Donald's ear, and he turned to recognize William Rhodes in the dungarees.

'What are you doing here?' shouted Donald, one eye upon the agility with which Lady Ormerode went, so to speak, over the top, and the other upon the tongue of flame which had pierced the roof, and was the herald of the end.

'It's my machine,' yelled William Rhodes. 'I've just made it, and I'm teaching these fellows how to use it. Had to come up and see how it went.'

The race was now desperate. The women were all clear, but the floor of the roof-garden was cracking and sagging. The diplomats went over, quietly and efficiently. Mr Huggins burst into the Marseillaise when his turn came, and sang it with a marked Lancashire accent. Part of the floor crashed as 'Becher's' Boldingham threw his leg over the parapet, but the main part was still holding out when Donald followed Mr Harcourt through the clouds of smoke and sparks. Half-way down he heard the poet mutter, 'Damn it, I'm thirsty.'

The last two to come down were William Rhodes, ecstatic over the success of his machine, and the Major-General.

The immense crowd in Park Lane was delirious with joy, and applauded each rescue with wild enthusiasm. At intervals the plaintive voice of Esmeralda could be heard saying, 'Hasn't anybody got a camera?' At last a Press photographer arrived, and, to the fury and chagrin of 'Becher's' and 'Snarks', the divine Esmeralda was photographed kissing William Rhodes.

Above the din a Lancashire voice was singing 'Madelon'.

chapter 17

After the long English winter, May had come at last. The trees in Royal Avenue were in bud. The shops were full of daffodils and pheasant-eyed narcissus, and violets and early tulips, and blue irises from the Scillies, and anemones. The air was clear. The Londoner's step was high and gay. The evening papers were already beginning to talk of the Advent of King Willow. The football season was almost three-quarters finished.

Donald was tired. He had been working steadily now for almost three months at work that was utterly unfamiliar to him.

He had not only been writing a book. He had also been struggling to learn the art of writing from its very beginning. He was beginning to feel a little jaded. The scents of spring, overcoming the fumes of petrol and the miles of soot and asphalt, peeped in at his open window and sadly interfered with his powers of concentration.

A morning dawned even lovelier than the rest. At 7 o'clock the sky over Lambeth was all pigeon-blue and mother-of-pearl and jade-green and citron and topaz. Small, billowy, dappled cloudlets with pale-pink edges were playing about together, knowing, perhaps, like children or kittens or mice, that when the storm-clouds and the black fogs are away the cloudlets can play. A cool little breeze was bringing fragrance all the way from Essex across the desert of stone and slate which mankind thinks is an advance upon a nest or a burrow. Donald lay in bed till he could stand it no longer. An extra-insidious puff of air arrived with a cargo, Donald swore, of the scent of roses and hay-making and honeysuckle; which, of course, was impossible, as the clover and the rose were not yet in bloom and no one hay-makes in May, with however torrid a fire the sun may shine. But anyway, the result was the same, for Donald uttered a loud cry and sprang from his bed, dived into a cold bath, hurled on his clothes, rushed into the street, and drove in a taxi-cab to Waterloo Station and took a train, choosing at random, to the town of Alton.

He walked a bit from Alton, and then lorry-hopped, in army fashion, as far as the straggly, red-tiled village of Alresford, where he got off for a drink of Hampshire beer, and then lorry-hopped again across the high chalky downs until the water-meads of Itchen lay below him on the right, and below him in front, the ancient City of Winchester, city of Alfred, once capital of England, perhaps even the Camelot of Arthur.

Donald got off the lorry at the top of St Giles' Hill and dropped leisurely down into the High Street, at the end of which is the statue of Alfred. It is a large statue, perhaps as much as a twenty-fifth of the height of the memorial which the later capital of England has built for Albert, and it faces up the steep, narrow High Street towards the Castle at the top, on the wall of which hangs the Round Table of the Knights.

Donald turned to the left and found himself suddenly reduced to the size and substance of a homunculus when he came round a corner upon the Cathedral, stretching its giant length, all grey and moss-green and pale yellow, across the grass like a sleeping leviathan.

Feeling very small and humble, he crept across the turf of the Close and timidly pushed open the west door and wandered in the dim coolness under that mighty roof, among the memorials to long-dead English soldiers, among the tattered flags of regiments, the cenotaphs of forgotten prebendaries, the brass tablets and marble sculptures, the brief rolls of honour of distant campaigns, the long list of virtues of ancient dames, the Latin inscriptions, and the tombs of cardinals and bishops, and the effigies of unknown knights. But in all that carved and sculptured splendour of the history of England, its wars, its wealth, and its religion, its princes and prelates, and its imperial conquests, there were only two memorials that touched the heart. One was the chantry of William of Wykeham, saved from Cromwell's destroyers by the drawn sword of a Wykehamist captain, a Cromwellian, who stood upon the chantry steps and, against all comers, defended the tomb of the Founder. And the other was the little old lady of College Street, who commanded no armies and attacked no religions, who was burnt at no stake and married no prince, whose life added no faintest ripple to the waves and storms of England, and no fragment of a line to its recorded history; who is, alone among mortals, loved by all and hated by none, and who is, alone among the Great, imitated by none and parodied by none. English of the English, heart of English heart, bone of English bone, kindliest and gayest and gentlest, her memorial is not so wide as a church door nor so high as Albert's, but it is in Alfred's town, in Wykeham's cathedral, near Arthur's Table, and it will serve.

Donald spent a few minutes among the scattered gravestones outside the west front looking for the famous epitaph to the Hampshire Grenadier who caught his death by drinking cold small beer.

'Soldiers, be wise from his untimely fall,
And where yere hot, drink strong or none at all.'

He found it behind a memorial to other soldiers who fought in a later time, and read the proud, magnificent sweep of its inscription, which sounds like the roll of titles of a Spanish king or a blast from Milton's everlasting trumpet . . .

. . . Who died in Flanders, France, Italy, Russia, Macedonia, Palestine, Egypt, Mesopotamia, India, and Siberia, or by the Dardanelles, or were lost at sea in the Mediterranean.

Thence his wanderings took him past the Judges' Lodging and the Deanery and the lovely Canonries and the dusty Elizabethan tithe-barn, through an archway into the outer world of laymen, and through another archway into College Street. The summer term had just begun and the street was crowded with boys and young men, all wearing straw hats. A few were draped in long black gowns which Donald thought were not half so picturesque as the scarlet of Aberdeen and St Andrews.

He visited the College Buildings, and listened to a description of them by the College porter, and carried away four memories – the loveliness of the cloisters round the lovely chantry, the darkness of the rooms off the Quadrangle in which the boys sat and worked, the Important Fact, repeated several times by the proud porter, that Winchester was nearly fifty years older than Eton and, indeed, practically founded Eton, and, fourthly, the extraordinary school motto.

Every other school or university motto he had ever heard of consisted of an invocation to an unspecified Supreme Power to allow the institution to flourish, or to prosper, or to wax strong – in general, to get on in the world. It was the natural thing. Old Boys needed a slogan to remind each other of their duty to their Alma Mater, of the happy days spent there in youth, and of their natural desire not to see the numbers diminish and the place simply go to the dogs. Besides, it made a capital toast at the Old Boys' Dinners when the diners could jump to their feet and raise their glasses and cry 'Floreat St Ethelburga's, Worksop', or 'Floreat St Francis Xavier's-in-partibus, Tel-el-Kebir'.

But the Winchester motto was the extraordinary one of 'Manners Makyth Man'. Donald walked up and down Meads, the old school playing-field surrounded with its red-capped wall of flint and chalk, and wondered about this motto. It was obviously impossible to make it a toast at an Old Boys' Dinner; it was obviously impossible to shout it at a school football match, even if the boys were organized in American fashion by a professional cheer-leader. Donald looked at the Chapel Tower, which was just visible over an exquisite, red-brick, Wren building, and thought that on the whole it was unlikely that Winchester employed a professional cheer-leader. It almost looked, Donald decided finally, as if Winchester cared more for what happened to her boys in after-life than for her own flourishment. Perhaps, after five hundred years of flourishment, that was a justifiable attitude, but it certainly was a little unusual.

He pulled out his note-book and jotted down a brief description of the scene before him, the architecture, colouring, landscape beyond the red-capped wall, and a few other details. The trees, not yet in full leaf, bothered him – in wind-swept Buchan there are few trees to bother anybody – and he stopped a small, black-gowned boy, about twelve years of age, and asked politely:

'Can you tell me, please, what that tree is?'

The boy took off his straw hat and replied with equal politeness:

'That is Lord's tree, sir.'

'Lord's tree?' said Donald, also taking off his hat. 'What is that?'

'It is called that, sir, because only men in Lord's are allowed to sit on the seat at the foot of it,' explained the child.

'I am sorry to appear stupid,' Donald apologized, 'but when you say "Men in Lord's" do you refer to the Peers of the Realm?'

'By no means,' replied the infant. 'Men in Lord's are the men in the cricket eleven.'

'Oh, I see. The cricket eleven is called Lord's because they go to Lord's to play cricket.'

'No, sir. They don't go to Lord's.'

'Then why are they called Lords?' Donald was getting confused.

'Because we used until quite recently to play at Lord's against Eton.'

'Ah! Now I begin to understand. Until a few years ago; how many years, by the way?'

'About seventy or eighty, sir.'

Donald kept a firm grip upon himself, and tried to speak naturally as he answered:

'Quite so. Just the other day. I see. And the boys in the cricket eleven—'

'Men,' interrupted the child firmly.

'I beg your pardon.'

'Men,' repeated the child. 'We are all men here. There are no boys.'

Donald, by now quite dizzy, bowed and thanked the man for his trouble.

'It was a pleasure,' replied the man, bowing courteously and removing his hat again and going on his way.

Donald, hat in hand, turned and watched him, and was immensely relieved to see the man halt after going a few yards, and extract a huge and sticky piece of toffee from his trouser-pocket, and cram it into his mouth.

From College it is only a step into Meads, and from Meads only another step through the gate in the flinty wall into Lavender Meads, and from Lavender Meads into the green expanse of Riddings', and from Riddings' to Dogger's Close, and from Dogger's Close, the last of Winchester's playing-fields, it is hardly more than a step to the ancient Abbey of St Cross which presides with venerable dignity over the Greenjackets' cricket-ground, and which still gives a free horn of ale to the wayfarer. Thus a traveller who has a little time to spare, and who is not trying desperately to cut the existing record for home-bred citizens of North and South Dakota for the 'doing' of the College of the Blessed Virgin Mary apud Winton, crosses the threshold of the Outer Gate of College and finds himself only beginning to awaken from his medieval trance in the Abbey of St Cross.

But Donald had not even begun to awaken from his trance when he left St Cross and wandered over the water-meads that the Itchen and its branches and canals have chiselled in the green valley. He had not begun to awaken when he climbed the first slopes of St Catherine's Hill, or when at last he reached the clump of trees on the top of the hill and found a little grassy slope which fitted his back like a deckchair at full stretch, and lay down and tilted his hat over his forehead and joined his hands behind his head.

At his feet were the glittering streams of the Itchen, that small, magic river of silver and dry-flies and trout. Beyond them were the playing-fields with their white dots of cricketers, and beyond them the tower of the College Chapel, and beyond that the slumbering leviathan, Wykeham's House of God. The air was filled with little sounds, the tinkling of sheep-bells across the vales of the chalkland, the click of cricket-ball on cricket-bat, the whispers of the fitful puffs of wind in the trees behind him, the megaphoned shouts of the coaches as the racing-fours went up the stream with flashing blades, and from across the valley the bells of the Cathedral, deep and far, like the strong clang of Thor's anvil in Valhalla.

Twenty or thirty feet below the grassy deckchair on which Donald was by now half dozing ran the circular trench which the Britons dug as a defence against the Legions. The line of the Roman road was clear, a chalky arrow, as far as the blue horizon. Saxon Alfred's statue might have been as visible through a field-glass as the pale-yellow Norman transept of the Cathedral was to the eye. The English school, whose motto puts kindliness above flourishment or learning, lay among its water-meads, and all around was the creator, the inheritor, the ancestor, and the descendant of it all, the green and kindly land of England.

Donald went on dozing until he was gradually aroused by the consciousness that something queer was going on down below in the valley. The landscape seemed somehow to be different. The little streams were not so twinkly. The grass of the playing-fields had become more like the colour of grey-white olive-trees than of new-mown green. The Roman road and the horizon itself had disappeared, and the transept's amber was fading fast.

Donald sat up and rubbed his eyes. A thick white mist was rolling swiftly up the valley from the direction of the sea, and the advance guard was already wreathing itself round the ancient town. The small sounds were no longer audible, and even the reverberating echoes of the bells were muffled, and their vibrations died quickly. In another minute or two the water-meads were covered with a great pall. The College Tower sank out of sight, and the fringes of mist lapped over the edge of the British entrenchment. Even the fitful breeze had dropped. The bell ceased. The silence was like the silence of eternal snows.

Donald lay back again and gazed at the white bank that eddied so softly across the spring marguerites and buttercups and dandelions. Although it had come with such a rush, it hardly seemed to be moving at all now. The eddies and ripples became even softer. Here and there the antics of a wisp which had slipped away from the rest became quieter and quieter, until gradually the great fleece of mist slid and swayed and rocked itself imperceptibly to a standstill.

He felt no surprise. The medieval spell of Winchester had not yet completely worn off, and he was too sleepy after his long day in the open air, and too tired after the months of concentrated work, to feel surprised at anything. When, therefore, the fog gradually flattened itself, and narrowed itself, and spun itself out into the shape of a snow-white road that stretched, as far as the eye could reach, towards the English Channel in the south and over the edge of the English downs in the north, Donald was quite unmoved. It seemed a perfectly natural thing for a mist to do. If a road could become suddenly a solid wall of mist, why should not a solid wall of mist sudddenly become a road?

It was a very reasonable place to have a road. It was a capital place to have a road. It was queer that no one had ever had the sense to put a road there before. It was an ideal place for a road. The mist was quite right to turn itself into a road. Mists are obstructive. Roads are beautiful. Especially a road that runs just at the foot of lovely grassy slopes like St Catherine's Hill, where a man may lie at his ease and watch the world and its wayfarers. That was the way to learn about a country or a people. Lie on the grass among spring marguerites and buttercups and dandelions and watch the country and the people passing along below. Ten thousand times better than rushing about wildly with a note-book hunting for material. Let the material come to you. That was the ticket. Let it come along its roads to you. All you have to do is to find a road and a grassy hill above it. And was there ever such a road as this – smooth and broad and straight and firm? Incidentally it was clever of the mist to have made itself into so firm a surface, after having been so soft before.

The only odd thing about the road was that there seemed to be no traffic upon it. From end to end, the snowy ribbon was unmarred by the little black dots which men are, when seen from a little way away, a very little way away.

But Donald was not worried about this. It was obvious that as soon as people knew of the existence of this road of roads, they would scramble to use it. All he needed was a little patience. So he clasped his hands again behind his head and waited.

He had not long to wait. A tiny black dot appeared over the downs away to the north and other black dots followed it, and still more black dots, until a perfect host of men came straggling over the horizon. The whiteness of the road was steadily obliterated, as if a giant painter were methodically running a black brush over it. The mass came nearer and nearer.

Donald wondered how long it would be before they reached him, and he glanced southwards to make a rough estimate of the distance, and saw that another great mass of men were coming up the road from the sea.

As the two columns came straggling towards St Catherine's Hill, a low rumbling sound began to fall upon the air. It was not in the least like the sound of marching feet, for it was deeper, and it had no rhythm, and it came in gusts, sometimes in a long, resistless roar like the fall of sea waves on sand upon summer nights, and sometimes with the short crash of a thunder-clap.

Soon Donald could see that, although they walked out of step, in groups and parties, mingling with each other and changing from moment to moment, with here and there a man by himself, although in fact they did not remotely resemble the disciplined advance of an army on the march, nevertheless, every single one carried a weapon of some sort, even if it was only a cross-bow or a bill-hook or a scythe. And yet none of them wore anything that might be described as a uniform; mostly they wore black suits or shabby corduroys, and they carried their weapons in a careless, amateurish way. The rumbling noise grew louder and more continuous. The faces of the two vanguards were now visible, and Donald saw that all the men of those two armed bodies of civilians were shaking and quaking and heaving with inexhaustible laughter. The vanguards met immediately below St Catherine's Hill, where the road had widened out, somehow without Donald noticing it, into a great broad open space, and in a few moments all the men were talking and laughing together. Nobody listened very much to anybody, but they all seemed to be in raging, towering spirits. They threw their weapons down apparently at random, and pulled books and scrolls and parchments and pieces of paper out of their pockets and chattered away and declaimed and recited; and suddenly and queerly and instinctively Donald knew that they were all poets. Once there seemed to be some sort of alarm sounded, for they all sprang to arms with inconceivable rapidity, and ranged themselves in battle array and handled their jumble of weapons in a manner that was the complete reverse of carelessness and amateurishness. When it was found to have been a false alarm, they shoved their weapons away again – one, a little fellow, stuffed a great meat-axe casually into one coat-pocket and hauled a quarto volume out of the other, and one arranged his Hotchkiss machine-gun into a three-legged table and sat down on the ground and began to write a poem upon it – and fell to talking and laughing and scribbling and shouting and declaiming.

Donald gazed and gazed upon the enchanted scene. Time did not move. The clouds above him were motionless. Even the sun, surely, had given up its mad race with eternity.

Then a faint dull clang filtered laboriously through the mist, and Donald lazily wondered why the Cathedral bell had begun again, and then he wondered how the sound had come through the mist, and then he saw that the edges of the mist were stirring softly among the wild flowers and the stray wreaths were once more playing at spirals with each other.

He sprang up and rubbed his eyes. Everything was changing quickly now. The road had vanished entirely, and the open space that was covered with the poets and their weapons was narrowing as the mist closed in upon it. The poets themselves were changing fantastically, for half of them were growing fatter and redder and jollier, and half of them were growing thinner and brighter-eyed and bearded, and, one by one and group by group, they were vanishing, but whether they were vanishing into the deepening, swallowing bank of fog, or whether by some curious trick they were vanishing into each other, Donald could not make out.

At last only two were left. One was the survivor of the fat men, the fattest and reddest and jolliest of them, with the kindliest and gayest and most gigantic of laughs. He had lost his weapon and was swigging away all the time at a monstrous jar of canary-sack which he carried under his arm. The second was the survivior of the thin men, and he was thin and had a small pointed beard, and his eyes were the brightest of them all, and he was full of silent laughter, and he was the gayest and the kindliest of them all. By some queer optical delusion, although these two men were really so very different, yet for a moment their faces seemed very like each other, and then for a moment both looked a little like Mr Hodge.

Just as the mist reached these last two, the Stratford man's eyes flashed with mischief, and he turned and said something to the fat man, who roared like a waterfall and then said – or at least it sounded as if he said – 'Shall we shog, Will?' – and then they linked arms and vanished, and below St Catherine's Hill there was no longer any trace of the passing of that absurd host of kindly, laughter-loving, warrior poets, but only what they have left behind them – the muted voices of grazing sheep, and the merry click of bat upon ball, and the peaceful green fields of England, and the water-meads, and the bells of the Cathedral.

Donald got up and yawned and stretched himself and went off to find some tea.